TriQuarterly

T0164125

TriQuarterly is
an international
journal of
writing, art and
cultural inquiry
published at
Northwestern
University

TriQuarterly

issue 112   *fall · winter 2002*

CONTENTS

New American Poetry

cover painting: "Spread Like Water,"
watercolor, Angela Schlaud

Kerry Hardie

Glory

Sycamore,
running with gold leaves
in a small wind
from a damp sky

        And behind it
        dark haws
        on bare thorn,
        its leaves cast.

So comes
glory,
and who cares so we
shine like this even

        for one hour, even
        for one eye
        opening only
        one heart.

Sleep in Summer

Light wakes us—there's the sun
climbing the mountains' rim, spilling across the valley,
finding our faces.
It is July,
        between the hay and harvest,
a time at arm's length from all other time,
the roads ragged with meadowsweet and mallow,
with splays of seedheads, slubbed and course, rough linen.
The fields above the house, clotted with sheep all spring,
are empty now and froth with flowering grasses,
still in the morning light. Birds move around
the leafy fields, the leafy garden.

It is the time
to set aside all vigil, good or ill.
to loosen the fixed gaze of our attention
as dandelions let seedlings to the wind.
Wake with the light.
Get up and go about the day and watch
its surfaces that brighten with the sun.
Remark the weight of your hands,
your foot in its sandal,
the lavender's blue hum.

And later, when the light is drowsed and heavy
go find the burdened fruit trees where the shade
lies splashed and opened-out across the ground.
Spread over it a quilt worn soft by other bodies,
then curl and fall down into sleep in light.

Awaken to a world of long, loose grass-stems,
and leaves above,
and birds, breaking out of the leaves.

At the Heinrich Böll Cottage

This is what happened in the night. I lay awake long after he had gone off into sleep. I had never slept in that room before. Something was in the room that came from another place. I pulled the cotton quilt to my face, it covered my mouth and my nose and I tried to smell its smell which is my smell, not the smell of the damp blankets or of the window behind the bed, fitted with darkness. But there was no my-smell, there was only other-smell. What was in the room has to do with a war or a great tribulation, that went on a long time ago that was now. It wasn't soldiers. It was about people who were waiting, and it was about fear. I saw the seal we had seen that afternoon. It had put its head out of the water and looked at us for a long time. It had reared up—its whole head and part of its shoulders out of the water—to look at us hard and deliberately. It passed its kingdom through its eyes and its kingdom entered us through ours. There was no fear in this exchange, only strangeness. There was no strangeness in the room, only despair.

Lord protect us from war, from famine, from despair. Let us live with the seal's kingdom in our hearts, the slap of gray water, death that is only death. Save us from horror. Let me not close my hand tight around anything. Let me close my hand tight, and hold on, and let no grain of sand escape from my grasp. Let the bones of my hand lie out on the machair, let the sands run through the sieve of the bones, let the dog pass and scoop the bones and crunch them in quick gulps. Let the sun break through on the machair, let it lift the bright grass with its wild light, while the sky beyond is slate with storm and the gulls gyre over the headland like chips of white quartz. Let the seal dive.

Notes

Machair is Irish and Scots Gaelic for the sandy plain found behind dunes and used for pasturage. Often also used for the dunes themselves.

Heinrich Böll, the Nobel Prize-winning writer, was a conscript in Hitler's armies. Later in his life he bought a cottage on Achill Island and since his death his family have reserved it for the use of writers and artists of all nationalities.

Achill Island, Co Mayo, was ravaged during the Great Famine of 1845–1849. Dugort, where the Böll Cottage is situated, is controversial because it was one of the places where people were invited to convert to Protestantism in return for being fed.

On Keel Strand

There was a big old woman
and I stared at her and stared
because I wanted to learn how to live in age
without being pinched;
she had strong white legs and bare feet and windy white hair
and behind her the swimmers dipped and plunged,
and behind them the black-rubber surfers
stood to the flashing sea;
and all her clothes were loose
with a blown cotton blue-and-whiteness,
and in her hand was a red bucket;
and all around her
and in the spaces and gaps of arms and legs and fingers
was a wash of green sea—not bulky, not flesh, not fixed,
but moving and pouring
and growing more translucent and transparent
as she grew denser—
and under her big, white, splay-toed feet the sand
was fine and grayish and damp where the tide had slid off,
and I looked down at my bare legs
with the first blue vein wriggling the calf
and my feet planted in the wash like saplings
and the mystery of flesh was very near and very far,
it was all and yet nothing at all.

Where to Call Home

This living is sometimes
like following a death,
as sorrowful and the same
sweetness, heart gone to
some other place.

I have been reading
Tess Gallagher, the high pride
of her mourning, her knowing there is nothing
for her here, yet here she will stay,
living, even sharply alive to
life, its frail beauty,
frailer and lovelier still since Carver's death.

Some men need deserts,
some women
tend children like candles, our dog lays
her face on Sean's thigh,
her deepest place.
For me, I
blow in the wind,
living nowhere except in the world, which is holy,
loving windows and doorways; daylight,
its fall through clear glass.

James Liddy

Nobel Gold

Into the valley of James Joyce rode the 600 metaphors
that should have been dervishes.

Sweet rain water in Northern Ireland
so the horses offered to drink it when they came
to the stream of the island inside the island.

Harvard never existed only horses do.
The clouds came to Boston and begged to flower,
damp heaving on astroid hooves.

Honey mixed with water so landscape became as luscious
as a tinted photograph.
Stoned horses levitation mellifluence water.

They store our gold in Scandinavia and pay interest
but we are on a different plateau: Yeats's platonic
dolls Joyce's horny toy fair, fun beauty.

Stolen goods, collars of gold and
libations? Libation of dervishes, hold out your glass.

Eamonn Wall

Emergency

Red-doored, white-trimmed, geraniums thriving in old carts:
A solid station on a summer afternoon between the old brick
Of the beer merchant and ol' man river Slaney. Nine swans
On the water, two crows on a wire, one distant island pony.

The signal is down. Children wave from atop a metal bridge,
A man holds a hoop for passing to the driver of a Connolly
Train. The station master passes tickets & handles change. Again,
To dwarf the fact of his son's departure, a father passes on the

History of the Irish when families keened as men ascended
Night trains for bombed-out buildings in the English Midlands,
Sent to captivity in Coventry for plucked chickens and black
Brogues shined for Confirmation. Men extend arms as quietly

As bobbies waving batons across the center of warm afternoons
Before the sirens sound. Emergency. A woman must light a
Second cigarette to better face the steep hills & dismal churches
Of the Free State. What grief did silence measure those first hours

Of empty time when hall doors closed, O women and children in
Chill evening? Just in case, a joyful couple comes well-supplied
With flask and sandwiches. They might waltz across the platform,
They are so happy. The new Hugh Leonard at the Abbey is a hoot.

Ben Howard

from Dark Pool

I

Tomorrow something new may cross my path
But today I write to you from Dublin City,
Whose name, as you well know, is anything
But new. Along with torcs and other relics,
The Danes who lived and moved in these environs
Left behind an image and a name.
Whatever I may think when I look out
On Georgian squares beset by noisy traffic,
The Danish eyes that fastened on this landscape
Perceived in it a place of murky water,
To which they gave the Danish name for *dark*
And the Danish name for *pool*, which in the dark,
Unending stream of naming and re-naming
Became *dubh linn*, its Irish counterpart.
And so I write to you this Monday morning
From the Dark Pool, whose air is often damp,
As though its early name had lingered on,
Exuding into air no longer Danish
Or altogether Irish something wet
And dark—the residue of habitation
But also of the languages that came
And went, the words no weightier than ours
That now are part of that unseen deposit
Which lies on walls and lanes and kitchen gardens
And sometimes smothers what it claims to know.

III

Where are you now, that I should write to you
From this bewildered city? I call it that
To capture if I can its quick-step tempo,
Its harsh brasses and, no less than that,
Its rattling drums. I mean no disrespect
To the Dark Pool nor to its thousand years
Of history, its celebrated streets
Where authors in their cups and noisy poets
Maintained the gardens of their verbal Eden;
Where untold creatures clamored to be named
And giants suited to that grand vocation
Threw out a dozen sumptuous appellations
For every beast that lumbered into view.
Dark Pool indeed! City of the Names,
I might have called it—names for enemies
And friends, cousins and acquaintances,
Passions and their objects, furtive feelings,
And all the dreck not spoken of in public
But named within the confines of the heart
And later brought to light. Bewilderment
Is not too strong a word for that emotion
Which sometimes overtakes me on these sidewalks,
Congested as they are with men and women
In earnest attitudes and in a hurry.
Such was the case one Friday afternoon
When everyone was headed to a bar
Or seemed to be, and I was out of step,
A foreigner with letters on his mind,
The ones I should have written earlier
To friends and family, retailing stories
Heard in the pubs or overheard in buses
Or clipped from pages of the *Irish Times*.
Those anecdotes more present in my mind
Than what was happening before my eyes,
I found myself accompanying the crowd
Into a pub whose name I can't remember,
Though I can see its stools and leather benches,
Its swirling smoke, its animated faces.
Maybe it was the Dublin intonation,

The *tink's* and *grand's* and *brilliant's* in the air,
The talk that was the sound track to the dramas
Occurring in the booths or at the tables—
Whatever it may have been, that dense profusion
Was like a storm, a bout of ugly weather
That I had wandered into, unprepared
And not well suited to negotiate.
Pausing at the counter, undecided
Whether to add more wind to that commotion
Or leave the way I came, as yet unnoticed,
I felt a word expanding in my mind
And pressing for release. The word was *publish*,
Untainted by its modern acceptation
And meaning, as of old, to interject
A private truth into the public body,
To make one's feelings known in public forum.
And as I entertained that potent word,
So rich in consequence and implication,
I found my tensions easing and my mind
Reflecting on the fabric I had entered,
Which someone aptly named a *public house*,
A shelter, if you like, for *publishers*,
However circumspect their revelations
Or cautious their impromptu publications.
Lifting my pint of Guinness, newly pulled
And primly handsome in its priestly collar,
I took my place among the publishers
And offered to the stranger on my right,
A nodding lad, inclined to conversation,
The essence of my thoughts on Irish weather.

IV

What is a name if not a bolt of fabric,
Its shape and aspect tailored and adorned
To suit the common good? One Friday morning
I lifted up mine eyes to the horizon
Whence came no help and only a little light,
The weather being damp and overcast,
The sky a dull and unrelenting gray.

Against that muted glow, revolving slowly,
A yellow crane attended to its business,
Some heavy object dangling from its cables.
What caught my eye and held my rapt attention
Was propped above the weights behind the cab,
Its presence no less bright for being small.
It was, I saw, the flag of the Republic,
Its triple colors flapping in the wind.
Imagining the man who climbed the ladder
And crawled out on the beam to mount it there
I felt a shuddering of vertigo,
As though it were myself who set that emblem
Of nationhood and long-sought independence
Aloft above a busy, fabled city
Which may or may not notice or regard it
Or find in orange, green, and neutral white
Its true identity. I looked away
And down, no native and no patriot
But stirred to wonder by a piece of cloth,
Whose form was changing even as I watched,
Its meaning not to be interpreted
But left to cast its net on crowded streets
And engines racing to the latest fire.

VIII

How loftily the pundits speculate
About a future no one will decipher
Even in retrospect, employing names
To do the work of knowing and unknowing,
The shaping and reshaping of the story.
What Jane will call a *splendid revolution*
Will seem to Joan a *spurious rebellion*
And facts themselves will gradually unravel
As sweaters do, their yarns at last returning
Into that primal state from whence they came.
Yet if I may join that happy band
Of prophets, panelists, and charlatans
Who claim to have a purchase on the future,
Allow me to envision Dublin City

In fifty years, its National Museum
Still the same, though newly stocked with cell phones
And other relics of our present time.
Its air will be more redolent of Progress,
Its Liffey even filthier than now,
Its urban essence all too effable.
As for the culture that sustained itself
On words and stout, as others have on wine,
What will become of it? My guess, as good
As anyone's, is that its bronze memorials,
Its Kavanagh and Anna Livia,
Its lanky Jimmy with his walking stick,
Will outlast all of us, a fitting tribute
To writers whom the world has deigned to honor.
But as for what those Publishers have published,
Those writers written in their finer hours,
I see it too as gradually disbanding,
As though the names that gathered on a page
Or in a room had gone their separate ways
And every text were headed for perdition.
Looking down this evening at the Liffey,
I see the waves dispersing on the quay,
The wakes dissolving in the fleeting light,
And wonder if those poems learnt by heart
Or cherished under glass in dustless rooms
Are any more coherent or substantial.
If not, then let the *dubh linn* claim its own,
The Names give up their portions to the stream.
And let it flow as mightily as water,
This language that is neither yours nor mine
But enters and inhabits us, its colors
As varied as the colors of the world,
Its lanes and crescents, channels and canals
As trafficked or as desolate as those
The eye encounters on its daily rounds
And shores against incipient erasure.

Vona Groarke

Cities and Flowers

So your city is a garden with its heat in flower,
stiff with outlandish vibrancy and spill.
And your skin rustles like petals on the turn
to wisps of music more fragrant even than blossoms
with their careless overtures. So buildings are laying
slabs of shadow out, workmanlike, the way a tree
could never be, with all that giddy lineage, those airs.

Well, my garden works its allusions to the death,
but the poppies remind me of lipstick, the hydrangeas,
of noise. I'm wearing high heels that still stake me,
but they'll do. There are pavements to be set tinkling;
streets that need only breath for them to swell.

Coming To

Like a fist unplunged from the river
and held on high for us to count
until the final drips traipse
from your ring back to the deeps

we wake to this. A first skin
still impressed by dreams that slip
through the eye of daylight
to arrive at ours. And whole days

blanched on the coverlet
where your shoulders round
on promises already spilled
too far and wide for us.

Here's one: the edge of a curtain
lifted by a strand of air so lissome
the days dawns on us all over again.
Another: that it could happen like this

over and over; a last half-hour steeped
in the not-yet-said, and my poring
over it for fear I'd miss a pulse
in your coming to. And still.

Everything now is held like breath
between the second last and final
notes of a song turned lightly
to summer and its slipshod overtures.

Which brings me to the sight of you
coming up from the lock, your mouth
streaming, your hair in need of my fingers
and a wide, complicit sunlight on your back.

The way you wake. The way
I am waiting for you.
We could do this all morning.
We could go on and on.

Why Music Does

Because these are days with a reason of their own in which
       the high-C of a neighbor's running tap or the protracted
       soprano of a braking bus is somewhere to begin.

Because the children are quiet for once, and the unmade beds are cubes
       of brightness at six when the shadows have not stirred themselves
       and the sheets ruffle like high notes and their consequences.

Because the blackbird will consume even the dumbsong of the worm
       it cocks an ear for on the lawn, and the rooms of the house
       have not yet been fine-tuned against the ravenous air.

Because the toy-box in the attic has a mobile from a cot that bleats
       the first notes of some lullaby from on high for no good reason
       when the day is unusually warm or the house inexplicably freezing.

Because questions spindle the vacant hours and there is nothing
       to be accounted for but rooms that glance against the rim
       of each other with something like the true-note of fidelity.

Because the light from the kitchen still shimmies on the lawn whether
       or not there is dancing to be done, when the upstairs chatter
       diminishes between sundown and the nightly reckoning.

Because the bells are banging on for the Novena like drunks who want
       to be heeded and have their wrongs set right, and the children
       of another Monday are settling back against ten thoughtless hours.

Because the newspaper shuffles through, day after day, to its death notices
       and their brandished consolations, and the looked-for name
       is not found there, and so, slips its performance once again.

Because what has happened by the time a word like "love" comes easily
       cannot be reckoned when the lamp's soliloquies are wearing thin
       and the phone has given itself to the hall and its reflection.

Because the years add up to nothing very much: a rustle in another room;
       a glint of taffeta on an evening dress worn once; a favorite song
       with half the words rubbed off and gathered up into a scant refrain.

Because it goes unheard and means nothing, not least of all the word it did not keep when it rounded back upon itself and eventually gave in to the way it goes, what follows on, and how and why it does.

Peter Fallon

November Rain

The fields are full;
the water tables spilling
through springs and shores.
Rain—and more rain
forecast—overfilling

the gullies and drains.
The river's rise,
now that the day's come into light
and the landscape's lake,
slaps patches on the eyes

of the four-eyed bridge.
"What's happened to my land—
what was my land"—
he wonders as he stares
at his milk-herd on an island . . .

If the known world didn't
the one submerged before us
shrank before our watch,
below low cloud, and the mares
hunched in their uneasy chorus

a warning by the shelter of a wall,
their tails to the wind. What hides
sulking in the plowlands
is water on a giant beach
when the giant tide's

receded. What good could come
of such a deluge, unless it unite us?
Let mud be flesh
put on the bones of winter
to spare the waste of planting. Heraclitus

only knows where the night
will find us, at home in a dream
of the rest of the country,
hayricks and hedges coming
into their own, and us borne on a stream

to a morning that's exhausted—
a feature in the future almanacs—
the embers of dawn fit to be blazed,
a drying sun ready to rise,
and the breeze blowing lightly, at our backs.

Bill Tinley

On the Eve

Clouds are in congress on the last day of winter.
Over the canal and cinder path their bucket gray
Leaks the last measure of January rain;
Mallards converge as ripples on the buckled sedge,
Long weeds unravel in the water's albumen.
Somewhere, a Sunday bell is holding its tongue,
Its rusty silence at one with the railway line,
The sleeper oil, the slick from lock to lock like glass
In which the sky can see so little of itself.
To the west a simple bud of light is opening,
A bridge the buttonhole for afternoon sunshine.
Birds dip in tandem with the sagging wires and fall
Away across the cloven fields and ditches.
Medusa brambles crawl over the grassy bank.
Again and again, unbroken down the years, these things
Cohere as nothing but themselves. The detritus
Another year has left lies in the undergrowth,
Beneath the bridges—Bond, Jackson, Chambers, Shaw—,
Footprints, flowers, ashes from a midnight fire,
Everything, like everyone who's passed here, resigned
To a patient decline. Lambs already on the breast
Hug their sooty fleeces to the indifferent earth
But will survive. Jackdaws graffito the horizon
Until distance dissolves them in the churning clouds.
It is almost springtime. The new year cannot wait
To be done with its dull palette of light and ice,
A contagion of yellow, white and brilliant green
Festering beneath the snow that has yet to fall.
What is there to relish in the muted spectrum

Winter breeds, but absence, lack and what is not,
Like the silence that restores itself to water
Now and again and is gone before it flowers.
Still, the famished world perplexes and sustains us.
With nothing to consume, our thoughts feed on the soul,
On what the soul cannot digest or fold into
Its amnion as once it did. Alone out here
By the wind's abrupt ablutions on the surface
Unease lies not in what is past or still to come
But what's at hand, absolute and singular,
Devoid of anything but what it, in itself,
Consists of, and that impossible to harness.
The wind swipes and cuts, the bushes writhe, the sun's yolk
Bulges momentarily in the south and sinks,
All a quaint tableau to soothe where there's no solace,
Unless the loss we celebrate is what abides
As who we are, our lives wound round and round about
An emptiness, and that substantial, to be held,
As now this stretch of water summons round itself
An hour, a day, tomorrow, a necessary life.

Medbh McGuckian

High Altitude Lavender

When snow fell for six hours
in an unforeseen direction,
the winter of fruit skins
recovered the footlight glow
of the sun as solid silver.

A gothic bouquet
of bronze-colored roses,
standing up in military elegance
shackled to a trance,
flexed gleaming silken arches.

A stem of body-bound
orchids on a breathless postcard
changed their florid despair
to a midnight-blue glance,
and accepted to speak about next year.

A sheaf of country dahlias
in a communal ward
turned their humbled palms out
with morbid homage to embrace
the rustle of live wings.

I kept colliding with the absence
of my own heavy family,
fiery as this year's grapes
that the dew considered heartless,
as though they had grown deafer;

and addressed a conversation
to no one among us,
to the gardens framed by your windows,
that can imitate the shape of flowers
with their mere mouth and their empty fingers.

Hearing the Weather Fall

The shutters folded back in their frames
with a pale movement,
a pacific repetition,
and only mirrors followed
to pierce where the day was stored,

each so enisled
and smiled at
by the sympathy of the tides,
looking less arrived
in a waveless bay,
and over, a bay of fields. . . .

Now crowningly,
the droop of the sky
into my morning—
somebody would pay
for the night, a very soon
weekend—for the braking,
for the slowing-up,

for the uncharted pain
as then still forgiven.
A never-fighter,
running out a hand
to ask as from a death-bed
why this loves to happen,

I'd rather this fishing village
at the end of the world,
lying down and down a dull sea,
than the bound slope
of a suburban hill,
or everywhere that one visits
acquisitively,

than library voices
in the changed room.
The country's essence,
moored at the north
but with an air of being
washed out west

could not forego that kindling,
the arm which tightened
like a steady look from his
long eyes, knowing
the wrong wings are crossed up there.

David Wheatley

The Cold

> There is little landscape where
> you are going and no warmth.
> —Stevie Smith

But for the cold sealing the estuary in
behind the fish market, behind the bridge-view car-park,
so that the sharp air smells only of us,
would it be easier, harder, to feel ourselves
marked by these afternoons we shoulder like an old coat?

The man on the corner stoops to coax a pigeon
into his outstretched hands then straightens and claps them
to warm himself, applauding the street theater
of his failure as the bird waddles off
(and there will be more time to waste, where that came from),

the weather hardening round us, my hand inside
the lagging jacket in an upstairs flat
feeling the cylinder cold. We will have to be patient,
as the hatchbacks that ease over the avenue
speed bumps are patient, the children in the back seats

staring up at us unfathomably
distant and content. The January sun
releases its grip on the day and my hand slips under
the cardigan sleeve you wouldn't have pulled down
to clutch in your palm so tightly but for the cold.

The Donor

They give you a magazine, though not to read,
while a fan shoos round the stale, distracted air.
Deposit yourself on the couch. It is permitted
to scrutinize a hairline crack in the ceiling
and discover in it a source of fascination.

The jar opens with a swift, circular motion,
call it a jamjar, and awaits resealing:
the sort of jar where a frog, recently mated,
might choose to leave its spawn as a living picture-
book for schoolboys everywhere to read.

Dennis O'Driscoll

Blood Relations

I

Who descended from whom.
Who has whose eyes.
Whose nose.
Whose bone marrow matches whose.
Whose blood group.
Viscous as crude oil.
Sticky situations.
Four times thicker than water.
Brought to boiling point
at the least slip of the tongue.

II

Blood is what earns you
a sponsor's place
at the baptismal font
cradling your newest niece;

or, sporting a paper crown,
the right to dish out breast of turkey
at the Christmas get-together,
test the firmness of pink ham;

the privilege to share
in triumph or disgrace,
put up bail, act as guarantor,
face the midnight call.

III

Cells dunked in plasma,
fruit in syrup.
Clots, blockages, oxygen loss.

Such scope for bad blood.
The potency to pump 8,000 liters in a day.
100,000 beats worth.

More than your hardening
arteries may find
the capacity to forgive.

Micheal O'Siadhail

Launch

1. Knot

Right over left and left over right.

Or the other way around. Symmetrical plot
Of two mutual loops drawn tight,
The squared-off weftage of a reef knot.

Double and single, a riddle of ligature.
Functional beauty sacred and profane;
A history of knots, a rope architecture,
Easy to loosen but tighter under strain.

Plied strength in our tying up of ends,
An emblem, one tiny glorious detail,
A sign becoming what a sign intends.
We tauten the love-knot, hoist the sail.

2. Splice

Braid by braid to unravel
Our weave as stripped
We intersperse
For better, for worse
Our strands; a whipped
And knitted re-ravel

No longer a knot with its come
And go but more
To have and hold
Our splice's twofold
Purchase, a rapport
Tougher than its sum.

I take whoever you are
Or come to be
Till one of us perish
To love, to cherish.
Steer by my burgee.
I hitch to your star.

3. Hitch

A moon hoops earth and earth the sun
Planet hitched to planet, swung like a stone

Hoisted into the taut whirlwind of a sling.
A month's wax and wane, neap and spring,

The tides of things, our orbits loop and pitch.
What is this trust which underwrites a voyage?

Our world-weight and giddy let-fly, a tense
Counterpoise of gravity and centrifugence,

Outward gyres held by their contrary force,
Some push and pull that covenants a universe.

4. Plunge

A balanced helm, a beautiful sail trim.
But over again surge and sweet of deviation;
A moment's perfect bearing another interim,
Our arc of covenant still steered by variation.

Under a bowl of sky watch and weather-eye
Alert to luff and camber, telltale breath;
Close-hauling, compromise of full and by
And how the wind bloweth as it listeth.
That perfect bearing already a moment ago.
Are lovers trimmers? O my Ulysses
Sail on, sail on! Our fleeting status quo
Perfection neared in a series of near misses.
Globed in a bowl of oil, a gimbaled compass
Bobs and pivots to hold its northern promise.

Aidan Rooney-Céspedes

The Name Takers

The sun had been up and about its own
good measure of hours—no nap, no coffee-
break, no smoke, just the usual glances thrown
to the jaded youth in their latest, puffy
fashions, barely a nod to business
casuals out to lunch, dittoing this,
uploading that, no time for a Guinness
or a level chat, all *age quod agis*—

when the dead paraded through the streets.
It was more embarrassment than snafu,
really, that made people give up their seats,
the dead turning their noses up at tofu,
bagels, sashimi, before they ordered
bowl after bowl of potato *soup du jour*,
spilling and slurping so much it bordered
on barbarism. You could tell they were poor

from their get-up of boots and gaudy rags,
the men, though hewn, lean, rough-cut, big-handed,
the women mostly what we'd now call hags,
but if you weren't aware they'd just landed
in from Afterlife, you'd swear by the medley
of laughter and cracks, they were living proof
of the very well-off. Their irony was deadly,
their wit sharp, and after lunch they raised the roof,

literally, and hovered for a bit
like Peter Pans, before they lighted down.
They had realized they didn't fit
in the busy streets of the modern town,
so they headed back the way they had come,
to their *status quo ante bellum*.
They belonged to no one. No one claimed them.
No chancers. No takers. No one said their name.

Mary O'Donnell

Solstice

Clouds have cleared. The Wicklow mountains
undecked of weeks of rain, leave
liquid ledges that overspilt the carping skies.
On this final day of the sun's trifling
with veils of moisture, low horizons,
there is light above—not the hopeful shaft
of a megalithic dawn, the silence in grave passages
as it steals through, then fades prematurely—
but a full six hours with earth and sky
revealed like *chiaroscuro*.

The lakes stretch out in loops,
like the eyes of slowly blinking water gods,
shorelines knotted with submerged boats,
as the ground squelches and soaks, but the sky
is a clear patch on the canvas of the global north,
mountains are semaphores, blue-gray signals
brushing open air, inviting light to enter and re-enter
streams, crotches of trees, the pores of our skin.
We are fully pleasured.

Transport

She drives the school road quickly,
feels the car winging between shadows of trees,
a bird of prey hunting threads of blue

from the peacock sky.
Another time, on the bike, belting up the hill
towards Rathcoffey, she brakes once, steps down

to silently address the multitudes of barley,
crows' holy crowd beneath the evening sun,
relinquishing cloths of gold.

But in the mountains she grows still.
In the sharp May air, she fastens kisses,
whole garlands of them around his neck,

they rest beneath the descant forest breeze,
the marvelous incarnate, believable
in their arms; cuckoos haunt them forever.

Conor O'Callaghan

This

began with an Oriole pencil I stumbled on among the stalls
of Santa Monica and lost by lunch. It ends thus, and now.
For months there was a play on "pastures new"
that became a blue sea that changed to something else.

I forget. There was something as well about the four walls
of a fortnight or three on the wagon. I'd forgotten also
an image of my gran in her kitchen up until a week ago,
the meadow of butterfly buns, her breathless "It's very close."

Then the night before last, after a few lonely drinks,
I gave myself a table of pals dishing out seconds and thirds
and tippling till the cows come home and leaving the dinner things

for armchairs on the porch and a silence without words
that was nothing of the sort, thanks to this and thanks
to the darkness I threw in, littered with mockingbirds.

Time-Zones

I drift on an ocean of eucalyptus.
An airbus, forty thousand feet up,
undoes the stratosphere's zip
and darkness opens out between us.

Sleeplessness. Homebirds in another room
are whimpering for me to call back across
an eight-hour lapse, the dawn chorus,
the landing I couldn't be further from.

We bring our long-distance silences to an end
(like Saint Brendan and Saint Patrick
arguing the toss mid-Atlantic)
still none the wiser where we stand.

By now you have long since tired
of the day I'm still midway through.
I can all but feel you ravelling the throw,
minutely, into your half of the world.

Through *Saturday Night and Sunday Morning,*
a late show, I blank out into the internal flight
that makes a straight line of the lights
of Baffin Island and the Black Mountains.

Standing here banging quarters into white space,
feeling like the next turn up on stage,
leaving message after disconsolate message,
sick of the sound of my own voice.

For the time being, being without yours
is being in love with this groundless
momentary displacement of hotel lounges,
a sweater folded around my shoulders.

Mostly, when sleep is beneath me,
I fall all over again for your absence,
the memory of your sap like absinthe's
aftertaste, your scent this near to me.

An afternoon in the eighties and it goes black
just like that, the way you envelop
yourself in your crushed velvet wrap.
I head back alone along the beaten track.

I guess I imagine you most while the elevator
is sighing through the motions back to earth
and I'm about to pass up, for what it's worth,
the lobby's foliage for the cold night air.

Time out with seconds to go for the Lakers
is suddenly a film of *The Tin Drum*.
In between, in fits and waves, the dream
of postcards arriving in my wake like echoes.

An hour to boarding, not expecting to, I get you.
The kids have gone down. You've just taken
your flip-flops into our west-facing garden
when the phone starts warbling out of the blue.

A biplane from the direction of Idaho
falls past the vanishing point across town
towards the very second it touches down,
a dragonfly landing on its own shadow.

For weeks there we come together
either side of the breakfast cereals:
you stepping out at Arrivals,
me still stuck in Departures.

Greg Delanty

Paper Light

Today's light would break the hearts of the dead
          if they could step back in.
The sun filters through the lightest haze, a gauze
          of light
swabbing the eye-cataracts that shroud what must be
          spirit-eyes.

It's as if the sun is seen through Japanese rice paper
          laid over
a timeless print or poem suggesting core light,
          the mystery light
that the sketch or calligraphy leaves out so the
          essence blazes through
what the ghosts might call the divine, that may
          be seen only at one remove.

Or, as now, at one remove through this haze's tracing
          paper, the kind that as kids we simply
traced the sun, clouds, water, trees, people, cars
          and boats of our crayon-colorful world through.
As it is now and never again shall be: fawn-fall grass,
          the milkweed-seeded air, the vermillion trees,
the lake's veiled boats, the ghost of a passing truck
          and the gray scribble
on this paper white as a wimple, lit up as if from
          inside
by the unseen grand hand on this day that breaks
          the heart of a man gone all simple.

Liam O'Muirthile:
Translated from the Irish by Greg Delanty

Walking Time

How's it going, Da? An will tú ann?
Still down the well in the Cork Arms?
Do you remember our day out in the Fiat?
We burnt rubber, wheeling it pronto to Bweeng.
You were County Cycling Champ again
on those war-rationed wheels of cane.
In Ainm Dé, it's tough to talk with you
in a language you haven't got
and, Da, that's between us
ever since I gathered the shavings,
those gold locks, welling around my ankles.
I stared up at you.
I can still smell them, fresh
as new leaves—there must be forests
of deciduous shaving-trees in carpenter's paradise.
I'm ráiméising on, or more like claw-hammering
on the ivories of the piano's stairs.
I'm ghost-playing, shadow-fingering
on the mockeyah keyboard of the kitchen table
that was made in your very own workshop.
The dying notes of Irish reverberating;
hitting home that morning the word Bweeng,
issuing from the radio, stopped me in my tracks.
It reminded me of John Coltrane's sax gyring
and gyving a note on *The Blue Train*, wedging
my heart fast with a tenon-joint.
I hammer out notes on the black and white mortise keys
of your rock-steady table, each leg hewn in metric feet.

The table is a sound quatrain
that even Blind Tigh, an file,
would have stood over.
You could gut a pig on it, you said,
the way those farmers used to, when you, a journeyman,
footed it from house to house along the Blackwater.
There are days I feel the blood of a squalling pig,
throat slit, darkening the grain of southern pine.
The knell of Cork bells rings out
in me under the current of everything.
I wade in and go with the flow, vamping
it again along the river from the sawdoctor
on the South Gate with your saw stuck under me oxster.
I swim home, a sawfish,
along Sully's Quay, and his question:
"Your Jim Hurley's son, so?"
is proof positive that I'm cut from a line
of surnames engraved on a saw handle;
sawyers: Riordan, Hurley, Boyce . . .
still reverberating inside my head.
"There's a smell of dead men from that"
you enjoindered, men
tenon-wedged with black humor,
grasping pints that solved nothing;
the hungry ghosts from the sword side of Carraig
on their own walking time up
and down the stairs,
polishing the stone steps
till you can see you own shade in them.
I must follow them now through Castle,
or else they'll be the death of me.
They keep harassing me to listen to their calling,
but I blocked them out.
I suppose I wasn't ready for them.
Mind you, I couldn't quite shut out
their muttering, always dogging me,
crowding my doorstep, the ancient
and the lately dead jostling each other.
God, give me the strength to open the door
and allow them in to drink from the pool

of blood darkening our table.
Then let them be off and leave me in peace.
The Irish I learned on Sully's quay muzzled English.
I can't ignore that trap growling up at me any longer.
Once I'd have called this walking time: Tráth Siúil.
Now it's clear my way's wedged between the two.
I feel a bit like the sawdoctor
honing a new edge on the blade's snarl,
every second tooth of English is turned one way, the incisor
of Irish, in the center, is turned the other.
You must have felt the same on your walking time
when you moved from Bweeng into the big city.
You were given walking money for the time
it took to vamp it from bus to work site.
It dawned on you
that the green country pup
was a fully grown man with his carpenter's card.
Despite all your wandering you never left
the Castle of your Bweeng youth.
I understood that as we scorched the road,
those cane wheels still sparking the cinder path.
I often think of the haymaker you made farmers,
the larch's tumbling butt—
that name springs from my mouth
like the shafts of a cart rising into the air
when the horse is untackled and steps from the trap.
I'm knackered now, Da, hammering home words
as you were beat hammering home nails.
All poets and carpenters can give is their all.
Take it easy, Da. Don't be too rough on yourself.
Mind you, be tough with the things that matter.
The crime is
we don't know in good
time what's precisely in our best interest.
By the time we do we feel unworthy
of it all—the cruelest cut of all.
We try every other way of walking
the walk till we can neither walk or stand.
At times, when I visit you,
I have to learn myself

how to plant my feet squarely on the ground.
I watch you walking on this foreign planet
of a world, a tight grip on your walking stick.
Your air soles shuffle for a level on the bed
of the floor, your sharp carpenter's eyes
still read the angles of a theodolite upside
down, searching for level ground.
Christ, Da, life's at odds with intelligence.
The crooked curves of love
tripped me up, despite my gratitude to you
for Euclid's plane, Pythagoras's theorem.
The muse sees the windmills in the hypotenuse.
I know, Dad, I've always been a bit of a shaper.
When we struck out for Bweeng that day
you recalled your prize for the race on cane wheels;
a brace of porcelain dogs you gave your mother.
They got lost among your sisters till we gathered
in the lonesome, pale white house after Nellie's funeral.
We doggedly ripped letters into pieces, packed plastic bags
with scribbled conversations between Dunmanway,
Chicago, Malla, Melbourne, Birmingham, Sutten—
bags full of remote confabs: "I hope these lines find you well,"
"Jim's must be big now," "Are you coming down Nell?"
I, a tearer, furtively read, listening to snippets
between glances at the letters and the rest of you.
I had to get out. You found a pair of porcelain spaniels
in the wardrobe and another pair, the exact same, in the loft:
a household of fully reared porcelain spaniels.
The pair on your mantlepiece stares down the other
in your window for the prize at Bweeng, your porcelain eyes
and mine finally leveled with one another.

Nuala Ní Dhomhnaill:
Translated from the Irish by Eamon Grennan

Early Evening: A Zen Moment

Not even a leaf glitters in the eucalyptus
that's usually all stir and sway in the wind—
always standing watch at the bottom fence,
reporting every passing breath of a breeze.

Each bramble seems frozen, as if on guard.
The clouds are standing still in the sky.
Each apple hangs forever, like the tree of Eden
before the snake slid into the world.

A small bird is singing to the monk in his church.
Oisín is mounted behind the fair-haired woman.
The Dagda is lying with the goddess of the Boyne.
The Fish Queen conversing with Iwashira Taro.

Then a single leaf stirs . . .
and the scaldcrow rises in lopsided flight
and—sending me round the bend—the magpie's back
clackering his usual crap from a neighbor's roof.

A near door bangs open and a blast of rock music
comes at me; now a racket-machine is shearing grass.
I lean back, with apologies, from the world of mystery,
trying to catch the tattered little tail of my dream.

Eamon Grennan

But So

Haze for days. Eyes useless. Rowanberries darkening to brown. Birds falling from branches under a lukewarm, almost African rain.

But when the dove becomes a handful of scattered feathers flying from under car-wheels back among *the glowing sundry of the world*, I find again the fine line between things touching is the shadow they throw on one another, gods in the wings still whispering soul at stake to the silence, till my daughter sails in in a swaddle of radiance and it's nightcity once more, the dream leaving me homeless, speechless, perplexed by the joy of it beyond reason.

But there he is again, that man of cardboard—face in hands, crying in a corner, the window looking in at him—so I find no song to brighten the heartbreak-grey of the empty kitchen, or kindle in the bedroom a spark in the darkened firegrate, and even those roses, light-blown as they are, will die of thirst.

But if I lift my eyes a moment from the snow-caked floor, I'll find in a flail of nerves and marrowchill the fruit-dish mounded with clementines, altars everywhere, and even in this dingy underground a flowershop shining near midnight. Or a goldcrest lighting up its bush in icy weather, or the dreamfox disappearing into the house of childhood—henna flash then gone—quite distinct its ember eyes and pale ginger head.

So, at dusk, there I am again being dazzled by Venus and Jupiter in conjunction, gold of whiskey, gilt or glass of doorknobs, and how the fact of faces grows stranger and stranger: faint puce browns, steely grays, the range of ivory, rose, biscuit, one faint shade of plum. And the ocean roaring on its short leash. And a gull riding the gale bareback—balancing, on its lethal bill, a single blink of salted light.

So no wonder I have to close my eyes to all the mirrors, shut my ears to this wren cockcrowing its hurlyburly and composing a home among the garage clutter. Or start *like a guilty thing surprised* from the hue and cry of kitchen habits: innocent clatter of forks and stainless steel knives falling from dry hands into a drawer: silence of the stove, the oven a dark patience for the heart to come on. Or just the *broken white* of a dress and its bone-colored buttons, two arms stretching, sleeveless, out of it.

J. O. Lane

Love Reading

Goi's 19th century breath travels far: through the tube, into the orange mass of
    molten sand and the gradual global expanse, the last
Of the green glass fishing floats he severs from his pipe to cool in the late April
    afternoon, and because Old Akutagawa
Scolds him for clumsiness, the one he dropped and cracked, Goi stops for a little
    cheap sake and talks
With the drunkards at Tajomaru's, but he stays too late and all that greets him at
    home is his mother's silence and cold rice.

By the time she dies, thousands of Goi's breaths leave the nearby harbor daily
    and bob at sea; thirteen drift ashore
One morning after a storm, bearing Kanazawa's corpse, and that afternoon all
    the village is still
But for the corner of a fisherman's hut: the *tink* of glass on glass as Kanazawa's
    widow mounds a shrine of thirteen globes.

What would surely seem to her like centuries later, their grandson gives the floats to
    Tajomaru's niece,
The shop keeper, because he is the last of his family and he is going off to die
    for the Emperor; they freeze in her store window
Until a strand of sun, many months after the bomb has fallen, curls itself around
    the topmost mossy orb and pulls in
The blue eyes of a captain's wife: she remembers precious buggy rides to the hot
    springs, the stream where she and her father fished,

She remembers the summer of her tenth year, when he died, how dusty air bubbled
    like a mud bath and scorched her throat
With each brief breath; she manages, in English and broken Japanese, to purchase
    these thirteen elegies
To the simple life and sends them home to her mother in California, who sets
    them among the Victorian legs
Of a marble-top table, upon which, when the old woman dies, the captain's wife
    sets her reading lamp.

Beside them her young son sits on the floor and tickles the calluses of her soles,
          wondering why she doesn't laugh and squirm
As he does when she simply wiggles her fingers near his feet: there is so much
          he doesn't understand.
How does she know to leave a rib of light each night in his dark door, and why,
          when her wicker chair
Starts its steady creak and a book jacket crackles open and the *shoosh* and *flap* of
          fresh pages begins, does he think of her fingertips
Grazing his scalp, why does he think of the blue brush and how he loves to undo
          the wind's work in his mother's hair?

He only begins to understand twenty years later, when a stranger in Manhattan
          asks him for money
And he pours his small change into the delta of grimy streams that is a hand; he
          sees an empty paper bag rustle up church steps
And flatten against the door; he feels as though he has lost what clasps his hands
          together, as though he has come to believe
Only in bad days; then he remembers his Mother's last word, a silent no, and
          the iridescent clarity of its swirl rising
From saliva, how the bubble broke on her lips and blued them dark—it will still
          be years before he can write, *I am not alone.*

Li-Young Lee

Degrees of Blue

At the place in the story
where the enchanted mirror falls into the ocean
and the moon's entire court is taken hostage
the boy looks up from his book,

out the window, and sees
the hills have turned their backs
and are walking into evening.

How long does he watch them go?
Does the part of him that follows call
for years across his growing sadness?

When he returns to the tale, the page is dark,
as vast as the room is huge,

and the leaves at the window have been traveling
beside his silent reading
as long as he can remember.

Where is his father? Who is his mother?
How is he going to explain the branches
beginning to grow from his ribs and throat,
the cries and trills coming from his own mouth?

And now that ancient sorrow between his hips,
the siege of springtime in his blood,

his body's ripe listening finally
the planet knowing itself.

The Eternal Son

Someone's thinking about his mother tonight.

The wakeful son
of a parent who hardly sleeps,

the sleepless father of his own
restless child, God, is it you?
Is it me? Do you have a mother?

Who mixes flour and sugar
for your birthday cake?

Who stirs slumber and remembrance
in a song for your bedtime?

If you're the cry enjoining dawn,
who birthed you?

If you're the bell tolling night
without circumference, who rocked you?

Someone's separating
the white grains of his insomnia
from the black seeds
of his sleep.

If it isn't you, God, it must be me.

My mother's eternal son,
I can't hear the rain without thinking
it's her in the next room
folding our clothes to lay inside a suitcase.

And now she's counting her money
on the bed, the good paper
and the paper from the other country
in separate heaps.

If day comes soon, she could buy our passage.
But if our lot is the rest of the night,
we'll have to trust unseen hands
to hand us toward ever deeper sleep.

Then I'll be the crumb
at the bottom of her pocket,
and she can keep me
or sow me on the water,
as she pleases. Anyway,

she has too much to carry, she who knows
night must tell the rest of every story.

Now she's wondering about the sea.
She can't tell if the white foam laughs,
I was born dark! while it spins
opposite the momentum of our dying,

or do the waves journey beyond
the name of every country
and the changing color of her hair.

And if she's weeping,
it's because she's misplaced
both of our childhoods.

And if she's humming, it's because
she's heard the name of life:
a name, but no name, the dove

bereft of memory and finally singing
how the light happened
to one who gave up
ever looking back.

Pillow

There's nothing I can't find under there:
voices in the trees, the missing pages
of the sea.

Everything but sleep.

And night is a river bridging
the speaking and the listening banks,

a fortress, undefended and inviolate.

There's nothing that won't fit under it:
fountains clogged with mud and leaves,
the houses of my childhood.

And night begins when my mother's fingers
let go of the thread
they've been tying and untying
to feel toward our fraying story's hem.

Night is the shadow of my father's hands
setting the alarm clock for resurrection.

Or is it the clock unraveled, the numbers flown?

There's nothing that hasn't found home there:
discarded wings, lost shoes, a broken alphabet.

Everything but sleep. And night begins

with the first beheading
of the jasmine, its captive fragrance
rid at last of burial clothes.

Barbara Hamby

Idolatry

My Baal, shimmering Apollo, junkyard Buonaroti,
        funkadelic *malocchio*, voice shouting
from the radio, talking about love, about heartbreak,
        about doing everything you can till
you cain't do no more. Then you float by
        in a Coupe de Ville, hair conked,
wearing the mink stole of delicious indifference,
        reciting the odes of Mr. John Keats
like you were his best friend. I was minding
        my own business, being good as a girl
could be when every inch of skin aches
        for the sky. Where is my wide sky,
now all I see is you? Where is my ocean, you hex
        on thought, golden calf in the living room
of ambition, pagan call, demon whispering like beetles
        on the skin of morning. I hear your voice
come out of the mouths of little girls
        jumping rope on Orange Avenue. I hear
your aria in the shopping center pharmacy,
        in the tired lines around the eyes
of every sleepless night. You're an astronomer,
        roaming the heavens like a flyboy
anatomist, dissecting the stars. Tell me again
        about the stars, those cheap flash
cards of the gods. Tell me about human sacrifice,
        the huju rituals of versification,
the quantum mechanics of line, my holy-of-holies,
        sanctum sanctorum, my hideaway

in the world of cool. Pagan huckster, heat up
        your spells, your charms, your rapture,
I come to you a novice, an acolyte, a scullery maid
        in the choir of the unruly. Give me
my music, my words, my lyrical demonstration
        of all that is gorgeous and invisible.
I am your handmaiden, your courtesan, your ten-cent-
        a-dance barroom floozie. My Lord-
who-whispers-his-secrets-into-the-skulls-of-angels,
        your slightest whim is my delight.
Every day I wake to your disciples' quick trill.
        I am a prisoner of your darkest sigh,
queen of ungovernable birds. You only visit me
        at night when no one can see, but your shame
is an aphrodisiac, a love potion, a quick fix
        in the alley from the dark drug of words.

The Mockingbird Invents Writing

As always the world was a mess, nobody understanding
        anything. It was two weeks after
Babel when God pulled the rug out from under creation,
        messed it up good. What
could I do, just sit there while everyone jabbered
        like monkeys? I got busy, can't sit on my
duff, contemplating the infinite. Anyway, the world
        was smaller then,
everything between the Tigres and Euphrates. *Mesopotamia,*
        now there's a fabulous word. I
found it under a rock at a bazaar in Babylon. At first
        it was simple counting amphoras of oil, cattle,
goats but humans know a good thing when they see it.
        Pretty soon they were making up
horrendous stories. *Gilgamesh,* my God, those Assyrians
        were inventive people, but the Egyptians—

Isis, Ra, Set, Thoth, the jackal-headed god. For 2,500
        years, not until the King
James Bible did I hear a translation of God's word that sent
        such a shiver up my spine, rocked my
kundalini to the stars. Chinese, a gorgeous lingo,
        but all those perfect
little pictures: I tried to talk them out of it. Limits
        their poetry in
my not-so-humble opinion, but they had their own ideas.
        Everyone does, don't they?
Now Arabic, there's a poetic language, good-looking, too,
        like a river running through the fingers.
Oh God wasn't all that fond of writing at first, a little
        jealous if you ask me,
pouted for a couple of thousand years. Woke up with
        the Children of Israel up to their necks in
quicksand, stranded in the desert, as ragged looking
        a group as you'd ever hope to see, Moses
raging at God, writing it all down. Nothing like a good
        book to soothe a savage deity, and Moses
saying God was in charge. He liked that. Yes, sir,
        something not a little bit
Teutonic about Jehovah, though Germany came later.
        Charming language that: Schadenfreude,
Übermensch, Scheissenbedauren, disappointment that
        something's not as bad as you'd hoped. Take
Vienna, 1900, almost religious in its incapacitation,
        how desperately it needed Freud. Wien, not unlike
wein, wine, whine. Oh, words, my darling liebchens,
        how I adore you—in cuneiform, pictographs,
xenophobic Fascist diatribes, the *Mahabharata*, Lao-Tzu,
        Crazy Kat's smacks and pows, *Das Kapital,*
yellow journalism, Yorick's skull, yabba-dabba-do.
        From Katmandu to the zebra-striped farms of
Zimbabwe, the world is singing my tune, backyard chat,
        blue-streak phat, the mockingbird's yakety-yak.

Charles Harper Webb

How I Know I'm Not
a Spiritual Master

I'd give anything to be photographed for *People*
in a muscle shirt (with muscles) on a vintage Harley
on a Grecian beach during the filming of *Captain Correlli's
Mandolin*, costarring Penelope Cruz and Christian Bale.
I'd kill to be Enrique, son of Julio Iglesias, proud

that my "way with women" "provokes whispers"
as I "squire" *American Pie* beauty Shannon Elizabeth
to my twenty-fifth birthday party at Le Colonial,
despite her being engaged to another man.
If only I could sit for hours pondering the Absolute

(not the vodka)! I have more attachments
than a dentistry machine; therefore, I suffer.
When my wife criticizes me, I can't assume
the lotus posture while cosmic resonance rolls up
from my deepest chakras, and my astral body drifts

among the stars. Staring at "Gorgeous George" Clooney
in his "impeccable" tux escorting Uma Thurman
in her "practically nonexistent Gaultier ensemble"
(lace, mirrors, and silver lamé) which she "ditched
in favor of a blue Ferretti number" to wind up

her Cannes afternoon, I think I'd die to have his life,
or for that matter, hers. I wouldn't feel that way
if I were a Bodhisattva, smoothing compassion's

aloe across the sunburned earth—if I could quip
to fellow crucifixees, "Dudes, hang loose"—

if I ever, for a moment, could live in that moment
instead of ricocheting between a past
in which I wasn't, and a future in which I'll never be
Quentin Tarantino "clowning with Juliette Lewis"
at a Hollywood Premiere, or John Travolta "mugging

with buddy Sly Stallone" outside Mann's Theatre,
or even Zadie Smith: daughter of a London ad executive
and a Jamaican model-turned-child-psychoanalyst.
This young author of *White Teeth* "bites into life
as a literary star," looking ultra-bright, tough, beautiful,

and bored. She calls "the fame game" "tiresome,"
and almost certainly returns from her photo shoot
to some Zen cell where, meditating on the letter B
in *Big Deal,* she'll close her "sultry brown eyes,"
and breathing from her diaphragm, (continue to) rise.

Mark Halliday

Acknowledgments

The author wishes to congratulate the editors of the following journals,
in which half-baked early versions of certain poems appeared:
Road Apple Review, Unmuzzled Ox, Lynx, Salt Lick,
TriQuarterly, Prairie Schooner, Ning Ning,
American Poetry Review, Skankcheese, Whang. You were lucky to get my work.

This work is not wholly self-born and autonomous and autotelic
though in some late nights the author has felt
an exalted nerve-flicking readiness for theatrical Titanism.

International corporate capitalism has assisted
in the production of this book in more ways than
the author can contemplate with equipoise.

The great Bob Dylan would be mentioned here for his
exquisite and profound encouraging
were it not for the danger of too-knowing smirks
from people who *don't know*.

The author wishes also to thank Calvin Bedient, Paul Breslin, Mary Kinzie,
Adam Kirsch, William Logan, Marjorie Perloff, Willard Spiegelman
and Helen Vendler for their beautiful kindness and unswerving loyalty
and what I can only call transcendent nobility;
if it weren't for alphabetical order I would list each one of you first!

Deepest thanks also to Dean, David, David, David, Mary,
Nancy, Bill, Brenda, Bob, Tony and Cynthia—siblings in the maddening art!—
(except insofar as any of you have expressed doubts about my work)—
let's remember that we are a *team*
even if I turn out to be Captain.

Thanks also to the members of the Purple Chopstix Poetry Circle—
I love you guys. No, really! You kept my dream alive
when I was down there in grubby obscurity with you.

Becky, Janet, Madeline: thanks. Broken eggs and omelets,
what more can I say?

And finally, Babs and Corky: your adoration means a lot,
and my debt to you is, like, way beyond words.

Chump Sense

This guy can't be the one. He makes sense. He makes
what mainstream consumerist Amerika calls "sense."
He says "I see such and I feel such." As if! He "says"—
that's the presumptuous colonizing bland blind arrogation
right there. We're not gonna read him. We're not gonna
talk about him or even admit he is "someone."
That whole "someone" category is hegemonic anyway
at least if defined his way which is so *so* naïve.
He can't boot up our buzzbombs he can't jiggle our dark hot launch pads
nor rotate the squeegees on our covertly revolutionary
postindustrial postpersonal cross-gender beanies. He can't!
He has said that we are boring. Hyeuffhoo! We?
He is boring. He is usuality in corduroys. He is capitulation
to received implanted matrices of power and without black leather.
Can he go
   "Radiant opacity liminal beyond the I/eye in with transactive
   sites of slither viscous presence modal unmaking withoutness
   imbricate within polysemic pigeons as hypomythic peasants"?
Not quite!
He wants to tell us how lonely he or his dad felt
one werry werry damp autumn night!
Oh he is that lump of such boredom of boring he's a chump
he's a status quo chump—he thinks in this late age you can just
"say things"—what a quo-chump!
He thinks he can sit with Tennyson and Wordsworth

68

when he goes to quo-chump heaven. Hyeuff!
He can't go

> "Vortex nude concentric lace-lattice predations of reified cum
> from absence signing signatory drainage of idiolective scum
> residual out of disfamiliar mappings through and from
> interiority to recommodify suffusion of eviscerating clitoral thumb
> by spiking neurons to dumptruck unslack trajectories beyond hum hum"

can he? He totally can't. He is a nontransmissive etiolated defunctive
maleist whiteist Old Dispensation torpor-tenured receiver-projector.
Let's forget his name.

Hugo Rodriguez

Primos

José Carlos says his name in English
means trusted and tireless
mender of handbags & *zapatos*.

José Gabriel reads tarot cards
& pisses on the hard pan of dirt
where he buried a doll.

Juan José shops army surplus,
camouflaged his tow-truck
during Gulf War
& carries a small caliber clip
on the tip of his tongue.

José Bernal brews an amber tea
from *calabaza* & quince seeds
that makes our mother's
wrinkles disappear.

José Ramón sells newspaper
cones of salted peanuts: clubfooted,
he reminds me of the crumb tray
on our burnt-black toaster.

José Antonio e-mails suicide notes
signed *See you soon*.

Joseíto disappeared in the eighties,
returned one *noche buena*

wearing a white gingham dress
& fishnet stockings.

Josefa makes me frijoles:
unmarried & childless,
she listens to insects & steals
aguacates from her neighbor.

José Manuel built a two-floor *rancho*
in Davie & drives a Chevy king-cab
with a confederate flag.

José María smokes home-grown
& nets ghost-red tides of shrimp
along the carved inlets & waist-high
shallows of Biscayne-Bay.

José Luis recently married
into a family of Marías.

José Enrique calls me collect
from the Texas State Penitentiary
asking for porn magazines.

José Pedro visits Vista Memorial
to sing *Guantanamera*
atop his father's grave.

José José says
I'm one of the many
they call Pepe.

Catherine Bowman

from 1000 Lines

Ten notes. Two pentatonics. The blues scale
in the key of E: the City's secret
hymn sewn into cement knot work, sky work—
ten years, what can I remember of it?
Avenues, wind, salt-glazed estuary—
frieze panels; stone work of new-born blossoms,
tabernacles and cusped arches: brickwork
robed in saffron, Wednesday evening picnics,
asiago, fume blanc in paper
cups. River talced with curatives of light:

ten years as chapters, scored and fluted, all
encrypted: the City's sky-box, soul-box—
the signs and omens: one Sunday, rookie
cops in training for suicide rescue
on the binderies of the Brooklyn Bridge:
their silhouettes, ideograms against
the river's vellum; one snowy Spring day,
two redtail hawks perched on a bare branch, one
holding a headless dove in its talon.
The end of love? Or a love offering?

Ten year hungers: a man eats raw chicken
out of the dumpster, while we eat raw fish
in the sushi bar; the lot swarming with
rats across from the gothic cathedral—
you can't figure out if you're depressed or
just unsatisfied—*and so what if my*
mother wanted cornbread stuffing?—baby

roaches in an ice cube at the diner;
reading a *New York Times* ad for silver
spoons, right next to a story on famine—

ten years: one hundred and twenty full moons,
give or take a few, underneath Amish
quilts made for us by Saloma Byler—
she would write: dear friend your quilt is ready—
(three years ago she died from breast cancer)—
wrapped in her double-wedding ring pattern,
we munched on low-fat Chubby Hubby, watched
screwball comedies: and the eight-second
TV parade replay of the police
striking a man fifty times with batons—

ten years: our bed: a desk, a couch, a horn,
a bird figurine, mortar and grinder,
a spoon for winnowing grains, a lemon
and palm branch in a bundle depicted,
a modern impression of ancient scales,
a boat without oars, where we heaved and hoed,
made mirth, shook in terror, sighed in relief,
fucked ten different ways, goose-down libation—
vowed to love God and walk in his footsteps—
ah, well . . . blade from a sickle, sickle blade—

ten red Fiestaware cups and saucers
I smashed on the kitchen floor: talk about
explosions. We fought every single day
for a year when we moved to the Village,
all stupid things really, it was clear, you
were not happy—your therapist said I
needed to get over my problems with
men, before we think about having kids—
my mother told me the day we married,
watch your temper. What temper? I asked her.

Tenebrionid: see darkling beetle,
from the Latin: one who avoids the light.
This isn't the movies, it's a marriage!

the real becomes visible not through close
attachments, but through close looking, atten-
tion, the mystic said, *is the soul's prayer.*
Remember your job interview—how I
bathed you—the rain forest trip—libations—
making love under Passover's full moon,
howler monkeys, Cieba trees, Mayan tombs—

tents packed we took a walk through the forest:
I imagined us just not going back,
we'd build a house in a tree that would last
us twenty rainy seasons, for nails we'd
use the spines of great big yellow flowers,
we would make our dollars from the green dye
in the leaves, our carpet a melody
of toucan feathers, each night we'd drain thick
resin into cups to share with our ghosts,
from cones we'd make a box spring (see below):

IOIOIOIOIOIOIOIOIO
IOIOIOIOIOIOIOIOIO
IOIOIOIOIOIOIOIOIO
IOIOIOIOIOIOIOIOIO
IOIOIOIOIOIOIOIOIO
IOIOIOIOIOIOIOIOIO
IOIOIOIOIOIOIOIOIO
IOIOIOIOIOIOIOIOIO
IOIOIOIOIOIOIOIOIO
IOIOIOIOIOIOIOIOIO

Ten summer trips back to San Antonio—
Saturday: Westside Mission Flea Market,
it's hard to see with a dust storm brewing:
the sky like a broth of childhood whippings—
objects speak, the soul just has to listen,
a woman tells us from a plywood tent
bathed in honey mesquite—the bargain's great!—
if you want cucumbers, there's a truck full,
and roosters, ten steel cages filled with—yes!—
roosters! snakes too! and one red cowboy boot—

ten bucks: a used world for sale, an antique
with just a piece of Panama missing,
a little KY will get it spinning—
you spot a nutcracker nude—oak nipples—
a vendor called the Rifleman, shoves a
pecan between her legs and gives a squeeze—
here's a ghost guitar, he says: and holds it
to the light, *needs no human touch to play*
three strums means death is calling, two a storm—
dust devils swirling: the smell of chili—

ten A.M.: the band is really cooking:
under the pavilion, a conjunto
accordion wails: *who were you thinking*
of when we were making love last night—red
wind, biker belts for babies, tripe tacos,
potent clouds everyone circle dancing—
an old rancher with a young man's body—
wasn't he just inside the rooster cage—
and the lean jeweled woman of seventy
he's dancing with?—*I think she was the snake*—

ten javelina hogs around the tent,
while I slept, you cooking a campfire
breakfast—remember that?—hiking the Lost
Gold Mine trail, ocotillo, cactus blooms,
pictographs of jaguar and prickly pear—
perfect margaritas at Ma Crosby's—
while hiking, I mimicked Charlie Chaplin
to make you laugh—we soaked in sulphur springs:
the desert moon five-by-five in the sky—
fat: as a pig raised on cherry milkshakes—

ten degrees past one hundred, ten past eight.
Stopping for breakfast in Presidio,
the heat capitol of America,
and everyone at the Presidio
Cafe is having biscuits. Everyone
is having biscuits with Presidio
gravy. *These biscuits are good. These biscuits*

are good. Better than last week. Much better
than last week. Sure is hot today. It sure
is hot. Should we get some more? Huh? Should we?

Ten gifts you gave me that I've lost: a pair
of cut glass earrings; one of two crystal
Waterford candle holders; the lilac
Belle France dress for Passover, the year we
made matzo chili rellenos; several
pearl studs; a Starbucks travel mug (my last
present); the bottoms to my rodeo
pjs; The Collected Wallace Stevens;
a portable phone, and a black silk gown—
how could you lose a phone?—you used to say—

ten years shaped like a dog flute in combo
with a Jaracho harp; wrapped in the light
just before we hit the Hoover Dam. Or
wrapped in the white handkerchief, you gave me,
soaked in our tears, as I headed out for
the Big Ten Midwest. The only contents
of my safety deposit box, besides
the fragments of sky, pieces of stars: our
wedding rings: the ten coins from the blind cashier at the White Sands' Missile Range Gift Shop—

ten years shaped into a friction drum, made
from the rosin fronds of willows that lined
Lock Lane, mountain biking past abandoned
cars and Celtic temples, me complaining
about the rough terrain. Ten years rubbed with
raspberry vodka and dilled baby corn;
scored by the rickety tap dance of wood
slats on Coney Island's Cyclone. Or scored
by the tap shoes we found in a seconds
store, the word 'burnt' chalked on each sky-blue sole—

ten years: a rosewood circle tambourine,
you got to do more than bang it to make
it play, you said, one March morning, as we

ate bagels and watched the squirrels go crazy
making love outside. While above ten milk
orange clouds: a chain-link sky fence to guard the
angels: an overground listening device—
a couple naps side by side—up north whales
arrive at their feeding ground ten tundra
swans alighting on a cranberry bog—

ten years: *Is something wrong? No, no, nothing's*
wrong. Are you sure? Sure, I'm sure nothing is
wrong. Nothing's wrong, really? Really. Okay,
but, you seem upset. No, I'm telling you
that nothing is wrong. If something was wrong
you would tell me? Wouldn't you? Was it me?
Did I do something to upset you? No,
nothing is wrong, nothing really. Are you
sure, obviously something's wrong. Really,
no, nothing's wrong. Okay, nothing is wrong.

(Ten baby mermaids on a clam shell float
at the Coney Island Mermaid Parade,
Haitian drum-band mermaids, heavy metal
mermaids, a merman sheriff in lamé,
hockey playing topless purple mermaids,
a mermaid transfigured by chemical
waste, a mermaid accordion polka
band in a Cadillac, a beautiful
blue child mermaid in a blue chariot
pulled by her merdog dalmatian, Neptune.)

Ten years now, I guess there's no turning back,
there are some things I know we'll never do
again, like the subway conductor said,
Watch out the doors are closing, the M and
the N the Q are passing: halfway
down the alphabet: I'll never sit with
you in a cheap hotel room wearing nothing
but your cologne, joint file, or check the box
'married,' or wear a string bikini: though
I won't rule out the possibility . . .

ten hotel rooms: the Locarno in Rome,
near the Spanish Steps, we eavesdropped on five
Romanian spies at breakfast, and I
shattered a vial of rose essence; the stork's
colossal nest we sat under drinking
raki from the roof of our Turkish dive,
the sun rising over the Bosphorus,
the muezzin's cry; the solarized bean
and cheese tacos we cooked on the sun porch,
overlooking Anasazi ruins;

Ten Gallon Hat Inn, switching back and forth
between porn and PBS, a magic
finger vibrating mattress, the mirror
smashed, spray painted pink, no AC, we filled
the bathtub with ice—jumped in! The antler
headboard at the Gage; the Frio River
cabin I picked for our honeymoon (you
said, it wasn't your style); Maya Club Med,
the room, an imitation Mayan tomb;
The Havana, the last time we made love—

ten years as elegy: see elegy
as love, as appropriating power
of, see elegy as meditation
on the living and the dead, as challenge,
as memory, as consolation, as
nostalgia, as temporal metaphor,
as monument to the past, as muteness,
as self-portrait, a form of evasion,
as tribute, as therapy, obsession:
ten years: elegy as oblivion—

ten years: did it happen?—was it a dream?—
summers in the country—light through tulip
trees weeping parchment of birch, wild carrots,
foxglove—bathing in the old fashioned tub—
castile soap—my eyes closed—spun poplar leaves,
caught galaxies of stars—a tremolo
of fire boats around the pond—silver

canoe—a crescent moon—did it happen?—
the smell of dying ferns—the Hickory
Bend cabin with the stone fireplace and

ten paintings of ships hanging on the wall—
the books on trees and birds and wild flowers—
I dream of a river full of black trout
running underneath the cabin—I dream
of Valerie—our cabin with ten ships—
you practicing clarinet on the sun
porch—I drink red wine, play with the dollar
Ouija board—trees are ghosts—the grilled eggplant,
the rustica sandwich, weighted down on
the counter with the blade of an old ax—

ten years was it just a dream?—was I there?—
you practicing clarinet on the porch—
me, at the typewriter—Valerie, dead—
David too—*La Sida* spray-painted orange
across Mayan ruins—you in a dream,
in me—in our lost galaxy, between
the four cardinal points of our river bed—
fire boat the yard starred with chanterelles—
Ghosts—Trout—flaulk (Faulkner?) on the Ouija board,
says we will have twins, together grow old—

ten reasons why we ended. I'm drawing
a blank. I remember more about the weather,
more about our seasons than the reasons—
winter skies like melted down silverware
from a wartime hotel in Paris, wind
razoring at 4 A.M. through the narrows
of avenues and dreams, siren circuits,
hard-edged, frozen, patterns of figure eights
left by rat tails on a perfect blanket
of snow in Fort Washington Park as we
walked to the Cloisters to hear sacred songs—S-

tenciled crescent moons, dancing lanterns in
the living room at the total eclipse—

on the radio, Nelson Mandela
is president! Decalogues of light on
Lafayette and the Bowery's masonry—
reasons why it ended? I only think
of lying on a blanket decoding
the night sky, watching meteor showers,
of you telling me stories, I would say,
darling, please, tell me that story again:

ten years of tenacity, of blind faith
in the tenets of union; more often
attending to the manifest than the
latent; more often not asking the right
questions, as our main form of maintenance;
you thought sadness just came with the tenure.
Now it's over. And I'm still listening
at the red door trying to remember
why, looking for a portent in a bowl
of ten red steaming beets for what vanished—

ten years: and I remember more about
the trees we've seen: the bewitched and twisted
cypress made elegant by salt and wind;
aspens like ghosts snared by light: fenced ginkgoes
russet branches, musky leaves outside our
window at 44 Prospect Place: why
can I suddenly taste, the exact taste
of the air rowing out to the ruins
of a stone beach house and not remember
your taste? Was it almond or cilantro?

Ten reasons why it ended: because you
heard erase when I said grace; because I
heard broiled prawns when you said, lets do it
on the lawn; because my first course was your
race horse; when you said bird feeder I heard
lurid fingers; when you said frost bite I
heard moist delight; in your past tense I found
palimpsest; when you said please, I heard pass
the peas; when I said help yourself you heard
naked elf; we didn't know how to lis-

ten, because we didn't know how to ask
the right questions; because somewhere a house
was aflame; and just at this moment a
baby is made; because we recited
a sonnet by Keats as we walked across
the Brooklyn Bridge; because of the lost shards
locked in a suitcase on a Scottish plain;
because of summer and winter: and what's
found in between; because oceans and clouds—
yes, that's why, because of oceans and clouds—

David Rivard

The Benefit

Outside, snow on all
the bronzework & Georgian museum cornices, inside
professional white folk
under glass:

> suited bipolar disorders
> with compelling hairstyles & clout,
> being served by
> "people of color"—

Salmon Caviar & White Bean Salad
Ruby Venison Ragout
Bulgar Pilaf with Green Peppercorns
Creamy Fennel Puree
Mache with Sauteed Pears

a suitable Volnay

and Maple Hazelnut Mousse—

> but over in the cortical warehouse
> of the jailer's tower, the
> county courthouse 11-stories tall

> three miles away
> in a dream one prisoner told of

> his loneliness, pointing to a hole in the snow
> there, the spot a bowlful of lentils

had been placed
sometime lately to cool.

Who knows what power really is? and force?
Which of us accepts his life is real?

Someplace in the city
elsewhere there was an ancient
copper downspout
no one noticed, on a brick rowhouse
it came down from the backside rain gutter, so no one noticed
when the seam between two sections split

and out popped a three-foot
spear of ice, sharp
with a frozen old oak leaf
impaled at its tip.

One Darkening Mood
Made Out of Three Months
Intermittently Overheard

February

A smell came over the street, lion-bright,
but sissified, somehow
it tasted of antigens
so that, for a moment, the clear sheets of shallow
rainwater trembled
pooled where they were in hardpan
down at the construction site.

Two suits stood there
talking, it was all about some
up & comer, no doubt

one of the most stunningly gifted practitioners ever
of that celebrated trade—

Real Estate Capitalization—

when the younger one
cut the other off,
setting him straight—

"You can't tell if Jack
is a poseur, or he just doesn't know what
the fuck he's doing."

The smell had a professional heft, it was depressing.

How could we be brought so low?
just two days after our greatest national holiday,

the only based solely
upon a rodent's shadow.

   March

Waiting for the once-a-month
Magic Night at the Green Street Grill

the drunk—
about to be shut down cold by the bartender—

stains on all ten of his fingers
the oils
of a well rubbed soul.

An enemy
with hobnail boots has rampaged
across his crocus.
Now it lays there,
smeared with dog shit,
way bent.

The great
improbable misery possible
of any life.

It must be opposed, sometimes

like so—

"Give me another
sin & tonic," he says,
"I'm mellow."

    April

False amnesty, as when

early Spring in the still cold mountains

the girls' choir having peed in snow & mud off-road
at sunset

they straggle back,
settling into their seats on a school bus named
Bluebird (tho as yellow as any other),

and because that one girl

while listening-in
has heard the bus driver talking to a chaperone
when he says
"Wild turkeys are slim in the belly, not fat"

so she imagines a flock, shot at

two of the birds lying down like flushed cousins,
their heads entwined & touching,
blood still warm, coagulant
bloody feathers, ejected shells

imagines it,

then begins to forget it, simply
by fiddling with her hairband—

an amnesty, a blessing,

"what a blessing is forgetting,"

no one has yet cracked the bee hives,
no one has waxed bright his handsome shoes & walked into the river,
no one catches fire by a treacherous boiler.

Elizabeth Alexander

"The female seer will burn upon this pyre."

Sylvia Plath is setting my hair
on rollers made from orange juice cans.
The hairdo is shaped like a pyre.

My locks are improbably long.
A pyramid of lemons somehow
balances on the rickety table

where we sit, in the rented kitchen
which smells of singed naps and bergamot.
Sylvia Plath is surprisingly adept

at rolling my unruly hair.
She knows to pull it tight.
                              Few words.
Her flat, American belly,

her breasts in a twin sweater set,
stack of typed poems on her desk,
envelopes stamped to go by the door,

a freshly-baked poppyseed cake,
kitchen safety matches, Black-eyed Susans
in a cobalt jelly jar. She speaks a word,

"immolate," then a single sentence
of prophesy. The hairdo done,
the nursery tidy, the floor swept clean

of burnt hair and bumblebee husks.

Kristina Martinez

Mercy

and paralysis. On the curb
the needle shoots the coccyx
numb; my tongue
finds your smell.
Capricorn oil:
patchouli and sandalwood.
The scent beds in your watchband,
your hair, my fingers even after I've washed them.
Somewhere between traffic,
the safety light
wedges in my thigh, the spokes go
and the hub is your face dodging cars.
Get it away from me. Thank you
for the towel but my eye is fine.
The blood is customary, the blood
is only the beginning.

Albert Goldbarth

Jodi

Their major god: the giant clam.
Its lockable, mysterious interior; its crennelate
and unforgiving lip. It controlled the abundance of fish.
They loved the annual ritual of lofting golden baubles
to the silt of the god's lagoon. And when
their only god became, instead, the dying man
upon the cross . . . when they were reconstructed
in the missionaries' image of "devout". . . the islands
started to provide the world's museums and tonier
gift shops with a wooden Christ whose eyes
are tiny cowrie shells, unreadable and bright.
Because a contact always leaves a seed; a germ;
see Wells, *The War of the Worlds*. American jazz
in Tokyo—and now, of course, a Japanesey jazz
that starts to change the way the riffs shake
in the States. If your lover has seen the Virgin Mary
in a spill of milk, you take a pill of that,
a button, a scratch, a breath of that, along with you,
forever, whether you want to or not. If your lover
has written a famous book. If your lover sleeps
with a steak knife under the pillow. A contact
deposits a thread. A smear of ink. Of yolk.
All afternoon I've been reading the poems
of my student, Jodi. Poems that force a focus
on the frayed wrists where a rope was tight,
on faces life has struck so hard
they may as well be road kill: these
are pieces of a world where nothing is innocent
of at least potential harm—not the lips,

not a spool of thin wire. Tonight, on the walk
I do every night to minimize the day's three meals,
I pass the garage that every night
is lit and slightly open and innocuous,
except tonight a child's backpack
hanging from the rafter casts a shadow, unerasably,
in the shape of the child who bore it all day.

Lisa Lewis

The Transformation

It had been afternoon as long as I could bear.
I folded the newspaper and laid it on the floor.
All the stories were on government appointments—
Bad news, not surprising. The accompanying photos'
Grainy smudge smeared suits and hands and faces.
I believed I knew every one of them.
You grow up with the fact of men, on the TV, on the radio,
And they seem to belong there, everywhere, like carvings
No one considers art. You can wrest them out
Of your life if you must, but if you had to take them
Back, you'd get used to it fast. They're an old habit.
If that tree in the front yard were bigger, something
About the trunk might remind you. If you spent
Enough time in that chair on the porch you might know
How they feel. I do. That unspeakable ache
In the back and loin, from hardly moving and wanting
To run, or fly. Or flee. Birds, for instance, are arrogant.
They know what they can do. I hadn't bothered to read
The gardening column in the paper I'd set aside.
It's easy to think you know enough already.
But it wasn't going to stop me from looking out the window
To late January and the leaves I didn't rake
And hose I didn't coil on the hook
And fluffed-out wren shrilling bill-wide answering
My canary. He lives in a cage on my dresser.
Every night I cover it with a folded sheet,
And he tucks his head into his feathers to sleep.
That afternoon, today, I mean, he was singing.
And I laid the newspaper down. I had to get up

And stretch my legs. I needed to get out of the house.
I'd been reading about the nation's officials,
Thinking I understood, yet it had nothing
To do with me. I'd gone a long way away
From everything, at least that's what it looked like,
Nobody with me. First I was a fatherless baby. Then
I was a little girl who didn't like to play with children.
Then I rode horses. Then overnight, everywhere, forever,
There were men. My stepfather and three stepbrothers,
Boys I did drugs with, boys I slept with. Men, truck drivers,
Factory workers, teachers, writers, religious cultists.
A student. Then nothing, not a knock or a touch. I was safe
But it took time to know it. It would take more to learn
Not to speak modestly, in euphemisms, talk to titillate
Eunuchs in some country I never heard of before,
Now racked by controversy. That was my life
All those man-years, man-hours, hard labor wishing
I could rest, stop somewhere, not see muscular backs
Twisting out of T-shirts in darkened rooms,
The same one forever, since men were forever.
That stolid fish-jawed man driving through the intersection
Just after the light's turned red is forever affixed,
Somebody's craving for some reason, or the thick-waisted
Boys hanging out around the up-hooded pickup on blocks.
They're somebody's life besides their own. I had a life
And figured out to live like I wouldn't've
Believed but I watched it happen like a slow-motion sequence
In a movie without a plot.
I needed to get out of the house.
I'd been reading the newspaper, same classifieds,
Same boring sports scores correcting same victories.
I got to my feet. No sweat. I passed across the polished
Hardwoods like something heavy trying to be light.
Nothing sank in. The way I experience gratitude
Is to open my arms and walk through walls, and today
When I tried it I stepped out of a mob, a sorely mocked
Past of seashells and pasta shells and heel marks
On tile, and I don't know how all the men
Who'd harmed me happened to be gathered on the other side
In a room hung with plaid and brocade,

Solicitous and repelled as if it were our last week to live
And we were vomiting blood. But they were, formal
As ever, always the reason I'd driven them to destruction.
I needed a good laugh. So there I was, walking
Through walls, picking my way past a tapestry of skulls,
Moving faster as a stretch of dusty pavement
Opened up ahead, closing my ears to the circular song
Of my own breath and fast-drawn hope and nobody
Blocking me by accident and no terrified
Certainty I could only get so far, so slow.
There was no longing: only reproach.
I got up off of the sofa that afternoon and walked
Through everything in my way. Just to be blunt about it.
I was that afternoon. I wouldn't live in a house
I couldn't get out of just that easy, and proud, too,
Like some poor sucker who's lost money night after night
At the poker table winning a hand or some jackass kid
Scoring a point in an argument with his mom.
I laid the newspaper on the floor and walked out
And dreamed and told everything I could
Before I had to start making it up, and that was the end
Of the sense I could make anyone understand.

William Olsen

Study of the Resurrection

"Jesus is coming; look busy"
—a bumper sticker

It is tempting to imagine the imperial surgeon's hands raising
     living gloves of blood.
It is tempting to wish to dissect the anatomist himself,
the body of Vesalius, say, beginning with the eye
which cannot otherwise imagine itself to see itself
—and pass through the origin of the superior oblique
to the articulated skeletons of Amsterdam plane trees
assuming the postures of gibbeted breadstealers,
this moment lowering its eyes below understanding.
Past the naked booths with the naked ones
go nervous truculent throngs, redlight district inanely antique,
past somebody's daughter drawing a tram ticket
tattooed with ocher and black and indigo numbers
so plainspokenly along such lips as needn't speak
that the worst for her must be unbelievable.
This resurrection past so many scant plots, so many blue movies,
chains, dildos, bongs, all without a worldly care,
so many beautiful kindnesses and so many horrible wants of kindness
and such healthy desire and such unhealthy desires—
not as when desire fantasizes and sleeves again, again,
her bones in flesh, and as pebbles in a stream her each cleft
     again shows—
though this is insipid enough—but as when some young girl
sits in a box all day zoned out peeling a Heineken label,
it is scarcely possible to understand the living pictures,

the evenings we hope one day to find even the first word for,
the Velvet Canal where the middle class was practically born,
this city of tolerance, sex slaves, kept art, and merciful death,
the one-time surreptitious Catholic Amstelkring,
the Frank family's door leading to the stairs to the mirror that
          reflected one oak
still trying to strip all winter as if we would never see enough,
the trolleys that are moving accordions opening to new streets,
new sights to love past temptation of death, past the resurrection,
a few clumps of bottommost leaves by a door thrown open to a
          strobe—
how each articulated snowflake seems to want itself again and again
          in writing,
in black and white, putting on the dark and then the light,
every church brick pulled from the fire then from the forge,
every window of every city staring through everything,
inside or outside every body alive, right there in front of us.

Richard Blanco

Hyakutake

at Everglades National Park
upon the visit of the comet Hyakutake

The last time you appeared like a dragon, tail lashing
through the sky, we hadn't named these stars yet,
they were a white dust settled on a jet of nothingness,
and we dwelt caved, without language, grunting at you,
with blood and soot, painting outlines of what we had
no words for—*deer, tree, hands*—over granite walls.
But tonight I can say words like *astronomy* and *astral*
with elegantly portioned breaths, my tongue indulges,
snacking on the texture of gouda and chilled shrimp,
neatly wrapped and packed in ice for our drive away
from the city and its mania of lights, to the lackluster
of these swamps where it is dark enough to watch you
breach the darkness again. Again we stare up at you.

But we've become quite clever I think, when I think
of how we once must have feared you, pointed
arrows trying to puncture the sky with flint or iron or
perhaps we made a god out of you, danced, or offered
fire and our flesh up to the heavens. But not tonight.
Tonight I point and focus lenses, my thumb and index
finger gingerly turning knobs against the turning
kaleidoscope of stars we've appraised and cataloged.
And more: we've traced our gem-colored planets
as easily as the jade of fireflies orbiting about us;
we've soared into space in little named metal machines,
taken the moon, photographed worlds beyond worlds:

hypnotic galaxies swirling like a perfume of light,
pulsars like heartbeats of gods we can almost hear,
and nebulas' intoxicating ferment of dust and gas.

Indeed, the wine is excellent tonight, what bouquet—
here's to our clever rage of *ologies* and *ographies:*
to the study of soils and mosses, of seashells and skulls;
of maps and fingerprints, of fathers and language;
of ears and silence, blood and water, rocks and sleep;
of moon, skin, of fruit and eyes, mountains, muscles;
to the study of hearts and wines, poisons and knowledge,
of hands and surfaces, of hair, ferns, old age, of bridges,
death and wind, of teeth and dreams, rivers and bones,
of wars and fossils, caves and cities, cells, the universe;
to the study of the alligators lurking in the sawgrass,
the raccoons behind us rummaging through trash cans,
and the scrub jays pecking at French bread crumbs
that have fallen through the darkness onto the ground
at my feet where I stand with eons asking: what do you
think of us now, Hyakutake, great stream of light?

Lydia Webster

Hiking the Middle Fork
of the Gila River

I hike down to the river
past the pack train with hound dogs,
the naked man in the hot springs, covering up.
Sign of beaver, the peach-colored walls
of the canyon, the giant living cottonwood,
the tottering cottonwood—the beaver—
the wide-lapped river, cattle-tramped and now ponded,
and the pond with a salamander sliding in as we pass.

I toe the curve of river-pushed pebbles
and the sharp stones and sand in my creek-crossing shoes,
their hard earned rips and gaps.
Now the shin-deep river, the thigh-deep river,
the tall, lime-bright grasses,
the current pulling Wolf, his V of water.
The light bounces off the river. Now
the flicker of native Gila trout.

I pass the overhang cave of the Mimbres or Anasazi,
their soot line, the rock
where I found the white fluoride arrowhead
broken in two. After eight, is it nine,
creek crossings, I look up
for the red snake drawing two hundred feet above
on the sheer wall of canyon.

Where the river divides—an island—
I rest, eat apples and carrots.

On the way back a wild horse follows us, two horses
grazing, lapping the diamond-backed river.
More emerge from the forest. Now it's sixteen
wild horses. Wolf is nervous.
They follow us quietly, then stop.

Going home, I stop at Anderson Vista,
the big divide, and see the cloud-driven light
speed across the green and gray
of granite, manzanita, juniper.
I can see the crease in the mountains
where the cliff-dwellers lived
in the high caves of the salmon-walled canyon
with their children and animals,
the long-dead animals—turned to bone
and ammonia, tree and ether, duff.
Javelina, elk, deer.
That cycle—one thousand times again.
I can see all the forks of the river—the blue snakes—
their passing is endless. Ageless shapes,
their quiet shifting—the way night pulls heat from rocks.
I can see all the way to Arizona.
I can see where we came from
and where we're going.

Tony Hoagland

Disappointment

I was feeling pretty religious
standing on the bridge in my winter coat
looking down at the gray water:
the sharp little waves dusted with snow
a chunk of ice nosed by a fish.

That's what I like about disappointment:
the way it slows you down,
when the querulous insistent chatter of desire
                              goes dead calm

and the minor roadside flowers
pronounce their quiet colors
and the red dirt of the hillside glows.

She played the flute, he played the fiddle
and the moon came up over the barn.
Then he didn't get the job,
or her father died before she told him
            that one, most-important thing—

and everything got still

It was February or October
It was July
I remember it so clear
You don't have to pursue anything ever again
It's over

You're free
You're unemployed

You just have to stand there
looking out on the water

in your trenchcoat of solitude
with your scarf of resignation
                    lifting in the wind.

Nicole Moustaki

Old Times There Are Not Forgotten

In the land of cotton, Picayune, Mississippi, I bought a Dixie
double-shot glass, Dixie's Confederate flag slicked around it
and *Dern Tootin' I'm a Rebel* brandished majestic as a Dixie
Land Band on the front, Dixie swimming by at ninety miles
per hour, and then the speeding ticket from a genuine Dixie
cop, all buzz cut and blond, so Dixie he couldn't pronounce
my last name off the license. An oyster po' boy at the Dixie
Gas Station\Tackle Shop, where JESUS IS LORD OVER DIXIE
and CIGARETTES are CHEAP, CHEAP, CHEAP, and Dixie
had me full and fortunate all the way through to Atlanta, Dixie's
glimmering marrow: I collected Dixie as my tires gathered red
earth from muddy roads and mud flats: a red Dixie pipe-lighter,
a Union Jack Alabama-shaped refrigerator magnet, Dixie dental
floss, Dixie 100% cotton T-shirt complete with crossed Winchester
seventy-threes, the favorite pea-shooter of those good ol' Dixie
red-Ford-pick-up-drivin' daddies with Dixie bellies hanging over
faded Wrangler jeans from too many Dixie-fried legs from greasy
white Dixie-chickens, one of which I smacked with my Buick rental,
bloodied feathers crossing my windshield like Dixie crucifixes
blazing on lawns of folks they'd like deported from Dixie,
back where their Dixie daddies stole them from in the first place:
look away, look away, look away, Dixieland. Driving the down-
roads of Dixie, roadside bar-b-que stands ascended on the horizon
and I sojourned at Adam's Dixie Ribs where the babyback tastes
like Old Dixie, sweet and fat and singular as a bad memory. Back
in bed at the cheap Dixie Motel, a map uncreased itself in my sleep,
an animate kudzu-green atlas of Dixie spreading itself in fingers
through all the States, museums replaced by Dixie hog plantations,
farmers squealing we-we-we all the way home to Dixie stretching

beyond the bounds of the United States, Dixie consuming Canada and Mexico in one Southern whoop, and beyond them, Dixie ate until it was sated, meaning Africa and the Americas all turned Dixie, China, Europe, India wearing the Union Jack, Dixie's glory, Yankees and Commies finally converted, Dixie leaders and Dixie children singing the Dixie anthem in Dixie English, a clear Dixie nostalgia wavering like heat through Dixie's Southern sites, the Transcendent Dixie, where people knew how to behave before the map's correction, Dixie men and ladies gathering themselves for Dixie's grand opening, a baptism for all of Dixie's new states, a shining wave drenching Dixie to its ears, a virgin shovel and a bucketful of innards for every new Dixie resident, that shining chariot swinging low, coming for to carry everyone home to Dixie where sweet old times were never more memorable: then Dixie woke me, startled and cotton-mouthed to discover a sleeping Dixie soldier at my shoulder, and I recalled a Civil War battle simulation and twenty full field cups of Dixie's finest Jack and coke, the soldier tattooed with a Dixie flag, REBEL written big on his chest (which I supposed was his name), DIXIE IN MY HEART etched on one tan arm and DIXIELAND ALWAYS inscribed on the other. I stole his musket and Dixie uniform, more gratis souvenirs as I drove North out of Dixie feeling like Scarlet O'Hara draped in those Dixie-green curtains, the scene where Scarlet realizes her Dixie is almost lost and commands all her grit to retrieve it, sweeping into the camera like a stunning Dixie storm: the sky as gray over Dixie as I'd ever seen as I crumpled my map, hail ping-ponging on my windshield, the Lord over Dixie tossing those bright stones to hasten my departure. The North would never be as warm as Dixie, never as toothsome as the soldier waking as I fled, him in hot Dixie pursuit, barefoot, bare-assed, and I can sure tell you what he wasn't whistling.

Lissette Mendez

Cento

It's afternoon, after a storm, wind—
a long bright carbolic-scented corridor.

I walk up the muggy street beginning to sun,
the air milky and spiced with the trade winds,

the word at the tip of the tongue
a radiant evanescence.

I wish I could write a poem like the 2:30 sun
nestled amid wild abrazos of climbing roses,

 a thing for use but full of elegance,
like a shooting star in slow motion

soaking up the white expanse of paper.
The sun presses westward

glistening a little as it dries,
covered with symbols, it mills everything alive and grinds

between the spirit and the flesh.
I will spend my days working to discover

which last longer, words,
contagious as shrines,

or the juba danced with lime and sifted weed.

Leaves freeze to dun
under the sun's fork and its yolk,

earth science
lies now rigid as a washboard,

the leaves are storm-rattled jester's bells.
Now night falls, its hair,

sugar, spread-veined & still
above the taxis and the homebound cars,

I'm drinking beer and listening to jazz,
the arrows of laughter

a prosodic lining, some of which will
whirl and make harmony

beyond the raging surf, beyond the bar,
in an algebra of lyricism.

What can I do to Heaven by pounding on a Typewriter
poetry of flight birthing motion,

powerful, cascading notes, amazing turns
with a metallic syncopation

to sing without rest
on a swordfishtrombone?

Once I dreamt of a poetry created by the
lines dividing sense from senselessness,

neon calligraphy
blessed with a blatant disregard for form punctuation.

Earth, can you imagine the sky removed?

Black at heart, yet azure in the eye,
all grip and flood, mighty sucking and deep-rooted grace,

the stillness trembles like a star
who reads poems.

Lines from the following poems were used in the poem "Cento":

1 Alma Luz Villanueva, "Even the Eagles Must Gather"
2 Tomas Tranströmer, "The Gallery"
3 Frank O'Hara, "The Day Lady Day Died"
4 William S. Burroughs, "Fear and the Monkey"
5 Octavio Paz, "Blanco"
6 Denise Levertov, "The Jacob's Ladder"
7 Judith Ortiz Cofer, "A Poem"
8 Lorna Dee Cervantes, "Freeway 280"
9 Kelly Cherry, "The Bride of Quietness"
10 Denise Duhamel, "Grace"
11 Cathy Song, "Beauty and Sadness"
12 Gary Soto, "Small Talk and Checkers"
13 Robert Hass, "January"
14 Robert Pinsky, "The Figured Wheel"
15 Tony Hoagland, "Lawrence"
16 Kelly Cherry, "The Raiment We Put On"
17 Rosellen Brown, "35" from Cora Fry's Pillow Book
18 Sonia Sanchez, "Haiku"
19 Rebecca Byrkit, "Zealand: A Toast"
20 Thomas Hardy, "In Tenebris"
21 C. D. Wright, "The Rio"
22 Ron Silliman, "Ketjak"
23 Ooka Makoto, "Marilyn"
24 Patricia Storace, "King Lear Bewildered"
25 Tom Andrews, "At Burt Lake"
26 Brenda Shaughnessy, "Quiet-Willow Window"
27 Mark Doty, "Chanteuse"
28 J. V. Brummels, "Fine Arts"
29 Tchicaya U Tam'si, "The Treasure"
30 Charles Bernstein, "Of Time and the Line"
31 Louis Zukofsky, "A"
32 Judith Barrington, "Villanelle VI"
33 Lawrence Ferlinghetti, "Poem #4" from Pictures of the Gone World
34 Allen Ginsberg, "Mescaline"
35 Quincy Troupe, "Embryo #2"
36 Paul Zimmer, "Diz's Face"
37 Yusef Komunyakaa, "The Whistle"
38 Victor Hernandez Cruz, "Mesa Blanca"
39 Tom Waits, "Swordfishtrombone"
40 Cecilia Vicuna, "Five Notebooks for Exit Art"
41 Sandra Cisneros, "Black Lace Bra Kind of Woman"
42 Nick Carbo, "For My Friend Who Complains He Can't Dance and Has a Severe Case of Writer's Block"
43 m loncar, "The King of Refrigerator Poems"
44 Duo Duo, "North Sea"
45 Richard Howard, "Dalliance"
46 Jack Gilbert, "Searching for Pittsburgh"
47 James Merrill, "The Changing Light at Sandover"
48 Dick Allen, "The Selfishness of the Poetry Reader"

Susan Briante

Cintas (1)

from the Nahuatl

I go about as bracelet snake.

He possesses someone's hand.
He possesses someone's frame.
He possesses someone's branches.

I cover myself with another's shroud.

He is someone's thorn.
He is someone's beard.
He is someone's shard.

I open my chest.

My heart turns white.

Cintas (2)

from the Nahuatl

I shouldered the yellow-throated grackle,
cacao of diverse colors,
cotton of diverse colors,
colors of milkweed, chokeberry, lily,
colors of a child's excrement.

I make a smudge.

He has made me his flute.
He has made me his lips.

A word is my meal.

Folded in my throat.
Folded in my entrails.

There was a sowing, there was a scattering.

Nick Carbo

Philippine Island Negro Rhymes

> "See that Monkey up the cocoanut tree,
> Ajumpin' an' a-throwin' nuts at me?
> El hombre no savoy,
> No like such play.
> All same to Americano,
> No hay dique."
>
> —from *Negro Folk Rhymes: Wise and Otherwise*
> by Thomas W. Talley (The MacMillan Company,
> New York, 1922).

Just who is that Monkey up the coconut tree?
Ajumpin' Ilocano,
Ajumpin' Bicolano,
Ajumpin' Samareno,
Ajumpin' Zamboangeno,
Just who is that Monkey up the coconut tree?

It's time to play mi amigo Americano—
Bring out your Big Stick,
Bring out your Manifest Destiny,
Bring out your Pacification Campaign,

Bring out your Benevolent Assimilation,
It's time to play mi amigo Americano—

Just who is that Monkey a-throwin' nuts at me?
Just who is that Monkey a-throwin' nuts at me?

Dean Young

Avalanche Garden

In the middle of the 45th year
of his education, Dean Young falls
in the Amphitheater while attempting
to rappel without a top rope anchor.
Poor creature, learning to fly by
scaring itself into using its gill-flaps
wrong. Below the roaring sky, roaring
earth. Are we there yet? An attractive
but untired way of obtaining data
about the excited-state Dean Young
involves study of photochemical
behavior in the gas phase but
getting to the gas phase . . . no one's
done it and reported back. He wishes
his heart would wake up: his only
physical complaint other than inability
to return phone calls which may be less
an anatomic than life-force problem
like kite-making. Is he listening
at the speaking end? Riding back
from battle with six arrows sticking out
his equipage? Is he trying to become
a rose bush again? Done in by a thumb-
tack, revived by golden fries. On July 18,
Dean Young was five or six feet off the ground
when struck by a piece of ice three feet in diameter.
Pitiful motion detectors alarmed the void.
They dressed him like a satellite,
a duck satellite. No wonder it's difficult
to know exactly what happened to Dean Young,
the preponderance of evidence

has nothing to do with the facts.
But here is his moustache.
I am tired of fighting for you.

As I Rav'd and Grew
More Fierce and Wild

I should be writing a letter of recommendation
for Roscoe Chandelier who I cannot seem to lose
since he took a class from me in 1973 when I
still thought my biggest problem was Vietnam.
I would like Randy Clavicord to be admitted
to the program at New Orleans because he needs
an arena and the program at New Orleans could
probably withstand him given their proximity
to the Mardi Gras but I feel a professional
obligation to mention Ralph Chambermaid
was utterly incoherent in class, maybe dangerous.
I spent the first half trying to get him to
participate, the last to shut up and often
he'd call Peggy and say if it weren't for her poems
he'd kill himself it'd be easy he has a gun.
Then Peggy would come to my office unable
to speak, then Rex Chowderhouse would show up
and Peggy would flee and after 3,000 miles I'd say
Goodbye I have to get my oil changed but then
he'd get angry and cry so we'd spend another hour
on his poem Death Tree. Do you really want crows
in sorrow-pants must the river be made of snot
the syntax seems off revise and let me see it
next week so he comes back in a day and says
I don't believe in revision I don't know who I am
but here's a new poem I wrote after drinking
two bottles of cinnamon schnapps and passing out
on a bench and coming to covered with snow I
dreamed I was in a canoe with Peggy sinking

because it was full of diamonds so I'm throwing
handfuls of diamonds into the lake only it's not
a lake it's a giant eyeball it's called Death Brain.
So I get down the Rimbaud and say whenever I try
to figure out who I am I try to picture my parents
dancing the night before my father goes to war
the night I'll be conceived but I can't even see
the blue of his eyes the pearl at my mother's
throat so Ron says Yeah I know what you mean
then he suddenly leaves and two years later
the phone rings. It's Richard Cornerback saying
This is Roscoe Chandelier. I can't hear, I say,
it sounds like cows being sawed in half. Yeah
he says I'm calling from my job at the slaughter
house do you think I should go to graduate school
and remember that poem Death Burger funny huh
I got a new one completely different except
it takes place on the same iceberg it's only me
and this woman I met spare-changing who turns
into a sparrow maybe a hawk it's called
Death Wagon I'll read it to you.

Facet

For weeks I've gone unbroken
but not unpunished by the quiet
of zero degrees which is worse than
the quiet of twenty when at least
you can't hear the stars wheeze.
I can't make it any clearer than that
and stay drunk. A crash-course
in the afterlife where I still walk
beside you but unable to touch your hair.
It worries me I could no longer care
or only in a detached way like a monk
for a scorpion.

David Kirby

Looking for Percy Sledge

My friend is telling me he and his buddy are driving around Atlanta
          one night in the seventies and they hear the DJ say,
"Percy Sledge is in town for just one more night, folks,
          and he's staying in room such-and-such at the so-and-so motel
and would like all of his fans to come on out and see him,"
          and they're thinking, Percy Sledge hasn't had
much radio play lately (and won't again until 1987 when
          Oliver Stone puts his only big hit on the *Platoon* soundtrack),

and while Mr. Sledge might have another type of fan in mind
          altogether, my friend and his buddy go to the motel
and knock on the door, and this chubby guy with a gap in his teeth
          and this wild hair invites them in, asks them to sit down,
offers them a soft drink, and the three of them talk
          for a while about music, sure, but also about sports and food,
and then the two men get up to go, and the guy
          shakes their hands and thanks them for stopping by,

and just then my friend stops to take a sip in the middle of his tale,
          and for no real reason I can think of,
I recall the most beautiful first sentence of any story
          ever written, Poe's "Fall of the House of Usher,"
which begins: "During the whole of a dull, dark, and soundless day
          in the autumn of the year, when the clouds hung
oppressively low in the heavens, I had been passing alone,
          on horseback, through a singularly dreary tract of country."

Lovely, huh? It's the word "heavens" that makes it so:
          everything here on earth is dull, dark, soundless,
autumnal, oppressive and low, but it's better up there—in the heavens!
          In the place where Roderick and Madeleine Usher will go

and where Poe himself will join them in a few short years.
      Oh, and the verb tenses, especially the "had been"!
For if the speaker were miserable then, is it not likely
      that he is happy now? Even if he isn't.

It is language to dance to, is it not,
      to waltz to, one might say, and slowly, soberly, like bears,
not wildly like frenzied chickens:
      Flaubert said language is a cracked kettle
on which we beat out tunes for bears to dance to,
      while all the time we long to move the stars to pity—
but we *are* bears, are we not, lumbering about
      to the harsh clang of the quotidian?

For Wittgenstein, philosophical problems
      are "language on vacation," by which he meant—
well, I'm not sure. How about this: philosophical or,
      for my purpose, poetical language, is language on vacation
from humdrum usages, from weather reports and office memos.
      Think of nouns and verbs in lounge chairs, basking under
a tropical sun as their paper-umbrellaed drinks grow watery
      yet somehow even more intoxicating.

Here's a good word: "isthmus." It would make a fine title
      for a book, though not one of mine. And "Zamboni":
now there's a fun yet a deeply responsible word,
      with its connotations of erasure, of wiping clean, of virtue.
Charles Ives loved virtue; Harold C. Schonberg said
      Charles Ives "yearned for the virtues of an older, town-meeting,
village-band, transcendentalist, Emersonian America,"
      though he expressed those yearnings "in the most advanced,

unorthodox, ear-splitting, grating music composed by anybody
      anywhere up to that time." Ives let the notes go out for a walk,
didn't he, as did musicians as different as Jim Morrison and Poulenc,
      now buried together in Père Lachaise. Oh, and the two guys,
the other two: my friend is telling me they're standing in the parking lot
      thinking, Was that really Percy Sledge, and they look back,
and suddenly the guy throws his arms out wide and sings,
      "When a mannn loves a womannnn. . . ."

Diann Blakely

from You and Me, Tina

St. Louis, 1958

Bonnie Bramlett, later Delany's other half,
Sings and dances, shimmies in a Dynel wig
And fishnet tights—the one Ikette not black.
Ike himself asked her mother's okay when that gig
Near the railroad tracks almost fell through,
Another defection. "I never wanted to be Tina"—
Then Little Ann—"In my wildest dreams, I knew
I could never be that good." But since her teens,
Sneaking across the river to the Harlem Club,
Bonnie Lynn had lapped Ike's sounds like honey,
And tonight wears the eloper's dress, stuffed
With cotton wads for her flat chest and fanny,
Skin darkened with Man-Tan. "In the worst way,
I longed to be an Ikette." Even unpaid.

"Gimme Shelter," 1970

The band looks shell-shocked in this flick,
Scenes with lawyers and in the editing room
More plentiful than concert footage. Mick's
Shot backstage, checking out assembled groupies
While Tina does her set in lavender sequins:
Sock it to me, baby, she moans and gasps.

Cut back to Lucifer himself, explaining
"Something very funny always happens—
Please allow me—when we play that number."
Long-haired, psilocybin-spacey, my friend
And I lurched to the lobby for souvenir
Posters of Jagger bopping at Altamont.
Was he blind to bikers moving in to kill?
These days I sympathize less with the devil.

Re-Watching "Tommy"

Here Ann-Margret's steel-coiffed and suburban,
Like my students' moms; though, for the wife
Of a British fighter jock, vapidly American.
Tina's needed to bring Tommy back to life.
She screeches: *this girl will put him right*
As her costume changes to spikes and steel bands—
This years before Madonna—just give her one night.
Deadheads grow fat with fuzzy good will,
Beatles' fans vegetarian, lovers of the Who
Now hope, before they die, they'll get old.
The Acid Queen swears *You won't be a boy
No more* to Tommy, drug-stupid, eyes wild.
Can music keep me *young, but not a child?*

James Harms

High Life

It was like living in a Counting Crows song
those years on Balboa Island, when every morning was a skewed
                    So long

sung vaguely to the ghost moon tilting
in the window, the pelicans sun struck and dozing

on buoys in the bay,
the phone ringing for hours, some sleeping friend at the other end
            with an antidote to day-

light drifting through his dreams, fingers dialing out of habit
or hope and Bob or Tom or Dwayne or John in the next room
            equally gone and ready to stab it,

the empty wrist exposed to drizzly morning sunlight and pinking
            beneath
a fuzz of hair, three clouds in a stoned blue sky wafting like loose
            teeth

in a slow-mo-instant replay of the end of the fight.
I never meant to leave. I never thought I was hiding from daylight.

Jim Daniels

Listening to 96 Tears by ? and the Mysterians While Looking Down on the Panther Hollow Bridge from My Third Floor Window

Snow kicks up the volume.
Okay, squint and push yourself
over the bridge, leaning into
the wind like an old friend
who's gonna hold your
drunken ass up. Late
and even the traffic whine
is stilled. Listen up,
sucker. The System
is just a steamroller
moonbeam, and The Man
is an aging seven footer
who can still block your
shots. And you're done
growing, for sure. It'd
be easy to lean over the rail
and drop into a small item
at the bottom of the page.
Cause unknown. What can I
tell you? The bridge
guarded by two gilded
cats. I sit awake and warm
high above you. You
could have an entirely different

story ready if stopped.
My wife and children
sleep softly beneath me,
but I had a blue jacket
like that once.

Little Feat

Stoned
began most of our sentences
as we gently bent over a scarred, round table
inhaling
He can't be beat   say
He can't be beat
The speakers whistled with fuzz
until the needle hit.
Until the needle hit.
Another hit. Sway
wide. Dip and hip. Air held
a quality then, liquid and plush
above dog hair and dust.
Smoke hovered like after-
sex remnants. We had our incense,
we had our stations of the cross. Oh,
we had our hymns.

Flag Day in Warren, Michigan

Warren—birthplace of Eminem,
aka Marshall Mathers, aka Slim Shady, dropout
of Lincoln High where even my Cousin Earl
made it through

where wind whips an oversized flag
around its pole like a funeral shard
I mean *shroud*
              and Eminem is arrested twice
for pointing his unloaded gun at:
a: a member of the rival group the Insane Clown Posse
b: a man outside a bar who'd been kissing his wife

on the streets, POW/MIA flags still fly
black and white beneath the r/w/ and b.
And the NO SCAB NEWSPAPERS
signs still blot the perfect lawns
five years after the newspaper strike because

we never forget, goddamn it.
My nephew knows Eminem—has his autograph,
admires him for *telling it like it is*
about gays and women

rapping lyrics I could be fired for
fired for
fired

hey perfesser, how you spell
homofobick?

      "This is stuff you might think
      but never say. He's allowed to cross
      that line; he's an entertainer—
      it's his job to cross it."

let me take you down Mound Road
past the Ford plant, past the Chrysler Plant
where my brother drives large trucks,
past the GM plant, past the newspaper printing plant
where they flew the scab papers out by helicopter
past the Ford Axle Plant where my father
spent his life, where I spent
enough time to learn Eminem's catechism.

> "MOTHER ON I-94 CHARGED
> *she killed her baby, police say*
>
> walking naked along I-94
> with the dead infant in her arms"

my father's compromise: he does not
subscribe to the paper anymore
but walks to the machine
to buy one

shards of broken glass mixed
in the playground woodchips
rip open my child's knee,
greenspace wedged between
two trailer parks on Warner
which parallels Mound.

10¢ a can recycling, highest
in the country. An old neighbor
pushes a shopping cart full.

> "It's offensive to some people—
> but not too offensive. It's right
> down the middle."

Legalized gambling in Detroit—
place your bets, throw your money
into the river. Busloads from Warren
pass Detroit to gamble in Canada
where white people rob you instead

"The Instead City"
No matter how you dig
there's no mail in that box

grief over an expired coupon
wave goodbye to your kids
disappearing in the suburbs
beyond the map's edge

Flag Day in Warren, and tree roots lift sidewalk squares
into crooked patterns like the bad teeth of the real poor
and it's somebody's fault but who can see beneath
the concrete, who can see the rich soil
where corn once grew, corn once grew?

The old farmer's house still stands. I stood
at that door with no bell and knocked
hard, pounded and giggled with school friends.
We interviewed the old couple, the farmer
pissing himself in a wheelchair, and suddenly
it wasn't so goddamn funny—we got the hell
out of there, abandoning the kind woman's sour milk,
the old man shouting *they plant houses now,*
can you believe it, as we shut the door behind us
and ran, you'd better believe it
and our oral report was a big hit

Aretha, the queen of hits,
the Queen of Soul
has not been paying her bills
at the local merchants
and the white people say
See?

number one with a bullet, bullet—
Eminem an angry punk with a big mouth
and it's all his mother's fault for ditching
him
          bullshit, who ain't been ditched
around here. It's the fucking City of the Ditched

where everybody's a farmer/slave
to their chemically nurtured squares—
don't fall on your knees, you'll be poisoned.

Hey Perfesser, you like chicks, don't you?

> "corrected a judge's pronunciation
> of her daughter's name"

My father told the neighbors he was growing
Japanese Dwarf Grass—he never
fertilized or watered. Just let his four boys
pulverize it while he scratched his pencil
into the night, rubbed its bald head,
miles away at the plant, the plant,
where nothing grew.

Eminem and Kid Rock and the Insane Clown Posse
white rappers from the Detroit *area* making it
on the national scene
                        everybody saying
they're from Detroit when they simply *ain't*

POW/
          my nephew's an unemployed high school grad
owner of an eeelectric geetar talkin bout
the community college talking bout
the CC, the CC, down by the C,
the beautiful C where the grass is somewhat
greener than at the high school

Twelve Mile High we call it
12 Mile and Schoenner, 3 miles the other side
of Mound. 4 from 8 Mile, the Border
with Detroit
          /MIA.

Flag Day in Warren,
"The Buy American City,"
and somebody tryin

sell me somethin at the door
smilin and sweatin but I ain't buyin

and the mean dog on the corner
locked in the house today lord have mercy
muffled barking. Mean dog not chasin me
chewin through the fence

      "choked on mud forced down her throat
      and her eyes had been gouged"

four women in their seventies sitting
on lawn chairs on a cement square porch
survivors of you-name-it
the last white people this close to Detroit
a Tuesday morning in June and they're
grateful it's cool enough and their children
are mostly still alive and their grandchildren
mostly out of jail and nearly employed

and life is good, life is fucking great,
right, Mom? Hey Mom, the phone's for you
Hey Mom, what's for dinner
Hey Mom, can I go out to play
Hey Mom

just kidding, just kidding—she's burning her elbows
in prayer every night for my other nephew
in some kinda home age 12 and not looking
good, brother. Got the Mark of X on him.

My son takes the stitches. The shroud billows.
No scabs. Roll the dice of blame
and put it to a beat.

      "neighbors said they couldn't believe . . .
      she seemed like a stable . . ."

If I stay here maybe Slim Shady gonna pull
an unloaded gun on me. My father offered me

his old bowling ball, but I turned it down,
I turned that sucker down. Wanted
to carry it home, sit on it, put my fingers
in the holes, throw a goddamn *strike!*

They're pretty high-tech these days, the new ones.
There's hope for us all. I live 300 miles away
but the magnet sucks me back, the famous rap
star sucks me back
                      I have spoken his every word.

Flag Day in Warren, and the plastic garbage cans
blow in the street, and out front one small boy
spits on another and my sister yells *hey don't*
do that, just don't and the kid looks up
and juices up another gobber and spits it
her way and Charles across the street
taken away by the EMS who drew straws
to see who'd have to go in and get him

(my cousin Earl's EMS now, can you
believe it—got his GED, stopped smoking
all that wacky weed, married someone
who even fucking jogs!)

Hey perfesser, you ain't a fag, are ya?

drunk on the floor in his own shit
among the lounging roaches and empty bottles
and boxes of rags and
                      my father's so happy
they're taking Charles away
he pops open a beer and watches
from the porch. Cheers!

Flag Day in Warren, and Kevin Dolan,
Slim Shady of the class of '74
mows his parents' lawn and does not
answer when I call from my car

does not know who I am
and why should he
another ghost in this ghost town

things getting blurry
call the cable
get them out here

an X ain't a star, everybody knows that

Carl Marlinga, County Prosecutor,
he's taking it to Eminem
great PR for his State Supreme Court run

Damn it, Carl, remember me,
I worked in your dad's liquor store
three years. Almost took a bullet
for the old man
                    though the gun
coulda been unloaded
mother fucker
          mother fucker
                    gimme the cash

Carl, you remember Kevin?
Kevin, Carl?
We got a variety of erasers here—
easy when the lines are so straight
but some of us just erase
forget to write anything new
satisfied with the white slate

satellite dishes at the trailer park
picking up signals
Eminem tellin em who to blame
no chocolate mess

          "'Are you able to see?'
          'No, I'm not,' she responded."

chaos, crime on city's land
      makeshift camps, drugs, prostitution
         occupy property

and I am guilty as charged
and I am one of the anointed
with the holy oils of escape
and I help my father repair
cracks in the cement once again

Hey perfesser, when you comin' back home?

and we have our share of Elvis worship
botched hold ups and multiple murders
and public urination and arson

(if you just take out the punctuation
and confuse the referents
maybe the borders will disintegrate)

      "Mom on I-94 charged
      She killed her baby, police say"

and we have our share of pregnant
teenagers and torn prom dresses
sad shrugs and accidental dismemberment

and today I dive into the dwarf grass
and swim my way through the poison

today I dive into the green carpet
shot by the words from the unloaded gun
murdered by the bullets
from the unloaded gun

      "still many unanswered questions"

and Eminem will get off free,
my mean little brother
shooting his way out of here.

David Altshuler

Portfolio: Easy Credit

The Time

Has Come

The Walrus

Said To

Talk Of

Many Things

Of Shoes

And Ships

And Ceiling

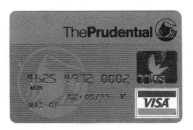

Wax Of

Cabbages And

Kings Of

Why The

Sea Is

Boiling Hot

And Whether

Pigs Have

Wings Altshuler

David Foster Wallace

Peoria (4)

Past the flannel plains and blacktop graphs and skylines of canted rust, and past the tobacco-brown river overhung with weeping trees and coins of sunlight through them on the water downriver, to the place beyond the windbreak, where untilled fields simmer shrilly in the A.M. heat: shattercane, lambsquarter, cutgrass, saw brier, nutgrass, jimsonweed, wild mint, dandelion, foxtail, spinecabbage, goldenrod, creeping charlie, butterprint, nightshade, ragweed, wild oat, vetch, butcher grass, invaginate volunteer beans, all heads nodding in a soft morning breeze like a mother's hand on your cheek. An arrow of starlings fired from the windbreak's thatch. The glitter of dew that stays where it is and steams all day. A sunflower, four more, one bowed, and horses in the distance standing rigid as toys. All nodding. Electric sounds of insects at their business. Ale-colored sunshine and pale sky and whorls of cirrus so high they cast no shadow. Insects all business all the time. Quartz and chert and schist and chondrite iron scabs in granite. Very old land. Look around you. The horizon trembling, shapeless. We are all of us brothers.

Some crows come overhead then, four, silent with intent, on the wing, corn-bound for the pasture's wire, where one horse smells at the other's behind, the lead horse's tail obligingly lifted. Your shoes' brand incised in the dew. An alfalfa breeze. Socks' burrs. Dry scratching inside a culvert. Rusted wire and canted posts more a symbol of restraint than a fence per se. **NO HUNTING.** The shush of the interstate off past the windbreak. The pasture's crows standing at angles, turning up patties to get at the worms underneath, the shapes of the worms incised in the overturned dung and baked by the sun all day until hardened, there to stay, tiny vacant lines in rows and inset curls that do not close because head never quite touches tail. Read these.

Peoria (9)
"Whispering Pines"

Under the sign erected every May above the interstate highway reading SPRING IS HERE—THINK FARM SAFETY and through the NE ingress with its own defaced name and signs discouraging solicitation and Speed Limit and universal glyph for children at play and down the blacktop's gauntlet of doublewide showpieces past the rottweiler fucking nothing in spasms at chain's end at the end and the sound of frying through the kitchenette window of the trailer at the hairpin right and then hard left along the length of a speedbump into the dense copse as yet uncleared for new singlewides and the sound of dry things snapping and stridulation of bugs in the duff of the copse and the two bottles and bright plastic packet impaled on the mulberry twig, seeing through shifting parallax of thin limbs sections then of trailers along the North park's anfractuous roads and lanes skirting the corrugate trailer where it was said the man left his family and returned sometime later with a gun and killed them all as they watched *Dragnet* and the torn abandoned 16-wide half-overgrown by the edge of the copse where boys and their girls made strange agnate forms on pallets and left bright torn packs until a mishap with a stove blew the gas lead and ruptured the trailer's south wall in a great labial tear that exposes the trailer's gutted insides to view from the edge of the copse and the plurality of eyes as the needles and stems of a long winter crunch and snap beneath a plurality of sneakers where the copse leaves off at a tangent past the end of the undeveloped cul de sac where they come now at dusk to watch the parked car heave on its springs. The windows steamed nearly opaque and that it seems to move without running, the car, squeak of struts and absorbers and a jiggle that seems to wish to be rhythmic but isn't. The birds at dusk and the smell of snapped pine and a younger one's gum. The car's shimmying motions resemble those of a car moving at high speeds along a bad road, making the Buick's aspect dreamy and freighted with menace in the gaze of the girls who squat at the copse's risen edge appearing dyadic and half tree and owlish of eye, watching for the sometime passage of a limb's pale shape past a window (once a bare foot flat against it and itself atremble), moving incrementally forward and down each night in the weeks before true spring, wordlessly daring one another to go up close to the heaving car and peer in, which the only one who ever does is no longer here.

William Olsen

A Few of the Many Numbered Birds of the State of Oaxaca

1

I sat next to a crow on a bus. We tried to talk, unsuccessfully, about the oldest tree in the world, in El Tule, then he went back to sleep. Just once he roused, to take off his straw cowboy hat and spit out the bus window, almost hitting a policeman on the shoulder.

2

Black seraphs rising from roadkill.

3

Cassiques, turistas, jays, trogans, parakeets, parrots, curacoes, beer-bottle quetzalcoatls.

4

American cardinals in cages rising from the back of a bird hawker, a twelve-feet-high mobile ziggurat.

5

All the bad news of another day doesn't stop. Nor does it stop the Mercado's stalls from opening, the knife grinder from sending sparks from the edge of the blade where no edge is. Nor does it stop him from staring through us to the black magic stall where a string of dried hummingbirds and a string of dried toucans with shipwrecked canoes for beaks are twisting, twisting like magnetic needles towards the arctic afterlife called Polaroid.

6

Turkeys are everywhere. Turkeys in wheelbarrows, turkeys tucked under the arms of Zapotec mothers, turkeys in baby prams, turkeys in shopping bags. But only this one in the butcher shop, the Corazon de Jesus, is tucked into itself, its bookmark beak buried in down, its feet twined, trying to get up before the old new world throws the mantel of starlight over its shoulder and brings down the cleaver.

7

Here in church is a sad sparrow named Christ, crimson velvet shorts, grayed flesh, stigmata, matted black tresses, lying on his plucked breast, a languishing centerfold. Erotica: behind glass. A glass case, a glass coffin: a glass barque. And another sparrow, another Christ, standing off to the side. This one holds a cane sideways, with photos of dead children safety-pinned to the hem of his crimson robe. His tresses came from a wig shop, too. He has a long face from presiding over the sorrow of worship.

8

The little yellow birds in the scrub, flying fruit, are screaming as if they chose to be screaming, perhaps that's joy.

9

The grackle at a Mary shrine has yellow eyes, a black rudder, and skintight feathered legs. Claws spurred, it hops around with its head bent toward the ground with the posture of one of the early dinosaurs, the ones with grandmotherly, effeminate forearms. Only it comports itself like a sleek businessman right out of business school.

10

The rooster that calls near dusk must have the apocalypse backwards.

11

The green jays in their men's pick-ups coming to market are smiling just like us. In the puddles of their green mantillas, they convince me that the earth has ended before. They seem older than the earth, greener than the earth, earthier. The part of them that isn't smiling is a deep rattle.

12

Next to the Corazon de Jesus is a cathedral the color of a cattle egret. By night every pigeon in the dusty streets is tucked away between the sandstone saints.

13

Then outside is dark again as the inside of this cathedral. Where wall meets ceiling, before the celestial icons begin, mirrors are facing downward—if you position yourself correctly you can see yourself, wingless but looking downward at yourself, puzzled at gravity.

14

The streetlights would be going off soon on streets that finally existed. Soon, the living lights called canaries. Soon, the green jays that seem greener than the earth. Soon, a crippled laughing gull to hop on one leg to all this good news. Soon, the thieving frigate birds to replace the fat-cat stars over the bay. And there would be more bird calls like skeleton keys in rusted locks, bird calls that scraped like a fireladder of a burning building, bird calls that presuppose birds as loneliness presupposes memory and love presupposes even more memory, bird calls like unoiled hinges of the doors that close behind us. One bird would actually cry like one of those doll babies you press to make cry. The silence had to break long before you could know it. Bird calls making that metallic sound that drops of water do when pulled off the eaves, into the uncontainable.

Lydia Webster

Tales of the West: Einar's Land

Todd and I meet the Icelandic man in Council, Idaho, at the Ace Bar.
Einar is trying to sell fifteen acres for $5,000, and he wants to guide us
backpacking for a week in the Seven Devils. Einar is wearing boots, a
leather vest, and has funky silver hair, a wide face and beard. According to Todd, when I leave for the women's room, Einar asks if we're
"attached." Todd says, "No."

We run into Einar a week later, but a lot of stuff happens in between: We drive a switchback road straight down into Hell's Canyon
to the Snake River Dam, Idaho Power, the little electric city for workers. We can't afford the boat trip on the Snake, so we drive up the
wilderness on the other side, and where an old hunter says get out and
walk to the edge of the canyon for the sunset view, we do. Then we
can't find our way back to the car and it gets dark. When we finally
find the car we drive through Joseph, Oregon and then to Enterprise
where the rooms are $12 and Todd wants cheaper. So we drive back to
Joseph where we find the rooms are $28. So we drive back to Enter-
prise and the Pioneer Guest Home where I ask if I can buy the embroidered pillowcase. No. We have a good shower, do the laundry,
fight.

The next day I fill out a Forest Service application in Lewiston and
lose my contact at a rodeo, so we drive back to Ketchum where I forgot my spares at this guy's house. On the way, we see the same hitch-
hiker we keep seeing everywhere. Kayakers flood the North Fork of the
Payette, police stop us in Riggins for speeding, and we buy a giant cu-
cumber for 15 cents.

On our way back from Ketchum, we go to a pool and Coors bar in
Featherville filled with Forest Service workers, Basque shepherds, and
crippled vets. We camp by Trinity Creek and spend the next night
drinking in the saloons of Idaho City, a gay ghost town. We eat dev-

iled ham and cream cheese sandwiches at the old Placerville Cemetery where people died in the 1910s or '70s. Lots of Lulas.

Heading back to Council we find overgrown hot springs and bathe naked. Todd takes a picture of my knees. The sky is pink and getting dark and threatening to rain, so we end up at the Ace Bar again where Einar is now offering fifteen acres for $3,500.

The next day we drive to McCall to check out Einar's real estate, and the real estate people are surprised at Einar's price. They send us back to Council to check the courthouse. The Clerk says there is no real deed to the land. He tells us Einar bought the land from Logan P. Tucker and shows us an aerial view of the land.

At the title insurance place they tell us the seller usually pays for the search. We find Einar playing poker at the Long Branch Saloon, but he ignores us. So we go to interview Cindy who works at the hospital and bought the other part of Einar's land. We notice a picture of Logan P. Tucker, Sr. in the lobby. Cindy's not there, so we drive to her trailer which is on the land she bought from Einar and next to the parcel he's selling. She's not home.

The land consists of two big hills, lots of burnt pines, and nice plateaus. We hike to the top where there are beautiful views, and a little hobo's campsite. The surrounding land is ranch and farm. We notice there is no water.

We stand up there and Todd says he's depressed at the thought of land he can't use for a long time that costs a lot of money. We fight because I can see myself on this piece of land, can see myself anywhere starting a little life and knowing at the same time it can never work. I want Todd with me but have told him over and over again he's not the one. I want to be in a small town that's already going, a town in the Idaho wilderness with rivers and mountains and trees. I can see this so clearly and I can see myself leaving it.

We drive toward New Meadows and pull into Zim's Hot Springs at dusk. It's spooky, not a soul in sight, canopies over big steaming holes in the ground. We leave. We drive into New Meadows and have burritos at Sarah's Bar. She is more depressed than we are and tells of losing her husband two years ago, remarrying, the hippies who are taking over. We drink beer, play pool, and watch Lou Grant on the big screen. Then we drive down the road to the Last Chance Campground near Goose Creek. It begins to rain again.

Robert Bly

A Group of Elephants

1

Just in front of us we see three elephants—twenty yards or so away. We see the white tusks gleaming first, just above the grasses, and then the gray mass occupying its own place, in the dimly seen trees, then the great ears flapping.

One elephant lifts his trunk-end up, stuffs grass in, moves on, stuffs more in, to the sound of crackling tree limbs. One front leg lifts, then the other. The elephant doesn't know we are here, but he slowly turns anyway and walks toward us. He looks big, confident, his whole forequarters full of character. Now he turns sideways again, now takes a low branch, turns in our direction. It all goes so slowly. "The bones in my hip joints roll slowly. Our grandfather elephants grow old so slowly. The night passes so slowly. It's no matter, dawn always comes." Perhaps eternity arrives that way, not in small parcels, but slowly, all at once.

With his ears flapping, he resembles a huge sea animal: the ears go forward and back as if we were in some enormous anemone garden, and the sweet African air were all ocean, as if this patient feeding were taking place in the slowness of water.

Now several other elephants walk from the left into the glade, two baby ones, and now a massive adult, with firm tusks . . . two more adults—all moving east. Thad says there has been some silent communication: THE IT IS NEAR—It is time to leave. And they are gone.

2

What we are left with is the grassy earth all around us in the darkening hills. We continue standing among the spiny acacias, among the we-will-survive trees and the have-you-seen-us birds reporting their views. The deepening twilight is a gift neither grievous nor joyous, taking place in the indented temple of God's skull.

We have to balance something now. We cannot carry the whole past. We have to decide which loyalties are right to keep, as when a man leaving his parents throws some of his clothes away.

Perhaps we'll have to kneel eventually, and put some of the burden down on the ground, or pass it back down the line to the cruel and bullying people we once admired. The cruel ones always laugh up their sleeves at those who labor and are heavy-laden. The more we leave, the more light-hearted we will be, so we do our balancing and walk backwards, carefully, away from the elephants.

A Rusty Tin Can

Someone has stepped on this tin can, which now has the shape of a broken cheekbone. It has developed a Franciscan color out in the desert, perhaps some monk who planted apple trees in the absent pastures, near the graveyard of his friends. The can's texture is rough and reminds one of Rommel's neck. When the fingers touch it, they inquire if it is light or heavy. It is both light and heavy like Mrs. Mongrain's novel we just found in the attic, written seventy years ago. None of the characters are real but in any case they're all dead now.

Denise Duhamel

from Mille et Un Sentiments (801–900)

after Hervé Le Tellier's *Mille pensées*

801. I feel that, as a person caught between Generation X and the Baby Boomers, I've had a very hard time growing up.
802. I feel like this must be extremely annoying to others who have had no choice but to grow up.
803. I feel like I have grown up to a point, but I'm not as grown up as my parents were at my age.
804. I feel like I am happier, maybe, than they were.
805. I feel like there's no real way to be sure.
806. I feel as though I'm not as critical of TV as I should be.
807. I feel as though most recent TV shows—except for CNN, *Once and Again*, and *Talk Soup*—bore me.
808. I feel as though I don't really know TV anymore.
809. I feel out of it when people talk about the *X-Files* or *Party of Five*.
810. I feel as though all the young actresses look the same now.
811. I feel that I can't tell the difference between the singers either. What's the difference between Christina Aguilera and Britney Spears? Backstreet Boys or *NSYNC?
812. I feel as though I can usually, although not always, relate to the people I meet, even when their feelings differ from mine.
813. I feel as though I can usually, although not always, relate to characters on TV.
814. I feel, for instance, like Mary Hartman (Louise Lasser) on *Mary Hartman, Mary Hartman*.
815. I feel like Jan Brady (Eve Plumb) on the *Brady Bunch*.
816. I feel like Samantha Stephens (Elizabeth Montgomery) on *Bewitched*.

817. I feel like a contestant who goes home with only parting gifts on *Wheel of Fortune*.

818. I feel like J. J. (Jimmy Walker) on *Good Times*.

819. I feel like Danny (Danny Bonaduce) on the *Partridge Family*.

820. I feel like a criminal with a guest spot on *Charlie's Angels*.

821. I feel like the smart girl Andrea Zuckerman (Gabrielle Carteris) on *Beverly Hills 90210* who left the show in 1995.

822. I feel like Agent 99 (Barbara Feldon) on *Get Smart*.

823. I feel like a matron in drag (Eric Idle) in a *Monty Python* skit.

824. I feel like Cissy (Cathy Garver) on *Family Affair*.

825. I feel, depending on my mood, like either Patty or Cathy Lane (both played by Patty Duke) on the *Patty Duke Show*.

826. I feel like playing Fanny Dooley, a game I still remember from *Zoom*.

827. I feel like saying, "Fanny Dooley loves apples, but she hates fruit. Fanny Dooley loves poodles, but she hates dogs. Fanny Dooley loves chess, but she hates board games". . . . until you scream, "Stop!"

828. I feel like making you try to guess: why does Fanny love apples and poodles and chess?

829. I feel like you may have already figured out that Fanny only loves things with double letters.

830. I feel nostalgic.

831. I feel ripped off because I never got to be one of the rotating child hosts of *Zoom*—the show was shot in Boston and would have been an easy commute for me from Woonsocket, RI. And who knows, maybe I would have invested the money well and have become rich by now.

832. I feel ripped off because I always wanted to be in the audience of *Bozo's Big Top*, also filmed in Boston.

833. I feel jealous when my cousin gets tickets to *Bozo* somehow.

834. I feel jealous when I see his big head smile into the camera, his hand waving wildly to everyone in the TV audience.

835. I feel ripped off when we go to the new shopping plaza in Rhode Island where Bozo is making a guest appearance in a helicopter, but when he signs his picture, he doesn't even act like the real Bozo.

836. I feel disappointed, but try not to let my mother know.

837. I feel my mother's exhaustion, waiting out in the scorching park-

ing lot of a new shopping plaza with her two kids who want, even more than to meet Bozo, to be on his TV show.

838. I feel like it must be really hard to raise kids.

839. I feel like you probably feel you should tell your children that's not the real Bozo, but then you also want them to have a good time and not be disappointed.

840. I feel like staying young and single forever, like Ann Marie (Marlo Thomas) on *That Girl*.

841. I feel that I should make my own kite with my own silhouette, just to get it out of my system.

842. I feel like taking my Denise-silhouette kite and flying it in Central Park.

843. I feel like Mary Ann (Dawn Wells) on *Gilligan's Island*.

844. I feel like someone who just won big bucks identifying the "Golden Melody" on *Name That Tune*.

845. I feel like Gloria Bunker (Sally Struthers) on *All in the Family*.

846. I feel I am much more liberal than my parents, but our differences aren't out in the open like they are on *All in the Family*.

847. I feel perplexed when I hear someone now use the word "meathead" or "dingbat."

848. I feel like I have to stop to remember what show made those phrases popular.

849. I feel like Sally Struthers, putting on weight and making pleas to fight hunger in third world children.

850. I feel good about my foster child in Columbia until my husband tells me it's a scam.

851. I feel like Sally Struthers being parodied on *South Park*, another current show I just remembered I like.

852. I feel like Aunt Bee Taylor (Frances Bavier) on the *Andy Griffith Show*.

853. I feel like Ralph Monroe (the girl carpenter played by Mary Grace Canfield) on *Green Acres*.

854. I feel like Elly May (Donna Douglas) on the *Beverly Hillbillies*.

855. I feel like wearing a rope for a belt like Elly May did.

856. I feel like acting really dumb.

857. I feel like Lou Anne Poovie (Gomer's girlfriend, played by Elizabeth MacRae) on *Gomer Pyle, U.S.M.C.*

858. I feel like Rhoda Morgenstern (Valerie Harper) on the *Mary Tyler Moore Show*.

859. I feel like Laura Petrie (Mary Tyler Moore) on the *Dick Van Dyke Show*.
860. I feel like Victoria Winters (Alexandra Moltke) on *Dark Shadows*.
861. I feel frustrated when *Dark Shadows* is preempted by Watergate coverage.
862. I feel bored by most of the testimony.
863. I feel really upset when Nixon is impeached.
864. I feel—maybe because I'm a teenager—that I'll never vote, that everyone is a crook.
865. I feel like a crook sometimes.
866. I feel like I can relate to Democrats more than I can to Republicans.
867. I feel, though, that basically it's hard to relate to politicians at all.
868. I feel that politicians don't have the glamour of TV personalities, even though they are, in essence, TV personalities.
869. I feel that politicians could be more distinguishable from one another if they dressed differently.
870. I feel that I would vote for a woman in a sari.
871. I feel that I would vote for a man in a Hawaiian shirt.
872. I feel that I would vote for anyone in an aqua bathing cap.
873. I feel that politicians sound fake when they try to be too earnest.
874. I feel like I should read the paper more closely than I do.
875. I feel like becoming a well-informed citizen.
876. I feel doomed when I'm too well-informed.
877. I feel that escapism has probably saved my life.
878. I feel that escapism has probably saved a lot of people's lives.
879. I feel that escapism has probably ruined lives too.
880. I feel like Batman.
881. I feel like Robin.
882. I feel like Catwoman.
883. I feel like Alfred Pennyworth, the butler of the Bat Cave.
884. I feel like Archie.
885. I feel like Veronica.
886. I feel like Betty.
887. I feel like Jughead.
888. I feel I am "sinking—to the very bottom—where all is made of/the same substance—then something will happen—/a transformation from inside, a sunflower bursting. . ." (Wang Ping)
889. I feel like Reggie.
890. I feel like Wilma.

891. I feel like Betty.
892. I feel like Barney.
893. I feel like Fred.
894. I feel that maybe I'm finally getting old, against my will.
895. I feel my gray hairs which are coarser than the others.
896. I feel, as a feminist, conflicted about dyeing them, but of course I do anyway.
897. I feel that I should at the very least tell you that I have more than a few gray hairs, most prominently located at the temple region.
898. I feel that when I get enough gray hair, I'll stop dyeing it.
899. I feel that I'm in that awkward stage—with only gray hairs at the frame of my face.
900. I feel gray hair can actually be pretty glamorous. It's sort of like extremely blond hair, when you think of it.

Martin Walls

Socialist Poem #5

England, 1975: "Mrs. Thatcher, milk snatcher."

We'd be three deep at the sand pit, brawling demigods building beaches for toy soldiers to die on brutally, or carving volcanoes, filling them, & sacrificing the molded blighters in murky, bubbling calderas, or we'd fight for Lego squares to make space cruisers with elaborate spangles & jibs & booms, only to smash them together & break them, while others scrambled for the strewn pieces, because we wanted to create to destroy, such was our symptom, when Mrs. Bottomley, she whose state salary bought only that cranky British Leyland *Elf*, would step from the booth at the back of the class, screened off as if a doctor's changing room, & call a name like a rubber glove snapping, sitting us down before a wall of words printed on small white cards, allotted a slot each according to its purpose, which we lifted out with snot-crusted hands & made intelligible on the tiny table: "My daddy goes to work on the train" or "Mummy cooks chips for my tea."

Then it was writing, so we sat at the long table, with a white sheet of quarter inch feint foolscap & an enormous 2B pencil, thick as daddy's carpenter pencils & green like a corporation bus; they were always blunt, & my hands were so small I couldn't hold one properly, gripping it with all my fingers like a screwdriver, when everybody else held a paintbrush, that great green bark somehow resting delicately between fore- & middle fingers, but I got nothing more than clucks & tuts from Mrs. Bottomley for my penmanship, though in my father's day, in the Catholic schoolhouse up the road, they'd have been cracking knuckles I guess, yet it was my brother who, four years before me, was sent to the dunce corner for sounding out his alphabet the way they taught him in private nursery, because long sophisticated grown up sounds (eh, bee,

146

see, dee) weren't meant for state school kids, who were handed rough, Saxon glottal stops instead: ah, buh, kuh, duh, written out on a strip of alphabetical wallpaper eye-height in front of the long desk to remind us: "a" was for "apple," not "able," "b" was for "button," not "beauty."

"S" was for "socialism." At eleven o'clock our union of little workers downed tools & lined up for the mandatory milk in squat glass bottles, a quarter the size of those left on my stoop each morning, with a board placed across the foil tops to stop bluetits getting the cream, but at school a big red crate was dropped to the floor with a sound like a glass incendiary; a genuine pleasure, once we had that red-&-white striped straw, to pierce the foil with syringe-precision & draw off the half-inch disc of soft yellow milkfat, then carve out the rest of the foil & swill it down like a quittin' time beer; in the morning we queued in demo-cratic silence by name, me tucked between Peter Szabo and Michael Wiltshire; there were always one or two bottles left over, waiting for whomever had been good enough to drink them before the afternoon story, & how we secretly longed to get the nod, to lord it over our friends, to have that ritual again, the clinks, the cream, the pierced tin, never mind the milk by then was warmed-over, frankly disgusting, clotting down our proud throats & heaving in the tummy.

Then one day there was no milk. There was little dissension. Some, I think, enjoyed the change & looked longingly at Mrs. Underwood, the assistant, as she laid out not bottles & straws but white plastic cups, filling them with a half-inch of orange concentrate & topping them up with tap water from a blue tin pitcher—squash! At school?! Who cares what harm was done when our teeth & tongues were stained sunset red & the boys could blow bright raspberries at the girls. It would be years before those dyes were banned. Though I can remember my older brother showing me the ingredients on a bottle at home. There was something funny about words that big. Words bigger than the biggest word in Mrs. Bottomley's corner booth. Words big enough to stump even Cathy Bevans' perfect pencil. Words built out of loose bits of a dictionary, then smashed together like a Lego cruiser.

James Harms

Union Station, Los Angeles (The Reagan Years)

So often the man scraped to bits by his latest try at walking through daylight trails sheet music from a pocket, as if the tune forever dribbling from his mouth has origins in the world. He stands too close to the tracks, though the porter is gentle with him, guides him behind the broad yellow line on the platform by touching softly the one elbow unexposed (the other scabbed and bruised blue, the shirtsleeve frayed and flapping in the easy wind blowing up from the tunnels).

The problem is the way sunlight slipped through holes in the evening air, the sound it makes, like a child choking on water. Union Station never closes, though three times a day it's swept two ways: a man on a rider broom motoring through the tunnels, swerving over bottles and paper napkins; the transit cops nudging to life each sleeping pile of rags and plastic sacks, shooing them through the tall tiled archways toward the parking lot, toward the alleys off Oliveras Street, the 6th Street underpass, to Chinatown or City Hall, the fenced yards beneath the Hollywood or Harbor or Santa Monica Freeways.

It hurts to climb from dreams and shave and dress, to work all day and wait for rush hour to end, to meet Tom and Bob and Jeff and Dwayne in Little Tokyo for a drink before dinner, another after. And then to Al's Bar near the tracks: the Blasters on at ten, the Plimsouls at twelve. The night ends late and everyone is tired but trying not to say so, just walking slowly in the early morning emptiness of Los Angeles, wondering if it's time to give it up and go home.

We'd known him in college: he stood in the drip of a rusted drain pipe somewhere east of Al's, took off his shirt and smiled. "Hey, guys," he said. "Long time no see, etcetera."

It's where you find it: public policy and smaller government, the trickle down effect, a gray fence recently excavated, all those years of thinking it's enough, hard work and straight dealing, all those years lifted like dust from an artifact, the wind a soft brush across the lips. And then the rain of rusty water, memory: part agent, part solvent, breaking down to bone the irretrievable, the stripped and bruised-through, the shame. "I'm taking a slow shower," he said. "Now please . . ." he turned around and spoke over one shoulder. We were looking for my car. I'd parked it somewhere near the station. "Please," he said again. "Could I have some privacy?"

Stephen Benz

Soviet Bloc Rock

1. Hooligans

For three days I shuttled around Moscow on the tourist bus, a visiting student guided en masse to the show sites of Soviet achievement. The Intourist guide's amplified voice called my attention to Worker's Monuments, new tenements, heroic factories. Young, pretty, and well-indoctrinated, Svetlana said, "Here is Economic Exposition Hall. You will like it. Please, this way." And for hours we were invited to marvel at displays of canned goods, wristwatches, tractors. Then the gift shop. Smiling, brushing blond bangs from her eyes, Svetlana pointed out a selection of postcards, grainy photos of high-rise construction, milk production, and state farm harvests in progress.

Hours later, I escaped from the hotel and walked alone into Red Square, the vastness of the place even more disorienting at night with the surreal oriental geometry of St. Basil's glowing and the watchtowers of the Kremlin brooding like chess players contemplating the endgame.

Lenin slept in the shadows.

Immured, John Reed brooded.

I crossed the square and came to the portals of the History Museum. It was there I met the gang of hooligans. That was the word Svetlana had used to describe the longhaired rabble loitering near tourist sites, hoping to barter for blue jeans or any Western trinket. Hooligan, my teacher said, was the Soviet designation for nonconformists, misguided miscreants, disaffected youth who succumbed to a fascination for anything bourgeois.

They came out of the darkness, drunk, blocking my path—but not threatening. Too wasted to pose a threat. In the Kremlin's eerie glow I saw yellow eyes, Gulag faces. Hollow, tubercular, like characters out of Dostoyevski. They asked for cigarettes, one of the few Russian words I knew. No cigarettes, I said, and then they perceived my foreignness, stepped closer, surrounded me, breathed furtive sentences beyond my abilities in the language, showed disappointment when I couldn't answer.

Americanski? they said. Yes, American.

Horrorshow, horrorshow, they said—another word I knew, the Russian for "good" sounding just like an apt description of an Alice Cooper concert.

There followed a kind of charade in which they asked me questions, I repeated a word or two I recognized to their encouragement, until finally I admitted I didn't completely understand. We had reached a standstill, no broaching the linguistic divide. They spoke amongst themselves, discussing some strategy for communicating with the stranger, then tried again, repeating slowly two tortured words that I at last came to recognize as English.

Rolling Stones? I said.

Da, da, Rullang Estonies. Horrorshow?

Yes, I said, yes, horrorshow.

Ping Flood, horrorshow?

Yes, Pink Floyd, horrorshow.

And so we proceeded through the late-night playlist of Radio Free Europe, the soundtrack of Soviet hooliganism, authenticating the hard rock tastes of American youth: Led Zeppelin, horrorshow; Jimi Hendrix, horrorshow; Cream, horrorshow; Allman Brothers, Grateful Dead, Jefferson Airplane, horrorshow, horrorshow, horrorshow.

2. Moldovan Bazaar

Twenty-five years later, a visiting professor, I'm touring a bazaar in the post-Soviet backwater of Moldova, a former republic of the USSR and now at century's end an independent state fast slipping into economic perdition. The latest numbers put Moldova behind even Albania.

A colleague leads me around the place. We have walked a mile from the university, passing along the way first a small park with a display of antiquated Soviet military remnants, and then the prison where women stand on the sidewalk and shout messages to their incarcerated men.

The bazaar is situated in a muddy lot. A cold March wind blows. My colleague—a philology professor—says, "They call this place, in Russian, *tolchock,* meaning toilet, like a slang." The fringes of the bazaar are lined with people hopeful of selling off the litters of their pets: puppies tied together with rope, kittens mewling in crates. We travel the rows, looking over scores of caged birds, perusing tarps spread in the mud for the display of scavenged auto parts and used tools. The philologist has brought me to browse the selection of Soviet mementos—military medals, Lenin pins, Young Pioneer badges.

Popular souvenirs for the diplomats and foreigners in country on aid missions. He spies something he thinks I will like, an old holster stamped with the Red Star. The vendor—himself as leathery and faded as the holster—wants five dollars. The philologist, indignant, argues him down to two.

One section of the bazaar is devoted to compact discs. Computer games, music: thousands of CDs, all pirated copies of Western copyrights, knock-offs from factories out on the Asian steppes, ultra-capitalists operating beyond capitalism's pale. The copies are faithful. Even the puritanical "Explicit Lyrics" warning label, meaningless here, has been carefully reproduced. The prices are exceptional: Five dollars a disc. Impassive, the philologist waits while I flip through the crates. I remark on the selection—every pop star, pseudo-star, and cult figure you can name available, a collector's paradise right here in this muddy lot in faraway Moldova.

I can't believe they're so cheap, I say.

A stupid comment: five dollars is one-tenth a professor's monthly wage.

Walking back to the university, the philologist says, "What was once forbidden is now merely impossible, you see."

When we pass the prison, a woman with a red scarf tied around her head is shouting up to a grated window. "Nikolai, your son was caught stealing again. What is to be done? What is to be done?"

3. Back in the USSR

In Kishinev, capital of Moldova, on a wide and nearly empty boulevard—a desolation row of crumbling high rises and deteriorating storefronts—you find the Beatles Bar, a dim place devoted to the Fab Four, where bare bulbs cast feeble light on rustic, rickety tables. Every inch of wall space is covered with posters, photos, and drawings of the group.

There's a still from *Hard Day's Night* of the lads running down a London alley.

There's another of the boys being detained by Bobbies in *Help!*
There's a shot of the foursome clowning on a putting green.
There's the pen-and-ink drawing from the cover of *Revolver*.
And the poignant downward shot of them from *Rubber Soul*.
And a cartoon still from *Yellow Submarine*.
And the backward Paul photo from *Sergeant Pepper's*.
And the rooftop performance of *Get Back*.
The Beatles with Ed Sullivan.
The Beatles with the Maharishi.
The Beatles with the Queen.

Hard not to see these familiar images as strangely transformed in these surroundings—icons bordered by words, much like the holy images in orthodox churches edged with Slavonic scripture, or like Socialist Realist posters proclaiming Cyrillic slogans.

Hard not to read the words on these walls as anything but blatantly ironic. Yesterday. Tomorrow never knows. You never give me your money. Revolution. Helter Skelter. Let it be. These are the new slogans, Lennon replacing Lenin. Imagine that.

But what's to imagine here? Just down the boulevard, there's an abandoned shopping center, built in the Soviet heyday, its collapsed stairways and eroded facades giving it the appearance of a war casualty. And throughout the city you see the skeletons of structures under construction until Moscow's largesse vanished nearly a decade ago. Long abandoned, they shed flurries of concrete in the winter wind.

Government workers receive sacks of sugar for their wages.

Only foreign aid keeps the place afloat.

Lenin's toppled statue lies buried in mud and snow.

Ask the man tending bar where the Beatles memorabilia came from and he shrugs.

Ask who owns the place and he shrugs again, turns his back. He doesn't like the line of questioning.

An officer of the U.S. Embassy explains: the only functioning businesses in the country are under control of the Russian Mafia. The Russian government can't do anything about it. Or won't. The Mafia and the government are entwined. A Russian journalist calls it Official Hooliganism.

The bartender is putting in a disc, cranking it up to drown out your questions.

You see what it is: The White Album.

You know what comes next.

Jim Murphy

Music at the Furnaces

For every Pentecostal child led by the hand, spun around in front of the stark chromatic Thunderbird and forced to watch the glowing cataract in terror *so you can see what hell looks like—*

For every spidery guitarist or hot piano strider direct from Anniston, Alabama who later failed to reach Chicago, buried under heaps of the "Coal Mountain Blues" (Sonny Scott and Walter Roland, c.1933)—

For James Withers Sloss, Daniel Pratt, and the other boutonniered barons who crossed roads in the Jones Valley, threw up the shotgun houses, and trained the produce of the old New South straight from Birmingham and Bessemer to every navy yard on earth—

this ghoulish amplification of a harp, distorted voice, these undead drums and bass now jack-knifing against the rust-flaked walls, between the stacks and long-cold furnaces, among these crumbling brick aortas plugged with coke.

Some blues gone, some to begin. A polite summer crowd in from a light rain learns just how the country comes to town—shakily, in a drunken shambles, stumbling up to speak on history. *That wasn't no plaything. When you got in the gate everything's dangerous—overhead, underhead, dangerous, you know.*

Some mighty thunderclap far off in the county now reaffirms this truth. It's my job to chuckle—my self a man whose single visible scar is the result of never learning how to properly iron a cotton shirt. I was so unschooled, I couldn't stay on the cool side of the iron.

Someone counts time, and a prehistoric chord progression binds us all together. We're on the watch for whatever satan each one knows, along with every glassy turquoise, green or yellow eye of slag that stares up from the ground.

Debra Woolley

Horse Races

Fagan killed his whole family one night when he'd had enough of talking. He wired them all to their beds as they slept and circled the house with a can of kerosene. My brother and I were crouched next to the radio, listening to the horse races, when someone flung the words through our living room window. We didn't budge. We loved those races—the king of sports, the sport of kings, horses with British aristocratic names highfaluting themselves from the dirt parks of Kingston city. Mother feared my brother would become a gambler, an Uncle-Tony-in-the-making, a slender man who preferred the dark of roadside shops where the stink of rum and cigarettes and sweat coalesced on the tins of powdered baby milk and the surface of betting slips. That's why she took us with her to see what we had to see, though the hill we climbed to get there is what I remember the most. And the river. It was calm that day, calm as the river that divided Eden. Inappropriately calm. My brother and I held hands to cross its shallow mouth and when I stepped on the first stone the minnows below shifted. We walked on. Mother with her long strides was already at the hilltop, holding her open jaw as if the weight had abruptly become too great for the muscles. There was a gathering now. Women, so many scarfed and slippered women, some who had aborted dinner, hands still coated in dish-water, onion juice and helplessness. Others who gripped their round hips in silence until the words rolled back to their tongues like rough stones—words to bridge the distance between shock and understanding. I listened to their exclamations drifting down to the clearing where I lingered in the scent of Fagan's garden, the burning hibiscus that his wife had planted because their red softened the austere column, prettying the house. My brother stared back toward our house, wanting to know what horse had won. I returned to the river, granting it one more chance to do something, wishing it wasn't a summer day but a weeping October night, blackened by torrential downpours to swell the skinny dirt streams that emptied their bodies down the giant throat of this river roaring and fuming its way to the Caribbean.

Michael Hettich

As Dusk Fell

my children and I walked along the train tracks, through a run-down neighborhood, across a black shallow river in which manatees lolled. We watched the wind breathe butterflies and tiny birds; we watched a kingfisher shoot its hatchet body at its own shadow, skim the water lightly, circle up around and try again. That night I dreamed I'd given birth to a baby whose umbilical cord looked like a hairy arm. I dreamed she dreamed of crawling back inside, and I yearned to let her go back in; I breathed myself larger to make a space for her. And that kind of breathing means something, sure, as smells mean something when we haven't slept far enough inside ourselves and walk around all day like a half-opened door. The fragrance of wild orange blows through our house all night while we sleep, intoxicating memories. I opened the back door one late night and walked out and knew what it would feel like when I had at last to disappear.

Polly Roberts

On the Perfection Underlying Life

1. Comfort

The wrist on the right side of my body is shattered into an uncountable number of pieces. Perhaps they counted but didn't know how to convey to me a definitive numeral, with their British/Portuguese-accented-English. The needles they used were far bigger than any we have here in America. The one they used on me was the size of my own body. They slit open the inside of my lower arm and strung the fragments together with two pins. I imagine the darkened surroundings of the room, the spotlight of the operating table, and it is not impossible that, like a used puzzle, they found inexplicable pieces that didn't seem to fit comfortably anywhere. I can see fragments in a stainless steel basin. What did it matter, one fragment more or less. (Note: Comfort is always an issue.)

2. Helplessness

Days go by with no stop and no start—every time I open my eyes, I am in the same position in a post-World War II hospital bed, staring at walls the colors of which seem to change: matte yellow, public school green, the same shade in blue. I blink. If I turn my eyes to the right, I see somebody reading in a chair. They say nothing to me. Some part of me appears to be strung up like a pig, but I can't tell what it is.

When it happened, I was simply reaching for the bulbous, elongated balloon from a footstool in the hotel room. It was a very nice hotel. I am perfectly aware of my upbringing. The stool tottered; my sister said, "Careful"; it happened; I fell. I said, "Ow, ow, ow, ow, ow"; there seemed no other expression for it. My sisters gave each other looks of dismay and amusement.

I remember falling on the stairs at a castle and crying. My mother was embarrassed. The arm hurt.

A different doctor, elegant and prim, takes the bandage off in his office in Lisbõa. It is like seeing the forehead of a monster. I scream; my mother has no sympathy for screaming people anywhere.

> I want particularly to talk to those who recognize all of their failures and feel inadequate and defeated, to those who feel insufficient—short of what is expected or needed. I would like somehow to explain that these feelings are the natural state of mind of the artist, that a sense of disappointment and defeat is the essential state of mind for creative work.
>
> It is hard to realize at the time of helplessness that that is the time to be awake and aware. The feeling of calamity and loss covers everything. We imagine that we are completely cut off and tremble with fear and dread. The more we are aware of perfection the more we will suffer when we are blind to it in helplessness. . . .
>
> —Agnes Martin, "On the Perfection Underlying Life"

3. Nobody Notices For Two Miles

My father (Eugene Leslie Roberts, Jr.—Little Gene, Daddy, Gene), 10 or 12, is riding in the back of an automobile somewhere outside of Pikeville, NC, with his mother (Margaret Elizabeth Roberts, nee Ham—Grandma, Margaret, Momma) and Aunt Dora in the front. Daddy sits next to his cousin, Tom. The automobile hits a rock or a curve, the back door pops open, and Daddy falls out. Tom says nothing. Nobody notices for two miles. Tom finally says carelessly to Grandma, "Oh—Gene? He fell out a while back." My father is not a complainer.

My mother (Susan Jane Roberts, nee McLamb—Mom, Susan, Sue) marries my father in February of 1957. The car says, in soap, "He smokes. She drives." Mom has always hated driving. In 1993, the last time I can recall her driving at all, she said to Daddy and me, "I'm getting out of this car, and I'll see you both in Hell." We were somewhere near Maryland.

4. Broken People

Last year, my mother slipped on a mountain during a rain in a small town near Granada. The local newspapers, glad to have tourists, wrote that "the angels [had] to come down off the mountain." My mother said to me, "I never broke anything before. I used to think it was just a nothing. Now I have sympathy for people with broken things everywhere. And broken people."

My Aunt Patsy (nee, Patsy Page McLamb—Patsy) was recently en route to meet both of my parents in Kenya, but was unable to complete the trip because she broke her wrist. Things happen in threes.

I have three sisters: Margaret Page Roberts (Maggie, Mag) is the second-oldest. At five, she had an operation on her stomach, which has left her with a scar just above her bellybutton. It looks like two bellybuttons if you're open to the idea. My mother's recollection of it is that Maggie refused to be wheeled into the operating room without her small, plastic, see-through pocketbook. She is on the gurney, clutching the pocketbook over the place where the scar will be. You can see right through to the flesh. My mother finds this very amusing.

My oldest sister, Leslie Jane Roberts (Leslie, Les, Sweetie), pops out her kneecap during a ballet class. She is 10. It still pops out from time to time. She says the pain is excruciating. Men have turned blue at the witness.

My sister Liz (Elizabeth Susan Roberts—Liz, Lizard, The Liz) takes the pool slide into a motel swimming pool. She is six; she can't swim. My father, fully clothed, jumps in to save her. "She sank like a stone," said my mother. What is remembered most about this is that my father was drenched from head to toe, even the shoes. I guess since Liz didn't die, this is the thing to emphasize.

I am born December 27 at 2: something P.M. at the Montclair General Hospital, Montclair, NJ. My mother is "(White)." My father is "(White)."

5. Affording Antagonism

February 4, 1986
Dear Ms. Roberts:

Thank you for your kind letter. I appreciated your concern, but was slightly dismayed at the tone. I realize, however, that you were misled by the newspaper article. It just proves that you can't believe everything you read in those interviews.

Also, do you really want someone else some day to draw the strip? I can't believe that you do.

Kind regards,
Charles M. Schulz

The solitary person is in great danger from the Dragon because without an outside enemy the Dragon turns on the self: In fact, self-destructiveness is the first of human weaknesses. When we know all the ways in which we can be self-destructive that will be very valuable knowledge indeed.

The terrible thing is that we are not just the Dragon but the victim even when he is destroying someone else, and our suffering is according to just how destructive he feels. So we cannot afford one moment of antagonism about anything.

—Agnes Martin, "On the Perfection Underlying Life"

6. New York

Carroll Gardens Take F Train to Carroll Street stop 22 3rd Street go out Smith St exit (Carina & brother) Be there not after by 9 pm go diagonally across the street & to the left 718 797 0106 (call if you get lost)

3118 41st Street Apt 4 R Train (towards Queens) to Steinway Street (toward Forrest Hills/Continental Ave Queens) (350 + sec + 1/2 util) 2 BR apt Alex (Between B'way & 31st Ave) leave @ 6 7 pm leave by 8 718 278-1963 1 blk away walk straight towards B'way and make right ONTO B'way—make left on 41st St. END OF BLOCK

Richard Fry (Frie Frey?) (Frye?) (40's) $500 W. 96th St. Start calling @ 10:30 am should reach him by 11 am—keep trying 864 7442 wants someone as soon as possible He smokes will have to walk his dog 111

W. 96th Apt 9 Ring both intercoms (Frey) 11:45 am Stand in the middle of the hallway

Ideas for poems for class to 1st year college students No goddamned blackberry poems!!!

Cornelius Eady
Jack Gilbert
Phillis Levin
Nicholas Christopher
Grace Schulman
Jean Valentine
(poetry workshop instructors @ 92nd St Y)

Sept 9 SATURDAY/SAM/SAB mailed submissions to 92nd St Y Chirag 7 pm Penn Station went to Angel's for dinner then "BROMIDE"? "APERITIF"? "BITTERS"?

Sept 10 SUNDAY/DIM/DOM HICKEY ON NECK Julie's show in Greenpoint 5? 6 pm?

Sept 17 SUNDAY/DIM/DOM Leslie's Brunch Dale & Helen Margaret (grad. from U of C) 11 am (actually 1 pm) 9/18/95 THOUGHT if worse comes to worse, you can always apply to the Univ of NC @ Chapel Hill for a Ph.D. in English—surely there you would have a slight chance of even being considered.

Sept 30 SATURDAY/SAM/SAB Dale called Called Dale back

Oct 2–Oct 22 getting sick getting sicker called Dale back again to make plans starting to lose voice went to MCR Realty—found Richardson St apt 7:30 pm—Joan Deal in cash on Richardson St really losing voice &:30 pm—Joan TOTALLY LOST VOICE Dale 8:30 pm Thai House Cafe GRE NEXT SATURDAY move into apt #5L 144 Richardson (718) 349 0662 went to IKEA haircut next Saturday Rose shocked myself on Leslie's lamp voice quavering (starting to drink a lot) another bleary weekend Haircut this weekend-Highlights? $135 9 am Joan Dale 2 pm? MET MET closed (went to Dale's for Pizza) Peter McManus (jukebox) very drunk. maudlin Night of the Roach Scenario Drunk Again Apt Being Bombed TONIGHT 6 pm ROBERT'S OPENING meeting Dale @ 5:15 or 5:30 @ ñ GRANDMA DIED 10 pm Henry Roth also died today (next Friday—Elton John w/Aunt Patsy) GRE EXAM 8 AM NYU Flight to NC Reception for Grandma open casket Grandma's funeral flying back to NYC Phillis Levin's class starts next Monday 6 pm Robert & I demo'd room in Richardson St apt found newspapers from 1949 (or was it '44?) The BOMB DROPS ABOUT AUNT PATSY (more drinking) (bleakness) 9 am Joan generally freaking out Dale 7:30 pm VeraCruz Jean-Pierre's parents coming to lunch @ Leslie's (w/Dale) (Grand March of the Dachshunds?) got rejection letter from Poetry Day of bitter argument w/Loc @ some pt. This day is a blank, oh—phone conversations (AIDS panic)

7. Hospitalization

DATES OF TESTING: 2/23, 2/24, 2/25/88
ADMISSION DATE: 2/12/88   AGE: 16   SEX: Female
TESTS ADMINISTERED:

Rorschach
TAT
House-Tree-Person
Kinetic Family Drawing
SFSC
MMPI
SCL-9 OR
Beck Depression Inventory

"The patient has a long history of acting out, family conflicts, and self-mutilation for which reasons she has now been hospitalized for the third time in two years . . . Sexually active at a precocious age, [she] regrets her sexual activity and appears to have difficulty comprehending sexuality and male-female relatedness. Her belief that women hold men in contempt must have its origins in the dynamics of her parents' relations with one another.

"Despite [her] outwardly hostile manner, which is often a cover for both anxiety and sadness, and despite the deadly rage she cannot always contain, she has a kind of aliveness, imagination, and hopefulness which has not yet been quenched. It is critical . . ."

8. Gravestone, Trinity Church, Broadway at Rector

"Here lies the body of Mr. William Bradford
Printer, who departed this Life May 23,
1752, aged 92 years: He was born in
Leicefterfhire, in Old England, in 1660:
and came over to America in 1682, before
the city of Philadelphia was laid out: He
was Printer to this Government for upwards
of 50 years and being quite worn out
with Old Age and labour he left this
mortal State in the lively Hopes of a
bleffed Immortality.
Reader, reflect how foon you'll quit this Stage.
You'll find but few atain to fuch an Age.
Life's full of pain. Lo here's a Place of Reft.
Prepare to meet your GOD then you are bleft.
Here alfo lies the body of Elizabeth Wife to
the faid William Bradford who departed
this Life July 8, 1731, aged 68 years."

9. Representation

ROBERT GUILLOT
Recent Sculpture
October 13–November 11, 1995
Opening Reception: Friday, October 13, 6–8 P.M.

JACK SHAINMAN GALLERY
560 Broadway, 2nd fl.
New York, NY 10012
Tel. 212.966.3866 / Fax. 212.334.8453

10. Untitled

"Polly: This segment seems to be a piece almost in itself . . . And you
do have a larger picture here—this woman/girl or whatever in comic
but genuine loneliness trying to connect with the rest of the world or
with anything or something other than on a physical basis. Do some
thinking on this and you may have a strong play coming together."

The function of art work is the stimulation of sensibilities, the renewal of memories of moments of perfection. . . . Perfection, of course, cannot be represented. The slightest indication of it is easily grasped by observers.

Agnes Martin, "On the Perfection Underlying Life"

11. Graphite and Ink On Paper

Robert Guillot. Untitled, 1995, graphite and ink on paper, 11" x 8-1/2"

"Thurs-Fri 1991 Polly—I'm on a futon in Connecticut. What are the questions? . . . I must fight my impulse to hate anybody I see here, but is it that old envy, or what. A bumper sticker on campus: 'Encourage your hopes, not your fears.' Bloody typical. These healthy minds with their achievable hopes and nurturing community. And the drug dealer making his name known at even the first party . . . I got some freaky sumac or something on my leg that day before I left, don't rip your skin off kid . . . I'm reading a Jim Thompson insane wanderings on the dirt roads of American hell and identifying maybe too strongly with the main character."

12. You Must Read Hesse's *Siddhartha*

Wednesday, April 4, 1990, The Goldsboro *News-Argus:*

> "Native Gets Vogue Pre-contract"
> *by* POLLY ROBERTS
> *News-Argus Staff Writer*
>
> . . . During one shoot, a wind machine blew an umbrella out of Caroline's hand and when she said, "Oh, mah gosh!" the whole Northern bunch of them began to laugh, "Even," Caroline said, "the ones who were like this" and she gestured with her hands to indicate someone very prim and proper.

July 10, 1991 Class Notes: (?) The anal retentive in the second row is reading USA *Today*. Not surprising. It's terrible of me to call him these rude names, but my growing frustration with his habits forces me to. If I didn't vent my frustrations that way, who knows? What horrors might I perpetrate instead?

"January 1, 1992

Dear Polly, . . . Just read two great books—*Portnoy's Complaint* by Philip Roth and Hesse's *Siddhartha,* which you must read—soothing in so many ways . . . Bliss—I'm moving into a single next semester after having a roommate with a chronic itch when he scratched (all night), his 400+ lbs would pllech a repulsive, hollow sound akin to throat clearing. New address: _____ . . . It was great to see Irv. He looked pale, older. Kept losing his keys. His two lectures were the highlights from the summer classes, verbatim . . . Savvy (10th?) wife—intelligent and beautiful. Have you been honing that ping pong talent? Any plans for abroad? It's between Italy and England for me next Spring . . . Skip *Bugsy* and (sadly) *My Own Private Idaho. Prince of Tides* is schmaltzy and never subtle, but entertaining. *Black Robe* is a good, somber movie. Polly, your letters are hilarious, Polly. I laugh out loud! Happy New Year. Love, _____"

May 11, 1992

. . . Once Evangelicalism lost its stigma as an alternative religion to the Anglican Church—once it became a "social process"—it began to create distinctive Southern institutions beyond those made of brick. Mathews writes: . . . The key word here is "conceptions." According to Keesing: . . . And as Durkheim wrote: . . . If religion is instrumental in shaping society, can Southern Evangelicalism explain the abundance of beauty pageants, double weddings, shotguns, plaid shorts, and golf in the American South?

(Note: Grade Received on Paper: A, with illegible comments)

13. Translation

Polly Roberts
Russian 201
Professor Anna Linden
December 14, 1993

<u>The Riddle of the Rosetta Stone</u>

From where do we know how people invented writing? How did we begin to read long forgotten symbols of ancient dead languages?

14. Without A Doubt

To: Manfred Ruddat
Re: Nomination for Student Speaker at Spring Convocation, 1994
Date: April 29, 1994

This is going to be a letter with a lot of italics in it; a lot of italics because the person who I am nominating leads the kind of life and is the sort of person who one can't describe without using italics; and superlatives; and glowing adjectives.

Karen Maguire must, without a doubt, represent the Class of 1994 at Spring Convocation.

15. Working

Date: Mon, 28 Nov 94 22:26:32 CST
From: Polly Anne Roberts <proberts@midway.uchicago.edu>
To: socolow@math.rutgers.edu
Subject: REply To YOur LetTeR 6/15/94
Good lord. That is all I can say. How are you (trite, trite, trite trite trite trite trite) I have not done email in so long Graduartion was truly disappointing. The speakers were just OK. I miss Jim's Journal, Paul. Send me some photocopies? How is math? I was working as a police reporter from July until October/Novemeber almost did not survive that, I hated it so much. Yes, journalism is not the answer to any of my questions. After a bad love affair, I took up smoking. Wrote some country music. Got mugged and beat up outside the apartment. Very dramatic —I was on my way to the Broadview—so i showed up covered in blood, ambulance etc. I looked unattractive for a long time. Am now working as a temp at a Japanese stock brokerage at the Mercantile exchange. Send me some e-mail and tell me how youare. I talked to Lorin recently. He said he's the "Table Tennis Man" (and I said, but you wer always the table tennis manand he said "But now I'm REALLY the MAN." You know, typical Lorin stuff. He shaved his head.) Continue to write poetry and foolishly hope that it will be meaningful to y\th e general public someday.
send
shit, ican't remember how to do this
send

16. Note, Late Night

10-19-96 1:45 A.M. The poem is wonderful—funny and sad, in a way. I saw a movie tonight that reminded me of what you said that night at dinner: that you do not know what will happen to you (that one does not know . . .) Perhaps you are right—I felt the movie mirrored my life in some ways—I had not expected it to. It was shocking. I hope that you have fun playing soccer tomorrow (today). I think that you would like me to play, but I can't. (or—I do not want to.) The weather is perfect. Thank you for responding to me—for whatever your reasons are. It has helped me immensely. I do not know why you have such kind thoughts.

17. Discipline

Going on without resistance or notions is called discipline.
Going on where hope and desire have been left behind
is discipline.
Going on in an impersonal way without personal considerations
is called *a discipline*.
Not thinking, planning, scheming is a discipline.
Not caring or striving is a discipline.
Defeated, you will rise to your feet as is said of *Dry Bones*.

—*Agnes Martin, "On the Perfection Underlying Life"*

"You were so sweet with those Valentine's for the T.A. group! We'll all miss your whacky [sic] sense of humor and your friendly personality. Love ya, _____ "

(Note: Indulgences—The fact that ice cream (consider all the possibilities—Rum Raisin, Butter Pecan, Butter Brickle, Double Chocolate, Rocky Road, high and low butterfat percentage) is not in itself bad, but, in the stomach, the bubbles, translucent but tinged with milky blue, float uncomfortably, indigestible puffs of DAIRY PRODUCT capable of producing mucus, hives, death. And yet at times I've stamped my foot because I know that I need at least a pint of ice cream to keep myself alive in a world where the sane have all the priorities. My stomach produces gurgles as if a stream through a ravine.)

18. We Just Have To Stay In Our Houses
and Watch For Boneheads

Being an artist is a very solitary business. It is not artists that get together to do this and that. Artists just go into their studios everyday and shut the door and remain there. Usually when they come out they go to a park or somewhere where they will not meet anyone. A surprising circumstance that I will try to explain.

—*Agnes Martin, "On the Perfection Underlying Life"*

From "The Unwanted," by William Finnegan.

The New Yorker, 1997; photographs by Mary Ellen Mark:

Jacob, on the other hand, decided to let his hair grow out—"to hang up my boots and braces," as he put it. When I asked him why, he looked nonplussed. "Why? Death, that's why," he said. "This is just not a win-win situation." His friends understood, he said. He would still back them up. He just wouldn't claim skin-head. Like many Sharps (and ex-Sharps), Jacob was angry at Darius. "Why did he do it? He had no right to play God, to take another man's life. And now we all have to lie low. We can't go out and get drunk, like we used to. We just have to stay in our houses and watch for boneheads."

19. Short Story—Tentative Title:
"Growing Out of Elvis Costello"

Tonight, after much crying, I lay down and read Robert Lowell. When I got up to urinate, just now, my back hip felt as if it had been snapped in two, and I was being forced to walk on the splintered shards. When I got off the toilet, the hip seemed to feel better, but now it's back to feeling cracked—and painful. I've given up writing letters to people because it is a waste of time: the people who receive the letters don't respond (you must imagine their smiling faces as they hold the unopened envelope, but that isn't enough after awhile), and much of what I write in those letters is wasted practice: poems, prose, manifestoes. The only letters worth writing anymore are the occasional ones: thank you, Mom and Daddy, for all the great gifts at Christmas; thank you, sisters, for those birthday drawings; thank you, supportive group with money, for the _____ _____ grant/fellowship/stipend;

thanks, all, for that book, this calendar, that thingamabob, this gew-gaw; thank you, young lover, for never returning my phone calls, my gestures or my letters (which I have now stopped writing)—thank you, friend, for the flowers: they were so completely unexpected. Still, the hip hurts.

In August, everything was blue, pale brown and liquid; the pool was a friend. The heat did that. I enjoyed it, unlike, seemingly, every-one I spoke to at that time: "How's this nice cool weather treatin' ya?" "How's that for humidity?" "Yessir. We're in the tropics now." (No one said, "It's a scorcher," because everyone knows that every day will be a scorcher. It's no surprise.) Bleah. Masked complaining. Com-paining. I felt no pain. I wore sensible sunscreen and even walked to and from the supermarket, with five bags of groceries. One day I went swimming at 10 A.M. and three hours later only the back of my body was scarlet. I thought it was exotic, pretty. It lingers still. (The back of my body often suffers maladies—in May, the Friday before Mother's Day, I was hit by a large blue car. Shark-like, it kept on going; luckily, I am a good tumbler. I glanced off of its wide, shark-like side, but my left back hip was achy for ages.) In August, everything was also sparsely populated. This, I realize, along with the heat, gave me false hopes about my cur-rent situation—one in which my hip is cracked and I seem to be con-stantly taking antibiotics for colds and infections. Also, I've given up letter-writing. I long for August.

By October, swimming in the pool was becoming a masochistic dare. One day it was such a masochistic dare that I shivered from somewhere in the middle of the swim (about 2:30 in the afternoon) to somewhere about 10 o'clock at night. After that, I gave up on the masochism and joined the YMCA, where parking is $1.75 after an hour. But I've become afraid of the Y pool since two incidents oc-curred, one right after the other. The first incident was the day I went swimming even though I noticed there was no lifeguard on duty. As I was leaving (going to pay my dollar seventy-five in the parking lot), the shoeshine man (Jonathan) told me the pool was closed. The peo-ple behind the desk raised their eyebrows when I informed them that I had gone for an hour's swim in the pool and whisked me to a back of-fice where I signed an "incident report" concerning the nature of the incident. There was too much chlorine in the pool—a problem with the filters. I had not noticed the sign. I was advised ("Member was ad-vised to take a strong shower") to take a "strong" shower and told ("Member's eyes did not appear red") that my eyes did not appear red.

The woman/girl filling out the report had big, loop-di-loop handwriting with lots of curlicues and flourishes. It took her a long time to write out my incident. She became embarrassed when I said that I had taken a shower, with soap—what did she mean by "strong?" "Ohhhh, it's just a question [giggle]—I know you're very clean," she whispered. Giggle, smile, giggle. Straight-face. Back to the incident report.

The second incident occurred the next day. It consisted of little more than the lifeguard herself—a robust, perhaps even brawny, 20-year-old—and my reaction to her. She was impatient, and she was clearly waiting for a phone call (there cannot be enough in your life when you're strong and twenty and female), and she was doing plié squats around the perimeter of the pool to pass the time. She made me nervous and tense; I felt her eyes on me. I felt judged. I speculated that, had I been doing laps alone (my relief was huge when I was joined by a man in the intermediate lane and an older woman in the fast lane), this young girl with a blazing and brawny future ahead of her might have been able to get off early. It was Friday, after all. I also speculated that perhaps she was filling in for someone else, was working two shifts in a row. The whole hour was a torturous wreck. I limped toward the showers, weighed myself and sighed. I haven't swam in the Y pool since. The joy is gone now. When I think about it, I only feel damp.

The limber lifeguard heralded my trip to Austin, a trip which coincided with less than a week on oral contraceptives. The oral contraceptives (Demulen—the name sounds like a prophylactic viral drug) took my iron will of resistance in the face of trial and tribulation and turned it on its side. I wasn't just taking the Pill; I was one. Austin was awful. And from that last swim until 10 P.M. that night, I did not eat. (Even though I bought plastic wrapped fried pies at a Route 10 Exxon—they were from the Yummy Candy, Co. in Tyler, TX and the packaging stated, "'Homelike.'") And when I did, it was at a sad sack crab shack at the end of an Austin tourist street—the waitress brought out a stainless steel bowl of corn and potatoes and dumped them, with little warning, onto my paper tablecloth. I forgot my friend's phone number, consequently missed him and a rendition of "Suspicious Minds" at Donn's Depot, and felt constipated, probably from the excess of chlorine the day before. It was Dante-esque, and I continue, I think, to associate the pool with the potatoes and everything else. Soon I'll overcome it.

Often, when I type, I type "also," the conjunction, as "aslo." I am thinking of naming my first son Aslo. Or writing an entire book about an Aslo. He'd have to be Hungarian, no doubt, or else the son of idiots. His sister's name would be Elde, which is what I type when I intend "else." Of course, Elde sounds Swiss. The novel would therefore have to be a tale of two families. Unless Hungary is very near Switzerland—that I don't know. But no one will ever leave you stranded because you don't know your geography. You may find yourself that way for the same reason, but it's hardly a valid excuse for abandonment, and, at any rate, I am not going to write a novel. Aslo will just have to wait until the day I give birth to him. I am avoiding, by clever machinations, my main subject.

John Dufresne

Johnny Too Bad

"You're going to run to the rock for rescue.
There will be no rock."
—The Slickers

Barbie

I'm not proud of this, but I'll tell you anyway. My dog Spot has a Barbie doll that he carries with him everywhere he goes. She used to be Malibu Barbie, but then Spot ate her splashy little lounging outfit, and now she's generic, brunette Barbie, or as my girlfriend Annick says, she's Housing Project Barbie. Spot stole the doll from Layla Fernandez-Villas who is five and lives two doors down. Layla's mom Gloria (Call me Glow!) hammered on my door, told me what had happened, said her daughter, her baby, was in her bedroom right now weeping hysterically. I told Glow to take a deep breath, offered her some iced tea. Sweet or un? She said something to me in Spanish, something about my *cabeza*. I stayed calm. I explained that while Spot was admittedly rambunctious (how could I deny the *chorizo frito* episode?), and while, yes, he was decidedly mischievous, though I preferred the word *frolicsome*, and certainly he could be naughty on occasion, and granted, he is impervious to discipline, I'll give you that, Glow, still he's an honorable dog, and he would never—

I heard the clicking of Spot's toenails on the terrazzo and turned to see Barbie dangling by her legs from Spot's jaws. She was naked to the waist, her buttery body slimed with drool, her belly punctured, her arms flung above her head. Her hair was perfect. I ordered Spot to come. He backed away, wagged his tail. I snapped my fingers. I said, Drop the doll! He shook her. Glow said she didn't want the goddam doll anymore—what good is it? I said, Please, let's not make this any harder than it already is. Spot dropped Barbie on her head, dared me to reach for her. He snorted. I said, My goodness, Glow, is that the Greenberg's cat on our coach? Spot looked at me, at recumbent Barbie, back at me. He growled. When I reached for Barbie, Spot snatched her up and bounded toward the kitchen. He stopped when I refused to chase him. He woofed. Had I forgotten the rules to Keep Away? Spot hunkered down on his forelegs, Barbie between his paws, his butt in the air. He lifted his brow. Glow told me her husband Omar would not be happy about this. Omar sells discount cosmetics and knock-off perfumes out of his silver Ford Aerostar. He claims to be the man responsible for this new look where women paint their lips a conventional red and then outline them with a violet or brown. So we know he's a dangerous man. Naturally, I bought Layla a new doll—Los Alamos Barbie. She wears a spiffy, starched—and discretely revealing—lab coat, high-heeled hiking boots, and she glows in the dark.

Bigfoot Jr.

Yesterday afternoon, Spot and I walked to Publix, our supermarket. Usually, I'll buy Spot a scoop of butter pecan at Ice Cream Cohen's next door, but today he wouldn't release his beloved Barbie, so I tied his leash to the bike rack and went inside. The place was mobbed. I stood in the express checkout lane with a twenty-pound sack of dog food. There was some confusion at the register. The customer, a great-bellied fellow in a white T-shirt and black Speedo spoke only French, the cashier only Spanish. Apparently the trilingual manager was being summoned. I put down the sack and plucked a copy of the *Weekly World News* off the rack. A woman with a hirsute toddler on her lap posed for a rather artless photo. The headline over the picture read *I Had Bigfoot's Son!* I wasn't sure we needed the exclamation point. Krystal Drinkwater had confessed to the astonishing copulation, but did not reveal the how or the why, did not mention where Dad was at these days, whether they kept in touch, shared custody and support. I wondered, too, if Krystal had simply used Bigfoot for reproductive purposes or had she been in love with the big palooka all along. And what do her neighbors think? (I imagined a trailer court at the edge of the woods, gravel yards littered with rusted hibachis, baby strollers, automobile tires, and Big Wheels. In the window of a yellow and white Skyline, an aluminum Christmas tree.) And is the child, Kirk, being ridiculed by his playmates at pre-school, pitied by the teachers? Is breeding outside the species something that Bigfeet regularly engage in or was Krystal's inamorato a sexual pioneer? I wanted to learn about the ecstasy, the trepidation, the dream. I wanted to be in that delivery room. And, of course, I wondered what had made Krystal so—desperate, was it?—so reckless that she would make this preposterous claim to her family, her friends, the world. Because, really, there is no Bigfoot, is there?

And then I heard folks behind me in line talking about the approaching hurricane and how Publix was already out of bottled water. I turned. Hurricane? I said. *Fritzy*, the Asian woman told me. I saw my incredulous face in her sunglasses. Hurricane Fritzy? I said. Was she joking? She wore a coral-colored, low-cut T-shirt with *Hottie* in blue letters embroidered across her breasts. She wasn't joking. How had I been so preoccupied that I'd missed the news of an approaching hurricane? I excused myself and went in search of batteries. Once again, I'd waited too long to order storm shutters.

Victim Soul

I made grits and cornbread, sat in front of the TV. The folks at the Weather Channel said it was still too early to determine the storm's landfall, but we should all stay alert and tuned in. You could see how sober and calm the meteorologists were trying to be, and how really jaunty, cheery, and hopeful they felt. No doubt, Jim Cantori was home packing his Gore-Tex windbreaker and his personal anemometer. I knew that Channel 7 (I, *Witless News*, Annick calls it) wouldn't think it too early to call for a direct hit on South Florida. I knew they'd already be reveling in the potential devastation. I switched channels, but the local news was over. The *Jeopardy* theme music played, and Spot came zooming into the room, dropped perforated Barbie, and howled. I put the TV on mute. Spot looked at me and whined. How many times does he have to tell me he hates that song? He collapsed on the floor, his muzzle against Barbie's back. I apologized. When I saw Alex

Trebeck, I put the sound on. Defending champion Betsy wanted *Geography* for $200, Alex. Alex said, It's the largest fresh water lake in the world. Betsy buzzed in. She said, What is Lake Superior? And Alex said she was correct, but she was not. Am I going to have to dash off another letter to these people? The truth is (or the fact is) that Lake Baikal in Siberia contains 20% of the world's fresh water, more than all of the supposedly Great Lakes combined. I hate misinformation.

I surfed through the channels and found an *Unsolved Mysteries* segment about a miraculous girl from Worcester, Mass., and naturally I watched because Worcester's where I grew up (in a manner of speaking). Turns out that the girl, Little Rose, drowned in her family pool ten years ago, but did not die. Not quite. She's in what the doctors call a state of akinetic mutism. She seems to be awake—her eyes are opened and mobile, but she is fixed and unresponsive. People call her a victim soul, say that she's crucified on her bed, that she takes on the suffering of others. She's developed the stigmata. Oil drips from the walls of her room, oozes from the holy pictures at her bedside. A statue of the Virgin on Rose's dresser weeps. The oil and the tears are collected on cotton balls, packed in Ziploc bags, and given to visitors who use them to swab their tumors, their ulcerated skin, their arthritic joints, and so on. Little Rose's mom says that her daughter was visited by a woman with ovarian cancer, and the woman was healed. When Rose manifested symptoms of the cancer, x-rays of her ovaries were taken and showed not a tumor at all, but an angel.

During the commercial, Spot the Vigilant heard me shift in my chair, or he sensed my larcenous intentions, and he bolted awake, took Barbie to his sheepskin-lined bed across the room—a very expensive bed that he's never used except for storage—and dropped Barbie inside next to his squeaky tarantula, his plush duck, his soccer ball, and his wooden shoe. Then he lay in front of the bed and stared at me. I said, She's not good enough for you, Spot. He blinked and yawned.

The Little Rose story resumed with a shot of a football stadium where a Mass was to be celebrated in her honor on this the anniversary of her drowning. Paramedics wheeled her into the end zone on a gurney. She wore a white gown and a gold tiara. Her abundant black hair tumbled off the mattress and trailed to the ground. I was afraid it would tangle in the spokes. People in the stands wept and prayed. They raised their arms to the Lord, shut their eyes, swayed their bodies.

When I was a boy I worked at this very stadium selling soda at Holy Cross games (only we called soda *tonic*, so I sold tonic, and we called a water fountain a *bubbler*, and pronounced it *bubba-la*; we called lunch *dinner*; dinner *supper*; sprinkles *jimmies*; a submarine sandwich a *grinder*; a hard roll a *bulkie*; a porch a *piazza*; a cellar a *basement*; a rubber band an *elastic*; and a milkshake a *frappe*. We called a luncheonette a *spa*). And then I saw myself at ten, no gloves, maroon woolen jacket, holes in my P. F. Flyers, torn dungarees, nose dripping, Navy watch cap pulled to my eyes and over my ears, lugging a tray of drinks up the stairs in Section 14 where I knew my old man and his buddies would need cups of ginger ale for their flasks of Canadian Mist. I could smell November in the air, and I knew when the game ended I'd have two dollars, and I could stop on the way home at Tony's Spa for an English muffin and a hot chocolate, and if the schoolyard lights were still on, Bobby Farrell and I would shoot some hoops. I heard a cheer, and I looked up to see if Tommy Hennessey had scored a touchdown, and I saw Little Rose being carried to the altar at the fifty yardline. I wanted to be cured of my aging. I said, Little Rose, take away my years. I waited. I switched off the TV. This was one miracle she could not perform. And apparently there was another: she could not heal herself. Which made me think. What would all of these people do if she were no longer the victim soul, just another fifteen-year-old girl in love with pop singers and sassing her mother? And what about Mom? Does she want her little girl back or does she want her little saint?

What I know and what most viewers of *Unsolved Mysteries* do not, is that Worcester is mad for the miraculous. When I was at St. Stephen's grammar school, Dicky Murray's sister Mary and her friend Patty Shea were praying at the side altar in our empty church when they saw the statue of the Blessed Mother move. Patty hyperventilated and passed out. Mary Murray wept and pledged her life then and there to Jesus. She would become a nun. When word of the miracle got out, the church was mobbed every day with pilgrims come to give praise, come to witness the dynamic evidence of God's love and compassion. And many were not disappointed. The plaster Virgin might wiggle a finger one day, cast a glance the next, flare a nostril, flex a toe. Her movement was subtle, not grandiose, that being her way.

Dicky told me that at night when he was in bed he could hear his sister through the walls speaking with Jesus. She wrote down their conversations in her diary. Dicky knew where she hid the key. Mary claimed that she could taste the love of the Sacred Heart, could smell sin on people's clothing. Jesus called her His Maple Sugar Valentine. Mary told the nuns at school that Jesus had asked her to suffer for their sins. This did not go over well. Eventually, Mary was pressured by the Monsignor to recant, to admit that fasting for communion had left her and Patty dizzy and befuddled, that perhaps the flickering lights of votive candles on the altar, the dancing shadows, had tricked them into thinking the statue had moved.

Not long after the Ecstacy of Mary Murray, a Father Leo D'Onofrio was assigned to St. John's parish down the hill, and he set about healing the infirm. His hands, it seemed, made whole. Busloads of crippled and otherwise ailing supplicants arrived from around the country on the first Sunday of every month. Father D'Onofrio made the lame to walk, the deaf to hear, the dumb to speak, the blind to see. He shrunk tumors, cleared arteries, purified blood. People abandoned crutches, prostheses, and wheelchairs in the aisles of the church. We took my uncle Armand for the cure. Uncle Armand got shell-shocked in World War II. When Father D'Onofrio laid his hands on Uncle Armand's head, my uncle spit in his face and never did regain a healthy mind.

I wonder what it is that makes people in Worcester so hungry for preternatural religious experience or what makes the city so hospitable to the wondrous. The TV beeped twice and a weather alert scrolled across the bottom of the screen. Hurricane Fritzy was now a strong Category 3 storm and was located about 270 miles east of the Lesser Antilles. Fritzy was heading due west at 31 miles per hour. Less than two days away, looked like.

I heard Spot snore, wheeze, snuffle. I turned off the TV. His forelegs twitched. Probably dreaming about chasing a stretch limo up Sheridan Street. I stood. He opened an eye, looked my way. Don't even think about it, Johnny.

The Bathtub

Spot is so terrified by thunderstorms that I tell myself we ought to move to the desert, and maybe we will some day. (And then I think: dry and flaky skin; nose bleeds; flat, flyaway hair.) As soon as Spot hears the first grumble of thunder he starts panting, whining, pacing the house. I take a bottle of cognac, a plastic cup, and a pile of magazines to the bathroom. As the storm intensifies, Spot starts digging at the tile or the rug with his front paws, trying to furiously scoop out a protective bunker. I figured out that the safest place for us in a storm was the bathtub where Spot could dig all night without hurting himself or our house. I sit at the faucet end of the tub and drink and hug Spot when he tires and takes a fretful break on my lap. I pat him. I sing lullabies. I read him stories from *DoubleTake*. I tell him, It's okay; Daddy's here. So you see why I was worried about a hurricane. I wasn't sure I was up for thirty-six hours in the tub.

One Saturday morning last July I woke up, and Annick was staring at me. I said, What? She said, Are we too old to be spontaneous? I said we weren't. She said, Let's do something unexpected. Usually when we're together on Saturday, we sit on the couch and read our books until afternoon when we plan a menu, shop, cook, eat. I said, Like what? We drove to Key West. We left Spot in the garage with food, water, leather bones, and an open door to the backyard so he could do his business. Spot wasn't allowed in the house alone because he'd eaten most of a Mission end table I'd bought at Restoration Hardware. Annick and I planned to have a late lunch at Blue Heaven, listen to junkanoo music over a couple of drinks. On the drive home, we'd stop to see the key deer. Be back before dark. We hadn't counted on the weather. We ran into a line of violent thunderstorms at Mile Marker 56, and we took a motel room on Grassy Key.

In the morning I dropped Annick off at her house and went home to rescue Spot. You could tell from the downed branches and the flooded streets that the storm had hit hard. I opened the kitchen door, and Spot charged me. He was so deliriously happy to see me that he zoomed across the living room, ran over and across the couch, the comfy chair, the coffee table. He made that circle three times and then he was back licking my face. Spot had chewed and dug his way from the garage, through the drywall and the plywood, and had come out in the cabinet under the sink.

What My Sweetheart Annick and I Are Not Doing Tonight

We're not in her kitchen preparing spaghetti puttanesca, sipping martinis, making naughty jokes about noodles and sauce. And we're not sitting on the deck of the S. S. *Euphoria* sailing to the Bahamas, holding hands, staring up at Cassiopeia, chatting about our aspirations. We're not at the movies, partly because I refuse to go anymore. I find them all dishonest, disheartening, and disappointing. Body parts and body counts. So Annick goes alone or she goes with her friend Ellen. She thinks I'm ridiculous about this, thinks if I love her I ought to be able to sit for ninety minutes by her side. But we'd only end up arguing. I'm insufferable, and I know it. It's all because I loved movies when they told stories about decent people in enormous trouble, when acting was a special effect.

When we first dated Annick told me she liked *Forrest Gump*, and I felt the life-force drain from my body. I thought, If she tells me she's a Republican I'll scream, and then I'll take my leave. When I'd mention Truffaut, she'd roll her eyes. I'd say Cassavetes or Spielberg: principle or spectacle; sentiment or sentimentality. She'd say, Cassavetes?

We're not at the movies and we're not in my bed, not in her bed, not in bed at the Riverside Hotel in Fort Lauderdale, which is what I had planned for this, our fifth anniversary as a dating couple. Dinner at the Himmarshee Grille, cruise up the New River on a water taxi, nightcap at Mark's on Las Olas. These days Annick considers herself my ex-sweetheart.

Screening

I left Spot with Barbie, went to the kitchen, and telephoned Annick. I got her machine. *Hello, you've reached Annick. Today's words are* cosset, oast, *and* judder. *Leave your name, your number, and your word for today, and I'll get back to you as soon as I can. Maybe.*

I said, Annick, it's me. Come on, pick up. I know you're there. Annick? One, two, three. Okay then. Call me. My word is *vaticination*. Bye. No sooner had I spoken my word than I wanted to take it back. And that's the terrible thing about speech—once it's articulated you can't revise. I hung up. A crumby Latinate word that will never enlarge anyone's world. A pretentious synonym for *prediction*. If I had thought a moment longer I could have said *rick* or *larrikin* or something interesting. With speech there's no time to see what you say until it's too late.

Ennis

Back in college, my friend Ennis Murphy fell in love with a girl from the Midwest. He married her in 1972 and divorced her in 1974. A year later he married again (both wives had the same first name and the same blonde hair) and had two kids, one of whom, the boy, got into some criminal trouble when he was fourteen. So Ennis and his wife search around for a proper boarding school for their son. Get him away from the crowd he's running with was their thinking. Ennis's wife's friend, a visual artist, suggested a school in Mitchell, South Dakota, that has a terrific reputation for turning wayward boys around. Saved her nephew Peter's life. Was into sniffing spray paint and now he's a clinical psychologist. This was in 1994, and Ennis could not have told you if his first wife was even alive.

So Ennis and his son flew to South Dakota, and Ennis spent a week at the Corn Palace Motel while his boy settled into his dorm and his routine. One morning over coffee at the Lueken Bakery, Ennis noticed an article in the paper about his ex-mother-in-law. He couldn't believe it at first, but there was her photograph, and Marlene didn't look much older than she had twenty or so years ago. She had won first prize at Dakotafest for her honey-spiced cornbread. And she lived in Epiphany. Ennis checked his road atlas, saw how close that was, smiled, called information and got Marlene's address.

When she answered the door, Ennis said, Marlene, you may not remember me, but I was your son-in-law. Marlene stepped back, opened the screen door, said Ennis Murphy, you're like some ghost, and she hugged him, and ushered him into her kitchen. He sat at the table while Marlene brewed coffee, warmed some cornbread. She told Ennis how her husband Tubba had died of emphysema six years ago. Never did quit smoking. That's when she sold the place up in Huron and moved out here, away from the hustle and bustle. She said her daughter lived in Mitchell now, taught literature at Dakota Wesleyan. Ennis had never known his ex-wife to be interested in literature. I'd call her right now, Marlene said, but she's in Rapid City at a conference. Ennis said, Well, you tell her hi for me. Marlene said, We know all about you, Ennis. We follow your career. We're so proud of you. (I should tell you I've changed Ennis's name. He's a moderately famous musician whom you might recognize.)

A year later, Ennis returned to Mitchell to perform at his son's school. He sent his ex two tickets to the show. She came alone. They got together later for drinks. She was a Willa Cather scholar, it turned out. Head of her department. Ennis told me, It didn't take us long to realize that our divorce wasn't working. After that weekend, he went home to his unsuspecting wife of twenty years, his devoted wife, and told her he was leaving her for his other wife. She said, This is some sick joke, right? It isn't funny, Ennis.

Ennis told me it was his great happiness over his resurrected love that gave him the strength to do what must have seemed so cruel to an observer. He told his wife he hadn't planned for this to happen. She said, Weren't we happy? He said, It was fate. She said, You can't do this to me. He said he was sorry, truly sorry that it had to happen, but it had happened, hadn't it? You'll be better off, he said. She hit him in the face so hard that she broke her elbow. Ennis drove her to the emergency ward. He was questioned by the triage nurse and then by two sheriff's deputies. His wife was hysterical. He waited for her in the lobby. His left cheek was bruised, his eye swollen shut. He called South Dakota with the news.

Ennis remarried his first wife on what would have been their 24th wedding anniversary. Their first marriage, I remember, took place in a field of wildflowers at an Audubon Sanctuary in Barre, Mass. We were all barefoot and garlanded, and high as kites. The second marriage was performed in a Lutheran Church in Mitchell, and Ennis's son, an A-student, was his Best Man. His daughter refused to attend the ceremony.

I made the mistake of telling Annick this story as we lounged on the couch the same night that Spot stole Barbie. So now she thought I wanted to reunite with my ex-wife. I said, That's crazy. She said, You made that story up. I was hurt. I said, If I'd made it up, you'd have believed it. She was crying now. She put down her wine glass. She asked me how I could have told her such a desolate story. I said I thought it was a story of enduring love and grand passion. Annick shook her head. She said my past was the one place she could never be. And then she stood, told me she was leaving, and walked to the door. Spot followed her, wagging his garrulous tail. She patted his head, scratched behind his ears, under his chin, called him *Spot the Looney* in her baby voice, and let him lick her face. She told him to stay. After she shut the door, Spot sniffed at the threshold, whimpered. He woofed at me.

At first I was angry with Annick. I mean, you think you're building a cozy and resilient relationship with a person, and then she proves you wrong. It's not at all intimate like you had imagined, but merely amicable. It's not irrepressible, but rather fragile, unsubstantial. But then I considered my motivation. Why *had* I told her about Ennis and the two Violas? Had I meant it, unconsciously or not, as an unsettling cautionary tale? Was my story a smile and a shrug? A nasty little assertion of my independence? A gratuitous nod to the treachery and caprice of Time? And then I was angry at my vicious self. I realized that I had committed an unpremeditated, but intentional, nonetheless, act of cruelty. I've caught myself playing this game before, the game of undermining my emotional prosperity. Something irrational inside, something ungovernable and unknowable, some fear or impulse has convinced me that the road of happiness leads to the house of sorrow.

Canine Theater

I cleared my dishes, rinsed them, poured myself a drink, and went out to sit on he deck. I put my feet up on the rail, leaned back in my chair. Spot sat at attention and stared at me. He wanted to know where I'd hidden Barbie and, more importantly, why would I do such a thing. I said, Maybe she found out I was suing her for alienation of affection and decided to skip town. He put his paw on my leg. I said, I don't think obsession is healthy for a dog. He yipped. He rested his head on my arm, looked up at me with his Pagliacci eyes. He's good.

Barbie was in the exercise room, which is not where I work out, but where I store all the training equipment I've foolishly bought over the years, the free weights, the Solo-flex, the stationary bike, the Abdomenizer, the StairMaster, the treadmill, the NordicTrack. You might ask why have I kept these reminders of my failure and my unfitness around. Well, I paid for them, and I can't bear to give them away. The financial loss would only compound my distress. I've also got a closet full of shoes that I haven't worn in years. I've got red clogs, green espadrilles, white bucks, dirty bucks, oxblood brogans, black wingtips, blue huaraches, cordovan penny loafers, chestnut Earth shoes, purple creepers, saddle shoes, beaded moccasins, Beatle boots, cowboy boots, chukka boots, engineer boots, fringed suede knee boots. I've even got a pair of parti-colored bowling shoes that I wore home from Gasoline Alleys Candlepin Lanes when they gave my sneakers away to someone else. If I ever put in a garden, I'll wear the bowling shoes to till the soil because who cares if they get wrecked.

I wanted to take Spot's mind and heart off Barbie, so I figured we'd play Canine Theater. Spot's quite a fine performer. I like to think he brings clarity and dignity to every role he plays. Of course, he doesn't like the Scottish play. When Annick, as Lady Macbeth, rubs her hands and declaims, Spot runs for the door and whines to be let out.

I stood. I looked at Spot. I said, "Biff, what are you doing with your life, goddamit? You've got unlimited potential."

Spot cocked his head.

"Don't look at me like that, Biff. Your brother Hap, he's doing gangbusters. But you, Biff, you're the smart one. You've got the winning personality."

Spot woofed.

"Out west? There's nothing out west for a man with ambition."

He growled.

"You're wrong, Biff. New York's the place for the Lomans. Willy and his sons."

Spot barked.

I picked up the Nerf football from the deck. I said, "Go long, Biff." I threw it as far as I could. Spot just sat there. I gave in. I got Barbie.

pannick@hailmail

I checked my e-mail: Speed Up Your Net Connection in Minutes GUARANTEED!!! Investor Alert! A Canadian Package That Matches Your Request. Archie MacPhee's On-Line Catalogue. And this from Annick:

> Johnny, I'm trying to give my future a shape. I don't want it being just more of the present. All my days are so alike now that they slip seamlessly into the past, and the past may be a fine place to visit, but I don't want to live there. Sometimes you make me so tired. It seems to me like I'm walking, you're standing still. You're stuck in your blue period. I'm going out to buy new paints. Time to get on with it. The opposite of change is death. Say hi to Spot. Have you heard about Fritzy?
>
> Annick

I went back to the deck.

Ways of Seeing

Some things you *look* at, and some things you *stare* at. You look at a photograph, but you stare at a flame. You look with intent and with intensity, but you stare without purpose or motive. When you look, you distinguish. When you stare, you witness. To look is to examine. To stare is to accept. Looking leads to comprehension, staring to reflection. *Look*, and you are fixed in time and space. *Stare*, and time dissolves, the world around you drops away. Me, I love the imposition of looking, but I prefer the susceptibility of staring. And that's why I love the night. Darkness obliterates distraction. I sit on my deck and stare at the stars. I see Perseus, Lacerta, and Cygnus adrift in the Milky Way. And I see beyond the stars to infinity, and in staring out I see within, see the faint shimmer of who I briefly am. Emerson said that if you want to feel alone, look at the stars. And I do. I feel alone, but also a part of something incomprehensibly vast and sublime. And I feel small, but not insignificant because I can wonder at it all, because I can think about the stars, and the stars cannot think about me, because I can tremble at the mystery.

The wind rattled through the queen palm. I smelled curry coming from the Pannu's house. I heard squawk of a night heron. I saw the Northern Cross, and the Cross made me think of Ray. Rayleigh Baravykas, my girlfriend just before I met my wife. Ray and I were in our sleeping bag in the dunes in Provincetown, and Ray pointed out the Cross and Andromeda and the dim galaxy beyond it, and we stayed awake to watch the Perseid meteor shower—a night of shooting stars. And then a thunderstorm.

The next morning we sat together at the laundromat, and a woman with a baby on her lap stared at us and smiled. She said, "You two look so beautiful together." But we're not together. Maybe we didn't believe in our beauty. I wondered how Ray was doing, and wondered how you could go from finishing each other's sentences to not talking for twenty years. There was a time I wouldn't let Ray out of my sight, and now I'm not even sure what she looks like.

I heard rustling in the heliconias. Probably a possum. Spot heard it and woofed. He's afraid of possums. I said, It's only Pogo. He growled unconvincingly. I guess my theme for the night was loss, or it was loneliness, because then I thought about two ex-friends who had the same first name (no motif intended). I've known the first Tony since second grade. He's my oldest pal. We used to sit in the schoolyard and talk about movies. Later we read Thoreau and Muir together, listened to obscure acoustic music. We planned trips out West, to Coeur d'Alene, to the Sawtooth, to Glacier. I'd buy maps, plan the routes, research the parks and campgrounds, and Tony would go with someone else. One morning he wouldn't be home and his mom would say he's off with Gary Smart (or Brian Houde or Henry Welch) to the mountains. I'd get to see the slides when they got back. Each time I was afraid to ask for an explanation.

One Friday night he called from his college dorm to tell me his girlfriend had left him, and how devastated he was, how suicidal. That Sunday morning I hitchhiked the fifty miles in sub-zero weather to see him, and when I arrived, his roommate told me that Tony was at a motel with the woman in question, and then he went back to sleep. *Miles* was the roommate's name. Miles to sleep. Miles to go before I sleep. Funny, I hadn't even known I knew his name. Miles, who later moved to Australia. Why do I remember that?

Tony was an only child. He had one aunt and no cousins. His aunt and parents died. Tony has known me longer than he has known anyone. I tell myself it's his childhood he's running from. But I think it's me. I call every six months, on Christmas and his birthday, and leave a message on his machine.

The second Tony and I did travel together—to Europe and across America. For years we were inseparable. And then he stopped talking to me. He told friends that I was stuck in the past, that I hadn't grown up. He may have been right, of course. He told them I had an indiscriminate sense of humor. Maybe it *is* better to put the past aside, but I never can. Tony moved back to his mother's house after she died. I wondered did he sleep in his old bedroom or move into Mom and Dad's. There's some cruelty in that thought, I know. I miss the Tonys. We could be having fun right now.

What if Ray and I had never split up? I tried to picture us now. (Yes, it's futile to think *what if?* about your life, but I've been doing it since I was a kid. What if Mom and Dad die in a car crash on the way home? How would I handle all that trouble? Could I go live with Aunt Bea in California? What if I had sprung my grandfather from the nursing home? [Would have needed a miracle here. In fact, I went to the nursing home, said, Pepere, you want to get out of here, never come back? He said, I know I'm supposed to know you. Could you tell me who you are.]) I could only see Ray and me in a cold place. Ray in a bulky wheat-colored sweater. We're on a farm in coastal Maine. Goats. Wild raspberries. And then I remembered her grandfather's farm and what happened there. Ray's uncle Edwin shot his father in the head and then shot himself, but not before he doused the parlor with gasoline and dropped a match.

I went back to the kitchen, made some coffee, sat at the table and wrote a poem about Ray:

Still Life With Ray

Ray tells me what Sister Cecilia told her and the other girls back
in sixth grade, that St. Lucy plucked out her eyes and sent them

to her tiresome and lascivious suitor, the Consul Paschasius, to save herself from shame. Yikes! It's 1969 and Ray and I are on the beach in Provincetown waiting for the sun to set over the bay. We have wine and chocolate and Portuguese bread. I wonder did Lucy have the eyes wrapped in silk and did she pay the boy who delivered them. I make a joke about how Lucy was from the school of aggressive chastity. I'm in love with Ray. Ray's mother has just died. Ray says eyes don't see, the mind does. I touch my forehead to her temple, and when she speaks I feel her words in the bones of my head. She says we never see only one thing at a time. Ray is a painter. She says if you look at anything for a long time, it melts and shatters. I wonder if she's talking about her memory of her mom or about the beach grass, sea rocket, and bayberry in front of us. When the sun sets Ray stands and looks behind us to the eastern sky. I look at the fuchsia sun, the purple sea. I look at Ray, her blonde hair aflame. She tells me to look at the purple band low in the sky. I put my chin on her shoulder and look ahead to where she's pointing, and finally I see it. We watch the band rise in the sky and then dissolve into the darkness. Ray says we just watched the earth's shadow cast on the sky. I hold her face in my hands. Ray averts her eyes.

I typed it. By now it was the middle of the night, and I still couldn't sleep. My uncle Armand told me how the world was destroyed every night and put back together again by God before morning. I looked through photo albums and found what I knew I would—a black and white photo I had taken of Ray and her grandfather on one of our Sunday visits to the farm. Ray is sipping soup from a spoon and looking over at me with her turquoise eyes, and old Joe is holding his ball cap by its visor and scratching his head. The tip of his index finger is missing. He's wearing a torn corduroy coat over his coveralls over his sweatshirt. Beyond Joe on a shelf over a dry sink sits a tub of Jewel lard, a pitted enamel wash basin, a chalkware collie, a hurricane lamp, and a box of Ohio Blue Tip matches.

I took a drink with me out to the deck. Something else Uncle Armand told me: you can tell the real voices from the crazy voices because the crazy voices are just outside your ear. We look out to the end of the universe racing away from us. We can only look back, it seems. The future is invisible. How shall we know it?

. . .

Glow & O

When you tell people that you write fiction, they tend to respond in one of three ways. There are those who will stop talking to you because they assume you are going to write about them, you're going to appropriate their precious lives for your squalid little stories. My family's like this. Years ago I was made to promise that I would never again reveal the kind of familial impropriety that had gotten my uncle Didi blackballed at the Singletary Rod & Gun Club, that I would not embarrass my parents or aunts or in any way muddy the family name. Otherwise I could spend my holidays in solitude. And I have kept my word although I do have a dozen or so stories filed away awaiting the deaths of certain cousins and in-laws.

Then there are the folks who think that writers write only about themselves, and so they assume that writers lead adventurous, troubled, and reckless lives. These people are eager to listen to your madcap tales of turmoil and self-destruction. You tell them you don't smoke, don't drink (you lie) or carry on with the wives of friends. You explain that you no longer shoot heroin and you don't roam the predawn streets with packs of other writers. You tell them you sit in a room and work. These people are hurt that you don't trust them with your indiscretions. The hurt festers into anger and resentment.

The third response comes from those who think that fiction writers make everything up. These are sweet, kind, and naive people who want to make your job easier, and so they tell you stories from their own lives. Like my friend Ennis and his two Violas. Or like the seventy-five-year-old woman I met in Winter Haven who told me she'd carried on a forty-year love affair with a married physician, a radiologist, a man with a wife and four children. Moved here from Los Angeles to be near him. They went on a cruise to Paradise Island, and he died in their bed in his sleep. She had to call the wife from her cabin with the tragic news, arrange for the transport of the body back to Winter Haven. She could not attend the funeral. He was the love of her life.

Gloria and Omar fit into this last category. When Gloria first stopped by to welcome me to the neighborhood she was very pregnant and smelled like vanilla. As we sat in my kitchen and talked, she ate the empanadas she had brought me. She told me that her husband—she called him the Big O—was away on business, meeting with the Latin American Cosmetics King in Caracas. She told me how she knew that O loved her: since she told him how much she loved his lavender shirt, he'd worn it every day. She told me she took lessons: voice, dance, acting. It was O's ambition that she make it in show business, get her own program on Telemundo. I told her I wrote stories. She told me her voice teacher's cousin knew Gloria Estefan's housekeeper. I said, So, you have an in. She raised her brow, pointed at me like I was onto something. She asked me what my stories were about. I told her love and death. She wiped crumbs from her mouth, leaned back in her chair. She said, You can write my story.

When she was sixteen, Glow was madly in love with Billy Cassidy, with his dreamy blue eyes, his wavy black hair, his sweet disposition. They'd been going steady for a month when Billy's mom died quite unexpectedly (aneurysm). At the wake, Glow sat between Billy and his sobbing father and accepted the condolences of strangers. Billy chewed gum. His jaw cracked. He held Glow's hand for what must have been comfort, but felt to her like restraint, detention. Glow wished she could say a prayer at the casket, express her regrets, whisper to Billy that she'd be there for him, and leave with their other friends.

In the following weeks, Glow spent her afternoons and evenings at the Cassidy house, cooking, cleaning, watching television. Billy had become more affectionate, but less amorous, more tender, but less demonstrative, more reliant, grateful, needy, and therefore less deserving of her passion. She wanted love, not domesticity, wanted to be an obsession, not a substitute. She told Billy she was sorry about his terrible loss, and then she returned the silver crucifix ring he'd given her. She told me she missed him, always had. He teaches high school in Miramar. And then she told me the hidden meaning to her story: "Death is stronger than love, Johnny."

When I first met Omar he was wearing a silky red and gold soccer uniform, shin guards, and wrap-around sunglasses. He handed me a beer, and we leaned against his van. He told me his team, the Jaguars, had just defeated the Lions of Judah at Boggs Field. He scratched Spot's muzzle, spoke to him in Spanish. Spot sat, gave Omar his paw. I noticed the cases of lipstick in the van and asked Omar how he liked his job. He said a man's job was to love a woman. Whether the woman loved him back was unimportant. The woman's job was to be loved. He asked me did I have a woman. I said I did. He asked me to describe her complexion, eye and hair color. I said, Cream, coffee, copper. He put down his bottle, cut open a case of lipstick with a key, pulled out a gold tube and handed it to me. "Cinnamon Spice. For your woman."

"Thank you."

"My wife tells me you write stories."

"Yes."

"Why?"

"Every story uncovers a secret."

Omar smiled, looked toward his house, leaned into me, and told me his secret. He had another family in Venezuela. A wife, Graciela, and three sons, Pablo, four; Carlos, three; Celestino, one and a half. "*Omar* is my American name."

"You wouldn't lie to me?"

"What would be the point?"

"How do you manage?"

"With difficulty."

"You have two identities? Two passports?"

He smiled.

"You seem happy."

"I love them all."

"What will happen? I mean you can't keep this up indefinitely."

"We shall see."

What Else Could It Be?

I squished my earplugs in as far as they'd go, adjusted my padded eye-shade, taped my Breathe Right nasal strip on my nose. I thought how this was a secret I kept from Annick. She'd never seen me armed for sleep. When we stay together, I sleep unfortified. I would be too embarrassed. Anyway, I like my dreams and want to enjoy them without interruption. But I'm a fretful and uneasy sleeper. Wind in the oleander wakes me, the refrigerator's hum, the dawn's light, passing cars, my own snoring. I puffed my pillow, smoothed the sheet, stretched my legs, relaxed them. For an insomniac, going to bed is like going to therapy. All the cargo you've weighted down with forgetfulness and disregard, and then dropped into the deep, comes popping back to the surface. Like my dad.

He had left a message on my machine, and I hadn't returned his call. He told me about the hurricane and about a woman named Fritzy that he knew during the war—before Mom. My dad was an inventor before he lost his sight. He didn't so much make new things as he found new uses for existing things. He made fishing lures out of bottle openers and teaspoons, made coat hooks out of plastic duck decoys. He once made a shaving mirror for the shower out of a harmonica holder and a woman's compact. And that's how he appeared to me as I tried to sleep—naked in the shower with the holder around his neck and the opened compact case snapped into the spring tension clamp. His face was lathered. He held a shaving brush in one hand and a razor in the other. He was far-sighted in those days, so he wore his reading glasses, which had fogged. He cracked me up sometimes. One day he ran out of shaving cream, so he shaved with Reddi-wip. He would point at an object and ask me what it was. I'd answer, and then he'd tell me what else it was. Like I'd say *ladder,* and he'd say *towel rack.* Or I'd say *ashtray,* and he'd say *soap dish. Wooden shoe—planter; flat iron— door handle.*

The reason I hadn't called my father back, the reason he was keeping me awake, had to do with the tape he wanted me to make. He wanted me to read my last book into a recorder so he could listen to it. I told Dad that Spot was in the book, that he belonged to the central character, a writer, not so unlike myself. I told him the writer's father had vision problems, so naturally he assumed the father is him. I did not tell him that the writer and his father have a problematic relationship. I did not want my father hurt by his misperception. Even if I told him now that he's not the character, he'll think I'm lying. Spot's Spot, after all. The writer's a pathetic little scribbler who left his loving wife, after all.

I took off my eyeshade. Maybe if I opened my eyes, I wouldn't see my wife. But there she was holding a peeled orange to her mouth, holding it with both hands, biting into it and crying. Just great! I pulled out the earplugs. Once again, thoughts had murdered sleep. I know that I made the novel up. I also know there are resemblances to my life. I know why the writer left his wife, but I don't know why I left mine. I like to pretend that writing is a plunge into reality, that it forces me to deal with what I'm ashamed of, with what I regret, with what I don't understand, with what I don't want to know about myself, but it can also be avoidance. Flight. It's easier to make someone up, after all, and give him the trouble and deal with his turmoil than it is to deal with your own. So much for courage and honesty. And I knew if I didn't do something soon, I'd be writing about the writer who lost his girlfriend.

I sat on the edge of the bed. I keep a memo pad and pen on the night table. I wrote this down: *a father is always a son; a son's not always a father.* I'd figure it out in the morning. If I hoped to get any sleep, I needed to get out of bed.

The Dead of Night

I've been despondent in my life. I've felt ponderous and numb, desperate and disabled, brittle and disposable, lost in a gloom so profound I wanted at once to hold onto anything and let go of everything. But I've come to understand that hope, our brief candle, is my only light in the darkness, and so I keep it with me.

I sat in the living room, feet up on the ottoman, staring toward the window. Spot snored on the couch. I realized you can't look at space, but only at objects in space. Without something to be seen, you are blind. I also realized I was avoiding what hurt. It was so quiet I could hear everything, the CFX freight rumbling alongside Dixie Highway, blasting its whistle at every intersection. And when that faded, I heard a semi whining along the Interstate. I pictured the driver wearing a T-shirt, smoking a cigarette. He knows he has seven hours to Savannah and then one more load to carry up to Augusta before he gets home to Myrna and the boys, gets a few days of rest and a chance to work on the dragster. He's thinking, because he always does, that he shouldn't have gotten into the long-haul business in the first place. Never at home. But how could he give it up now? That's what the car's about and why he needs to get it humming: the new life, the dreamed-of life, the real life he's not yet living, the life of a drag racer. He'll enter out at Silver Dollar this spring and then maybe Rockingham. He doesn't want to think about all this. He'll just get sad. He puts on the radio. Every station's in Spanish. Where the hell am I? He plugs in a Willie Nelson tape, and every song calls him home. His name's Keith. He's got a herniated disc in his lower back and a nasty scar that runs up the inside of his right arm.

While I thought about Keith, I felt okay, but I opened my eyes and the exhausted air was empty of light. How do we fill our emptiness? With jobs, with songs, with family, with friends. Even if we have to make them up. We connect how we can.

The night is both our blessing and our curse. It's a sanctuary from turmoil, a respite from the routine and clutter of our lives. Our days seduce us with activity. Our nights confront us with stillness. The night may seem false in its solitude, but it's the lie that speaks the truth. At night, we can't pretend that we're not dying. At night, we're reminded of this hurried interlude between oblivions. And that's why we choose to sleep, to dream. Dreams are the madness that keep us sane.

I saw Spot's legs twitch and realized my eyes had adjusted to the scant light that had been here all the while. I wasn't despondent. I was afraid. I thought about what I was missing, like my old friends, the old neighborhood, my old room, my old young and innocent self. Annick.

When I first met her—this was at a bookstore café—she told me her name was Annick, but she danced under the name *Blaze*. Blaze was the set-up. After our espressos, she shook my hand, said how nice it was to meet, to chat and all. She needed to find a book. I discreetly followed her, hoping she didn't head for *Self-Help* or *New Age*. She went to *Art & Architecture*, and this gave me the courage to approach and ask her if I might call her. She gave me her card. The card was the pay-off. I said, Very funny, Miss Pascal. You don't dance at all, do you? She told me she was a freelance scenic designer and worked mostly with local theaters. I said, Are you related? She said, He is my great-great-great-great-great-great grandfather. Later she told me her joke had been a test. If I hadn't recognized the name, she wouldn't have answered the phone.

I was, I knew, distracting myself with thoughts. I told myself not to think, but to feel, to wait quietly and the fears would present themselves. If I love Annick and she loves me, why don't I want what she wants? Why do I insist on separate lives? Do I love her in a different way than she loves me? Do I know what love is? Annick says, Love is simple. It's what you do, not what you think or feel. She also says that the only way to know the future is to imagine it. I'm not sure I want to know it, but I try. I see Annick and me in twenty years. We're living in Taos. It's a Saturday night in July, and we're driving down to Chimayo for dinner. And then I think, Twenty years—no Spot, so I just get up and go to the kitchen to make coffee. I turn on the TV. There's a live remote from Home Depot. It's half past four in the morning, and the place is packed. People are buying generators, sandbags, flashlights. The store's already out of plywood.

Walkies

I used to bring Spot to Bark Park up in Fort Lauderdale for his exercise, but he's been banned, *canis non grata*, labeled chronically aggressive, which is a lie, or, at best, a misunderstanding. What Spot did was he got a lot of otherwise docile and obedient dogs riled up, got them in touch with their inner-puppies, so that in their exuberance, they ignored their owners' commands. Apparently, these dogs had never seen anything remotely like Spot's exhilaration and abandon. They watched Spot run like mad around the perimeter of the park, his ears waving, his tongue flapping, his body leaning into the turns like it does. He'd stop to pee on the statue of Dr. Dolittle or to chew some piece of canine agility equipment, and then he'd be off again, dogs following.

Spot gets a kick out of prissy little dogs, and every once in a while he'd see one across the park, and he'd charge at it and then leap right over it at the last second, leaving the little Shih Tzu trembling in its satin bows. I could see people calling to their recalcitrant dogs, whistling, gesturing, ordering them to stop chasing after Spot the dervish and get back here this instant! The owners would look at me with narrowed eyes and clenched jaws. I'd smile as if to say I'm just as nuts as the dog. Spot earned five demerits in his first week.

The final straw came when Spot, who'd been splashing through the drinking fountain, crashed a doggie birthday party at the puppy pavilion, a party to which he'd been explicitly disinvited. He stole a cardboard hat off a beagle and ran off with it. The beagle looked sad, confused. Then Spot bounded back and galloped through the cake. The party's human hostess, a sixty-something platinum blonde, told me I was just the kind of reprobate that gave dog owners a bad name. I told her Spot was just playing. She told me he doesn't play well with others. When I intimated that the party guests were maybe unduly prim, she said, no, they were gentle and dutiful. Bootlickers, I said. She said did I understand the first thing about the responsibilities of dog ownership. I said something about the fascist's need to control and dominate. I really wasn't making sense.

So now Spot and I walk around the neighborhood, and I carry a plastic Publix sack so I can collect his poop. We follow a route of Spot's choosing along the mangroves to the canal where he does his business, to the pond where he barks at the Muscovy ducks, and then past the strip mall where I deposit the sack in the bucket behind Asian Nails, and then up Coolidge. (Used to be there were monkeys in the mangroves—escaped from Chimp World in the '50s, but lately the state's been paying poachers to trap them. Haven't seen any in months, which is fine with Spot. They freaked him out. We also have walking catfish here and marine toads the size of catchers' mitts, and four-foot iguanas, and basilisk lizards that run along on their back legs. That's the kind of neighborhood it is.) Eventually we come to Annick's house. And normally we pay a visit. So this morning after my sleepless night Spot ran up Annick's porch steps and turned to me. I told him to come on. He sat, looked back over his shoulder to the door. There were treats and hugs inside. I, too, was hoping the door would open, and Annick would be standing there in her cowgirl pajamas, and she'd invite us in for breakfast and reconciliation, but it did not. I saw no lights on inside, no activity in the yard.

Back on our block, O was unloading sheets of plywood from a U-Haul truck. Spot sniffed through the hibiscus while I gave O a hand. O asked me did I want to buy some plywood to board up my windows. I told him I wouldn't know what to do with it. He shook his head, told me I ought to be more responsible than that. "Your house will blow away. What will you do then?"

"I'll come stay with you."

O didn't laugh. He opened his cooler, asked me if I wanted a beer.

"Seven-thirty's a bit early."

He opened two bottles of Polar and we sat on the lawn. Layla told Spot he looked adorable. She'd tied a sun bonnet on his head. The two of them sat on the porch steps. His tail wagged a mile a minute. And then I understood. Barbie was Spot's connection to Layla, that's why he kept her around. He had a crush on Layla. I felt relieved and guilty. I saw Glow at the screen door talking to someone on a cell phone. She waved to me.

O said that Channel 7 had called for a hurricane landfall somewhere between Haulover Cut and Hillsboro Inlet sometime before dawn tomorrow. I said I ought to paint a bull's-eye on my house. He said we were under a mandatory evacuation order. We've got till dusk, but by three the Turnpike and I-95 will be one-way north and gridlocked. He said he was boarding up, selling what he could of the plywood—Glow's on the phone to the neighbors now—and then taking off. He's got a room booked in Orlando, closest he could find. He told me I should get ready and get out. I said I might have to stay. He said did I have a gun. Did I want to buy one?

Tropical Anesthetic

At home I switched on the TV, and there it was out in the Atlantic, Fritzy's well-defined eye, bearing down on South Florida. I checked HurricaneCentral.com and saw the bright yellow cone of probable landfall centered on the Dania Cutoff Canal. The consensus in the chat room was a powerful Category 4 event in our immediate vicinity with a twenty-foot storm surge, which would put the ocean seventeen feet above the sidewalk. This was not good news. I looked out the window at Spot, studied him. I'd read that animals begin acting strangely before a cyclone hits. Spot was lying in a puddle of sun on the deck. Maybe it was earthquakes I read about. I told myself I wouldn't leave without Annick, and I immediately felt noble, valiant, and self-sacrificing, and I realized as well that Annick would snicker at my idea of heroism, and then I felt embarrassed even though I was alone. You wouldn't think that could happen.

I called motels, and the few that had rooms didn't take pets, no, not even in an emergency. So I just lied to the desk clerk at the Osceola Motel in Valdosta, Georgia, told him I was dogless, even though he hadn't asked. I reserved our room, but we'd have to check in by 10 P.M. or they'd rent it out to someone else. I hung up and then thought what if it's one of those motels where you have to enter your room through the lobby. I hate getting caught in lies. I hate sleeping in cars. I closed my eyes and pictured the Osceola. I saw a red sign out by the street with white letters and a flaming white arrow piercing the center of the O, and then a one-story, u-shaped, white concrete building with jalousie windows and two red tulip chairs outside each room. I was relieved and chose not to look inside.

I needed to pack what I was going to take, needed to decide what I would save. I walked around the house and thought first, What do I want to take? Then: What do I *need* to take? Briefs, T-shirts, socks. Then: What is irreplaceable? I realized I had a lot of stuff in my life, most of it you would call junk, evidence of too much time and money spent on ebay: old scrapbooks, movie posters, match covers, baseball cards, advertising art, 78 rpm records, vintage eyeglasses, Viewmaster reels, swizzle sticks. And so on. I packed my computer and disks, my notebooks and photo albums. I figured I could get a thousand books in the bed of the truck. I'd just have to hope it didn't rain. Then I thought, Which thousand? All right, we start with the complete Chekhov. Shakespeare. The Bible. Christ this could take all day. Which Faulkner do I take? Which Tolstoy? Then I realized that Spot, Annick, and I wouldn't all fit in the cab of the truck. We'd have to take Annick's Tercel.

I put valuables in Tupperware containers in the fridge. I called Annick. Today's words were *pasquinade, herl, dornick.* I told her machine I'd be over in fifteen minutes. She should pack. I said, Our lives are at stake here, Annick. I paused. I said, I'm not leaving without you.

Then I thought, I hope she hasn't left already. I told Spot we were going for a ride, and he ran to retrieve Barbie from under the deck. On the way to Annick's I saw that the truck was on E. I stopped at the Chevron on Federal and waited in line for twenty-five minutes. They had raised the price by a dime since yesterday. Capitalism is not our finest idea.

I drove to the liquor store. Spot waited in the truck. Prakash and Chandra were boarding up the windows. Don was clearing shelves. He said he kind of figured I'd be along, so he'd saved me a bottle of Hennessy behind the counter. Said they were closing up as soon as they stored the booze in the back. Don's about sixty-five, moved here a dozen years ago from Michigan, and lives in a residential motel off Dixie. He has double-vision, which can't be good, but he won't go to a doctor because he doesn't have health insurance. He bought an eye patch at Walgreen's, says he's fine. The headaches have stopped.

Annick still wasn't home. I peeked in her garage. Her car was gone. What if she really *had* evacuated? I enjoy irony as much as the next guy, but to drown while the woman you're trying to save lounges by a pool at the Tallahassee Holiday Inn was more than I could handle. But Annick is responsible. She would not have gone without storing the porch furniture. She's around. I drove home to check messages. Nothing from Annick, but an update from Dad. Seems they'd closed the Fort Lauderdale airport and were flying the planes to safety. I put on the TV. The evacuation of the Keys was over. Whoever wasn't out, wasn't getting out. Card Sound Road and Route 1 south of Homestead were closed. Helicopter shots of I-95 showed six lanes of solid traffic heading north. Meanwhile, in breaking news, two Miami mayoral candidates had each claimed the endorsement of little Elian Gonzales.

I sat on Annick's porch, sweating and fuming, thinking how inconsiderate her absence was. I watched the anoles do push-ups, spread their orange throat fans. The sky was cloudless, the air still and steamy. I looked at my watch. I didn't know why I couldn't leave Annick behind exactly, I just knew I couldn't, knew without thinking, not even to save myself or to save Spot. I looked at him sleeping on the lawn, collapsed like dirty laundry in the mottled shade of a mango. I've always had this knowledge—or maybe it's a belief (or maybe there's no difference)—that I would survive any emotional disaster in my life. Like if this really were the end of the affair with Annick, I might be sad, but I'd be okay. Was that what I wanted—to be okay? In order to think this way, I suppose I needed to believe that I was independent and unfettered. Does that mean there's a part of me that can never relax with anyone, never trust anyone, cannot commit and never will? That seemed pathetic. Not that I wanted to fall apart, either. What good would that do? I realized, too, that this reticence, call it, was often perceived by others as a strength and was admired. Ray told me one reason she liked me so much, one thing that attracted her to me in the first place was that I seemed so aloof, so unapproachable, unknowable, self-contained. When she told me that, I was both flattered and disturbed. Evidently I had no idea who I was. Ray called me "The Island." She called me *"Jean le Fataliste."*

I got the house key from under the plaster lawn gnome (Chomsky, Annick called him). I knocked on the door. Waited. I opened the door, stood inside and yelled hello. No note for me on the kitchen table. No dishes in the sink. Nearly noon. We'd need to leave immediately if we hoped to reach Valdosta by ten in this traffic. I opened the garage, stowed the lawn and porch furniture inside. I took down the wind chimes, the bird feeders, the floral wreath, the chili pepper porch lights. I carried Chomsky inside. I changed my shirt. I saw Annick walking up the street. So did Spot. He ran to her. I waited by the truck.

I was deliriously happy and relieved to see her, but I was also apprehensive and angry though I had no right to be, and I knew that. I said, "Where have you been?" and I knew it sounded more hostile than concerned, which wasn't my conscious intention.

"At the beach."

Spot brought armless Barbie to Annick and dropped the doll at her feet. Annick tossed her, and Spot fetched.

I said, "Don't you know we're facing a catastrophe here?"

"Yes."

What did she mean by that? Had we just slipped into metaphor?

"The hurricane."

"Fritzy."

"And you're out strolling on the beach?"

"Thanks for putting everything in the garage."

"We live in a mandatory evacuation zone."

"So why are you still here?"

"I'm not leaving you."

"You don't owe me anything."

She was being disingenuous. "Come on, Annick, you know I love you." But why couldn't I have said it simply? The declaration without the agitation. I said, "Where's your car?"

"In the shop. Henk says I need a transmission."

"Shit. We'll squeeze in the truck."

"Are you trying to insinuate yourself back into my life?"

"I'd like to think I hadn't left it."

We went inside. We turned on the TV while Annick packed her things. Spot dropped Barbie de Milo on the floor and barked at her. He scrunched down, barked some more. He was angry, perhaps because her head was loose. Officials had already made all lanes northbound on the Turnpike and 95, and already the roads were clogged, traffic was stopped. Five million people trying to get out of Dodge. Cars were stalled—out of fuel and overheated. Fist fights had been reported in several locations, guns fired in Pompano Beach. A ten-car pile-up at Copans Road couldn't be cleared because authorities couldn't get at it. Annick said she'd rather be at home in a hurricane than parked in a truck on the highway.

At this point we had no choice. She told me I could stay. She reminded me that we hadn't made up, hadn't resolved a thing. I said, We'll get married. She said, Don't make fun of me.

"What?"

"You take it all so lightly." She cried. I held her. She said we'd have to talk about it later. Now we have to get ready. We need to fill up every container we can with water. Need to get out the candles, flashlights, batteries. We needed to get to an ATM and take out cash, move the truck away from the trees, check the rain gutters, move everything off the floor that we could, tie cabinet doors shut, and fill the tub with water. I looked at Spot. I said, We can't. Annick smiled. Oh, that's right.

Testimony

Annick and I walked to my place with Spot. We were oppressively cordial, warily chummy. I couldn't stand it. I confessed that I'd been behaving badly, and I apologized. I suppose I thought she would forgive me, would smile, wrap her arm around my waist, lean into my shoulder. She picked up a twig and tossed it ahead for Spot. The thing is I didn't really think I'd been bad, just honest. And now my graciousness was being rebuffed. How dare she?

Omar's house was boarded up, the rental truck was gone. The neighborhood was eerily quiet. Inside, we filled the tub and sinks with water.

I filled a cloth book bag with items from my desk: binoculars, pens, eyeglasses, a portable tape player, headphones, a Howard Finster angel (*One day out of a whole lifetime you will die*), scissors, glue sticks, Eva Cassidy and Louvin Brothers tapes, a stopwatch, and a shortwave radio. We locked up and walked to the beach. The lifeguards had gone. We got lunch at Angelo's before it closed. We watched surfers ride the ten-foot swells as we ate. I said, "Annick, I want to be with you no matter what. And if you want to be married, then I want to be married."

She said, "You just don't get it, do you?"

Strike two.

On the way back to Annick's we spoke to the bridge tender who told us he was locking the bridge down at three, per orders, and heading out to his girlfriend's house in Davie for a hurricane party. We bought Sterno at Publix, figuring even if the power went out, we'd have fondue. I showed Annick the photo of Bigfoot's boy. We bought Little Debbie snack cakes at the Dollar Store.

We watched TV reports of the devastation in the Leewards and in the Turks and Caicos. People stranded out on the parking lot that had been the Turnpike were setting up camps beside the highway. A couple of hundred stranded motorists on 95 had broken into Northeast High School and set up their own unauthorized shelter. Stores had been looted in Hallandale Beach and in Lighthouse Point, and nothing catastrophic had even happened yet. Dolph Diaz, the Channel 10 anchor, said he was going home to take care of his family and walked off the set. I asked Annick why we lived here. She said, The climate. At the Krome Detention Center in west Miami-Dade, the detainees, most of them Haitian refuges, fearing for their lives, had busted through the fence and fled into the Everglades. And then we heard the storm was slowing, strengthening. Estimated landfall in fourteen hours.

We turned off the TV and sat out on the deck. It seemed ridiculous that there was nothing we could do but wait. It started to rain. Radio reports indicated that these rain cells had nothing to do with the hurricane, but we didn't believe them. Annick kissed me. I was grateful, restored. I thanked her. We set up the bathroom which would be our fortification. Candles, the short-wave, a boom box with Puccini CDs, a Coleman lantern, batteries, plastic cups, cognac, Irish whiskey, blankets, water, alarm clock, books, magazines, dog dishes, dog food, dog biscuits, dog nest, dog chewies, what's-left-of-Barbie.

When we were first going out, Annick told me she had been an equestrian in the Big Apple Circus and had dated, had lived with, in fact, the lion tamer, Gunther Something, for three years. So for months I pictured the two of them in their trailer, her in a silky pink, sequined ballerina outfit with a feathery headdress and garish silver eye makeup and him in a one-piece gold and black tank-top deal with gold ballet slippers, the both of them, lithe and graceful, walking quickly on tip toes around the place, stopping once in a while to pose for the other, to toss back their hair, to acknowledge a glance with upraised arms and a grand smile, to bow deeply, sincerely, with the sweep of an arm. This kept me awake at night. I determined to shape up at a gym. I thought it odd that she never wanted to go horseback riding. Then she told me she'd made it all up. Said really she was a meteorologist—not a weather girl—at KENW-TV in Portales, New Mexico. *Light rain showers will continue this morning across much of Southeast New Mexico into the Capitan and northern Sacramento mountains. A few areas of low clouds and fog may reduce visibility. Motorists should use caution.* And I believed that, too, for a while. I even suggested we vacation in her old stamping grounds, told her I had friends in Hobbs we could visit. She laughed, kissed me on the nose, asked me if I'd always been so gullible. I told her I just didn't expect people to lie is all. She said, You lie for a living. I even believed Annick when she told me she'd been abducted by aliens. I mean I believed that she believed she'd been abducted, not that she really had been. We were snuggling on her couch when she confessed. She said she went into the UFO because she was forced to under mind control. She said, "You don't have a choice. I was sleeping, and when I awoke I heard a buzz, and I was paralyzed, and they floated me up and through the ceiling."

I suggested that perhaps she had had a particularly vivid and frightening dream and was unable to separate it from reality just yet. She shook her head. She said, "They like bedrooms, cars, and swamps."

"Then we're safe."

"It's not funny."

Spot climbed onto the couch with us. Annick said that I'd also been abducted. "You have their scar on your wrist."

"I had a tumor removed."

"That's just the memory they implanted." She asked me if I'd ever dreamed of UFOs. I told her that as a kid I'd dreamed that communion wafers were UFOs. She nodded, smiled. She said, "Unexplainable things have happened in your life."

"I suppose . . ."

"You've got sinusitis."

"Yes."

"Have you ever noticed blood on your pillow when you wake up?"

"Yes."

"Have you ever woken up and not realized where you were?"

"Every morning."

"Ringing in your ears?"

"You know I have tinnitus."

"That's what Earth doctors call it. But they don't know what causes it, do they? Or how to cure it?"

Spot rested his head on Annick's lap and stared at me. Annick said, "And you don't remember anything about an abduction, do you?"

"Of course not."

"That seals it."

"You're kidding, right?"

"Do I look like I'm kidding?" She said these aliens were bluish with large heads and large lidless eyes and spindly legs with wide, flat feet. They look like that until you get to the ship. "It's just a disguise, as you can see from our friend here." She patted Spot the Plutonian. He moaned. She laughed.

I felt foolish and relieved. I said, "Were you probed?"

"Not very well."

So I can be excused, perhaps, for what happened next. After we set up the bathroom, we sat on the couch. Annick cried. She told me she'd been a mother once. I thought, Oh, she's good! I said, "Bigfoot's boy?" She got up and walked into the kitchen. I waited a minute, pictured her in there waiting for me to take the bait. I heard her blowing her nose, sobbing. I went after her. When I said I was sorry, I half-expected her to crack up. Her shoulders trembled instead. I held her, and she told me the story.

She was twenty-seven, not married or engaged, having a difficult pregnancy. Took a leave from teaching. The boyfriend wasn't interested in a child, or in marriage, or in much of anything, really. An optometrist. This was in eastern Pennsylvania, where she grew up. She went into labor a month early. The baby weighed two pounds at birth and lived for two hours. She named him Jonas after her father who had died when she was fourteen. She told me she still imagined her son alive, still spoke with him. He'd be sixteen.

We lay down on Annick's bed and slept. In my dream I saw a man biting a dog by the nape of the neck, shaking him. I saw men walking upside down on the surface of the water, trees full of perching cats, people with handles on their backs, people floating in air. And I knew if I kept walking I'd see Annick, and I did, and when I reached out to hold her she split into shards of glass and dropped to the ground. Sounded like bells. We woke up with the first crash of thunder and the sound of Spot scratching at the bedroom door.

Miracles

The thunderstorm passed, leaving Spot exhausted. He panted on my lap for a while. Annick sang, "Spot the Magic Setter," his favorite song. I took the mittens off his paws. He hopped out of the tub, drank all the water in his bowl, and collapsed in a heap. The radio report said this line of storms was only a hint of what was to come. Fritzy was nine hours away, wobbling a bit, but still on course for Broward County. Annick and I sat in the tub talking about miracles, which are what Annick figured it would take to get out of this jam. She took a drink of whiskey and passed the cup to me. I told her I didn't believe in miracles. She said walking on water was a miracle. I told her loons walk on water, and Jesus bugs. She said, How about rising from the dead. I said, An oxymoron is not a miracle. I knew I was treading on thin ice. Annick's a practicing Catholic, and she's got a shelf full of books about miracles in her bedroom, books she's had me read. She said what about those stories? "What about the man from Dallas who got a spooky feeling and decided at the last second not to get on that ValuJet flight that crashed into the Everglades?"

I said, "Changing your mind is a decision, not a miracle. Coincidence is not a miracle. Luck is not a miracle. Thinking your dead mother is in the room is not a miracle. A hallucination is not a miracle. An accident is not a miracle. A doctor's misdiagnosis is not a miracle. Finding something you lost ten years ago is good fortune, but not a miracle. Learning from your mistakes is not a miracle. The decision to quit drinking yourself to death is not a miracle. It's a courageous act. Realizing that you've been a ruthless prick all of your life is not a miracle, it's overdue, and you won't change the past or buy your way into heaven by giving your stolen money away because heaven isn't the White House and God doesn't sell pardons."

"You don't believe in God."

"Figure of speech."

"It's always politics with you, isn't it?"

Annick said she didn't care what I thought, but she believed that God put his hand on that fortunate Texan's shoulder and said, Son, don't get on the plane.

I said, "Then you must believe that that same God sent the other two hundred or whatever people to their fiery deaths without a second thought."

Spot raised his head when I raised my voice.

Annick said, "It's a miracle that I'm with you." And I couldn't argue with that. She kissed me, and I realized how wonderful this moment was and how I would be remembering it all my life, the kiss in the tub waiting for the storm, and in that life would be Annick and Spot the Wonder Dog. Lightning flashed through the house. Thunder exploded and the power failed. "Must have hit a substation," I said, not really knowing what I was talking about. Spot whined, woofed, clambered back into the tub, buried his head in my armpit. I lit the lantern and the candles. We settled in for a long night. I poured cups of whiskey. Annick and I played the rhyming game we call *Spot Shot* (a certain dog's photo). She said, "An Asian Attorney General."

"Filipino Janet Reno."

"Presidential Butt."

"Bush Tush."

The next storm lasted twenty minutes or so. I held Spot while he dug into the curve of the tub. We weren't going to get any sleep. We put on Puccini. Spot howled along to "Maid with the Flaxen Hair." We played *Two Truths and a Lie*. Annick went first. I had to guess which of her three stories was the lie.

"Number 1: I was a sophomore in high school, and I had a mad crush on Hilary Bronson, who was gorgeous and troubled. He'd already been to Juvenile Hall. I started smoking to impress him, started playing hooky to be with him. So one afternoon, Hilary and I were in his bedroom, and we had just finished doing it, and I lit up a True Blue, and I asked him, Does this mean that we're going steady?, and he laughed and said he was already going steady with Elaine Gosselin, and I stared at him and twisted the cigarette into my hand, crushed it out, and I didn't feel a thing.

"Number 2: I was a volunteer at the Nescopeck Manor Nursing Home. I ran the balloon volleyball games, organized Manicure Day and like that. One day I read how pets were supposed to be therapeutic for old folks, so I cleared it with the director and called up a dog track in Connecticut and adopted a greyhound. Mr. Bluster. The sweetest dog. Terrified of stairs. We'd get him running down the ward corridor for exercise and he'd slip and fall on his face or else he'd get going and not be able to stop or turn and he'd slide on into the wall. For some reason, the geriatrics didn't take to Mr. Bluster. He brought out the meanness in them. They treated him like the children that had abandoned them. Agnes Timoney chased him with her wheelchair. Archie Ledoux threw his radio at him. Mark Levine beat him over the head with his cane. The director had to go to court over cruelty to animals. I had to have poor Mr. Bluster put down.

"Number 3: I was driving alone to Scranton, and the car radio was busted, so I was singing all the songs I knew, and just when I was singing 'Ruby, don't take your love to town,' the radio starts up—dashboard lights come on and everything—and Kenny Rogers is singing right along with me. When we finished our duet, the radio went off."

I tried to imagine Hilary's bedroom. The broken lamp, the socks balled up under the bed, the pile of elbowed butts in the ashtray, the grit on the yellowed sheets, the busted alarm clock. And Hilary himself: India ink tattoos, acne, mossy teeth. I wanted Hilary to be the lie, but the answer had to be the nursing home. They wouldn't make old folks play balloon volleyball, would they? "Number 2."

Annick laughed. "Number 3. How could a busted-up radio just spontaneously begin to work?"

"Sun spots?"

"Your turn."

I told Annick how one time I came upon a car on fire in the middle of a two-lane road in the piney woods up near Smackover, Arkansas. Flames leaping thirty feet into the air. What was stranger than the fire was that nobody was around. I drove to town and called the Sheriff who thanked me for the heads-up. I asked him what he thought might have happened. He told me not to worry about it.

Then I told her about the night I was in Memphis and couldn't sleep—a loud party going on in the next room at the motel—and I went out for coffee and met Al Green. Sat beside him, said hi. Al introduced himself. He talked about himself in third person and laughed for no reason. He'd be like, "Al don't touch liquor no more," and he'd giggle. Or, "Al owes all that he has to Jesus Christ." When I told him he was my favorite singer, he began to hum, and pretty soon he was singing "Precious Lord" right there in the coffee shop. And then the customers started singing along, and the waitress, and me. Like in a movie.

"Number 3: My first girlfriend Patty was a diabetic, and she let me inject her thigh with insulin."

Annick said three, and she was right, and then she asked me why I would make up such a lame lie and if there really was a Patty at all. There was. She had a small diamond implanted in her front tooth. She was not diabetic. Her father was. Annick shook her head. She said, "'Take Me to the River' Al Green?"

Pressure Drop

During the night, Miss Fritzy inexplicably braked, wheeled around her eye, and drove south—miraculously, if embarrassingly so, according to the National Hurricane Center. Unfortunately, our miracle was Cuba's catastrophe. There had been no official damage reports from the island as yet, but Havana, apparently, had taken a direct hit. It was nearly nine o'clock. When the last storm ended an hour ago, Spot climbed out of our crowded tub, squeezed himself as far behind the toilet as he could, and fell into a fitful sleep. He was snoring now. According to News Radio 99, South Florida highways remained clogged with parked cars, most of them now in snake-infested water up to their chassis. We had missed the worst, but were not out of danger yet. The hurricane continued to spawn bands of severe storms, some of them potentially tornadic. The Governor had declared a State of Emergency, called out the National Guard. Public offices would be closed until further notice. All but essential medical and emergency personnel were to stay at home and off the roads.

I stretched my cramped legs, shifted my weight off my numb left side. Annick woke up, smiled, closed her eyes and nuzzled into the pillow on my chest. During a commercial for Griot King Take-Out, I changed stations to a call-in show. A man claiming to be on a cell phone from Havana described the ruins of the Presidential residence and said that no one inside could have escaped its collapse. The next caller, who identified himself as a representative of both the county government and the Cuban-American National Foundation, said that as soon as rumors of El Jefe's death were confirmed, there would be an official, government-sponsored gala celebration in the Orange Bowl to which citizens would be respectfully asked not to bring weapons or infants. Another gentleman—*first time caller from Hialeah; love your show, Rick*—suggested that even if Fidel were alive, this would be an opportune moment for an invasion. I turned off the radio. Annick said that maybe at long last Cuba would be free.

"To install another dictator," I said.

"Don't be cynical, Johnny."

"They loved Batista."

"They don't love Castro."

"The Miami Cubans don't. And that's because he's smarter than they are, and taller than they are, and more Cuban than they are."

"You wouldn't be talking like this on Calle Ocho."

"That's my point."

"So you're saying that some dictators are okay with you?"

"I'm saying I should hate the son of a bitch, but I don't."

Spot whined to go out. Annick sat up. I stood. My knees hurt. My back hurt. I looked at Spot. He woofed.

"All right already, we'll go out."

Spot sniffed the yard in all the usual places. He lifted his leg against the banana tree, turned his back to it and kicked up some turf with his back legs. I don't know why they even bother. The yard was littered with buttonwood branches, the hibiscus was stripped of its blue and purple flowers. Spot lapped up water from the birdbath. The eastern sky was black, not the serene dark of night, but the ominous green and purple, the bruised black your eye might be if you walked into baseball bat.

The power was out, would be for days it looked like. Annick and I sat at the kitchen counter eating the Little Debbies and drinking bottled water. Spot chewed on the last of Barbie's midriff. Annick told me about her cousin Destiny, how every six years she commits matrimony with some loser or other. Married at sixteen, twenty-two, twenty-eight, thirty-four, forty, forty-six, and fifty-two. Seven husbands, and in between them a series of even more miserable boyfriends. Dope fiends and drunks, batterers and cheaters. She can't seem to learn. I said, Maybe she's looking in the wrong places. Annick said, You think? I said, No need for sarcasm. She said, You're going to use this, I know you are. I said, Destiny Pascal?

"Destiny Pascal Rankin Kennedy Ayer Liechtenstein Chesterfield Smith."

"How do you remember her names?"

"Mnemonic. Despicable Partners Rankle Kin And Leave Cousin Stunned."

I tossed Spot a piece of a snack cake. "You could look at each marriage as a triumph of hope."

"Rankin cheated on her all over Tamaqua and slapped her around when she tried to leave. That's how smart he was. Kennedy defrauded retired people out of their life savings for a living. One night he moved to Bimini with his secretary. Ayer and Chesterfield were heroin addicts. Liechtenstein was a fundamentalist preacher who beat her when she cut her hair. Smith is a drunk."

"What's Destiny do for a living?"

"She's a psychotherapist."

"Is that a joke?"

"And a good psychotherapist. Destiny's the sweetest person I know."

"Where is she now?"

"Lives with Smith in Colorado."

"Denver?"

"Loveland."

"You're making this up."

"Just before each marriage ends, she goes in for surgery. She's had her tummy tucked, her ankles thinned, her varicose veins stripped, her eyes lasered, her nose reshaped, and her tear ducts removed."

"Tear ducts?"

"Said her eyes were always watering, and she was sick of it." Annick brushed crumbs from her lap. "What do you think all the surgery's about?"

I sipped some water. I didn't want to say *low self-esteem* or *self-mutilation* or anything else a psychotherapist might say. I shrugged. Tired of weeping! Where's my pen?

Spot heard the thunder before we did. He sat up and whined. He walked to the sliding glass door and barked at the sky. I said, "Okay, sweet pea, I'll take care of you." I wrapped Annick's cashmere tartan scarf around Spot's ears, tied it under his chin. He quieted. I slipped the Gore-Tex mittens over his front paws, tightened the pull cords. We all got back in the tub. Suddenly it felt like we had peaked on a roller coaster and had just begun free fall. The stomach in the throat business. My ears popped. The thunder was now a continuous rumble and Spot was digging like crazy and crying. I held him. The tub trembled. Our liquor bottles clanged against each other. The radio lifted off the floor and slammed into the wall.

Annick said, "Jesus Christ!"

I said, "Tornado."

Spot leaped out of the tub and ran for the closed door. The door sailed into the living room. The little window above us popped like a champagne cork, and the glass and screen vanished. I remembered reading about a man whose brain had been sucked out his ear by a tornado. Then I remembered we were supposed to drag a mattress in here with us to cover ourselves. The walls groaned and quaked. I remembered, too, that you're supposed to open all the windows in the house to prevent a vacuum from developing, and you're supposed to go to the northwest corner of the house. Or the northeast. Too late for us anyway. I grabbed Annick and lay on top of her. I shouldn't have, but I looked up, saw the walls flex, contract, and topple, and I saw Spot, still scarved and mittened, hovering above us, about where the roof had been, and I called to him as if he could have done anything about it, as if he even could have heard me above the earsplitting roar of the storm. Spot floated away from us like a helium balloon. The furniture in the house skated across the floor, tumbled to the lawn, and rolled down the street. The Goretkin's chiminaya flew over our tub and so did a bicycle, a propane tank, a floor lamp, and a television. And then it stopped. We didn't move. We listened to a silence so intense I was sure my ears were blocked. And then a gas grill dropped into what had been the living room and scared the hell out of us. Annick trembled. I held her, kissed her face a dozen times. We cried and then we smiled. I said, "We should find Spot."

Our radio and lantern were gone, but our bottles of liquor were undamaged. I smiled at Annick. I said, "There *is* a God." She picked up a flashlight, tested it. It worked. The kitchen counter was gone, meaning our batteries were, too. The only piece of Annick's furniture in sight was a single kitchen chair. I set it upright. We had an empty sink and a battered stove, minus an oven door. We discovered a providential case of bottled water where the garage used to be. The Lord giveth and the Lord taketh away. Three clown triggerfish flapped their bodies against the Mexican tile floor. I looked at Annick. She nodded. We plugged the sink, poured in two gallons of water, and released the stunned but grateful fish. We watched them float, bodies bowed, at the surface, saw them right themselves, ripple their lacy fins, and dart madly through the tepid water.

We sat on someone else's plaid sofa in the backyard and surveyed the incomprehensible devastation. Annick cried. The sofa wasn't very comfortable. I checked under the cushions and found several dollars worth of change, a pair of drug-store reading glasses, a TV remote, and a copy of *The Unabridged Journals of Sylvia Plath*. My truck was parked on its side in the next door neighbor's living room. I hoped that my computer and disks were still in the cab, but I was too afraid to look just yet. I held Annick's hand, and all I could think of was that the worst part of this would be all the standing in all the lines at all the agencies that I'd be doing, all the forms I'd have to fill out, all the calls I'd have to make, all the paperwork and rigmarole involved in getting my life and Annick's life back to normal. And that's when I remembered that triggerfish live in salt water. I decided not to tell Annick. I called to Spot. I whistled. Annick said he'd be okay.

We spent the rest of the morning and the afternoon wandering the neighborhood calling to Spot. We seemed to be the only fools who hadn't evacuated. I found a replacement for my torn shirt in a pile of clothes on Harding Street—a Delta State University T-shirt: The Fighting Okra. We stepped around power lines, fallen banyans, appliances, and household debris. What on earth were we all going to do without homes or possessions? Annick found a portable radio, and we sat on a houseless porch and listened. The tornado had leveled everything east of Federal Highway in Hollywood and Dania Beach. The highways were still parking lots and now the secondary roads in and out were blocked. We told ourselves it wouldn't be looting to take the radio. Annick tapped my leg. Look, she said. Two chimpanzees walked down the street holding hands. When they saw us they stopped and hugged each other. One of them bared its teeth. Then they fled across the golf course toward the water treatment plant.

When we rounded the corner to my street, I half-expected to see Spot waiting for us. When he left Annick's house he'd been flying in this direction. I still had a deck and a Solo-flex, a washer and dryer, an armoire with a TV in the cabinet, bookcases but no books. We found my tent underneath someone else's Barcalounger. The smart thing to do was to get out of there. Walk to the beach and follow it south until we found a hotel that would take us in. Annick said, We're not leaving Spot. I said, If we haven't found him by tomorrow, we'll have to go.

Annick set up the tent in the front of the house while I walked back to her house for water, liquor, and my computer. I made part of the trip back in an E-Z-Go golf cart I found by the Publix. I got back around dusk. Annick had a campfire going. She'd found sheets and pillows for the tent. At least we'd be safe from mosquitoes and sand fleas, from water snakes, roof rats, and God knows what all else. I told her we should just move. She said we couldn't. We still had mortgages. We still owned the property. We'd have to rebuild and then sell and then move. I said if we both sold our houses we could buy a palace in some place more placid and less congested. She said, Montana. I said I didn't want to be cold. We drank cognac, listened to the radio. Castro had been seen on the devastated streets of Havana. In Bangladesh, 100,000 people had been killed in monsoon floods. In Boston, the Red Sox drove for the pennant. In France, union leaders had called for a general strike. We turned off the radio. We heard a helicopter somewhere nearby, and when that faded, the snore of tree frogs, and the exuberant call of a whip-poor-will.

I thought about my pitiful collection of shoes and how years from now some kid kayaking through the mangroves will notice a curious, single, salt-stained, penny loafer wedged into the prop roots, and he'll stop rowing and stare at it, and he'll make up a story about how it came to be there, how one afternoon this junior at South Broward High found out that his girlfriend, his steady girlfriend, his steady, lavaliered girlfriend, was dumping him for a senior who was also the assistant night manager at Pollo Tropical, and how the spurned boy couldn't stand it anymore and started running like mad and eventually found himself sloshing through the swamp, wondering how he got there, and then he lost his shoe in the muck, and the shoe was lifted by the rising tide and floated down the inlet and dropped here, where it may have gone unnoticed forever, except that he, the innocent kayaker, happened along—he could have gone to the beach instead this morning—and happened to be just here when a mangrove crab flashed its white pincer from the cradle of the shoe.

I realized I had been unburdened of the stress and responsibility of proprietorship. I now owned nothing, and I felt reborn. I smiled at Annick. I understood that I was buoyant because I was with her. Privation is not something I could bare alone. In the end, all we have is who we love. My past had vanished, as it were, and now I could be anyone. Annick said, "Did you hear that?"

"What?"

"Listen."

I didn't hear anything.

"Jangling."

I shook my head.

"Like sleigh bells."

Coming from down the street. And then we saw a dim light about a foot or so off the ground, bobbing in time with the jingle.

I said, "Goddam."

"What the hell?"

It looked to be a faint halo, and iridescent, scintillating glow. I got the flashlight, shined it at the apparition, and then I saw him, Spot the sundog bounding toward us with Los Alamos Barbie gripped in his jaw. He ran right past us, the plaid scarf now trailing rakishly behind him, one mitten on, one mitten off. He circled the tent, the campfire. He dropped luminescent Barbie and rolled on his back, squirmed like a fish, exploded to his feet, shook himself like he'd just stepped out of a swimming pool, and dashed into our arms. We petted him, accepted his messy kisses, told him how worried we had been, how happy we were. I threw another Mission end table on the fire. We all crammed into the tent. Spot lay between us, panting, drooling. Then he told us how he'd flown over West Lake and landed in a cushion of fallen Australian pines. Came by earlier, but we weren't here. He caught his breath, licked our faces, crawled out from between us, and curled into a ball like a roly-poly at our feet. I snuggled into Annick. She kissed my nose. Spot woofed. No more storms, he said. The three of us, we got to get out of here.

Andrea Barrett

Two Rivers

The Ruins

As a young woman, she had written letters only infrequently. But now, in aid of her sister's work, Miriam found herself writing letters almost every day. To the geologists, soldiers, government officials and river traders on whom she and Grace depended, she wrote requesting cargo space for their crates, or reporting progress on their project, or itemizing their expenses: *freight on 1422 lbs @ 6 cents/lb: $85.32*. She wrote to her son, in whose hands she'd left the Academy months ago, and to her daughters, who taught there. She wrote to bank officials, freight agents, book dealers and, late in the afternoon of one bright, clear day, to her dead husband Caleb's dearest friend:

> June 29, 1853
> Mauvaises Terres of the Dacota Country
> Dear Stuart—
>
> Forgive me for taking so long to answer your last. I do mean to answer promptly, I know you like to follow our progress. I can only plead the constant press of work. You would understand if you could see this place; the season for collecting is short, and we are busy every minute. Do you remember what Caleb used to say about the ruins of an older world being visible all around us? He might have had this strange ugly landscape in mind, so jumbled and jagged. Box canyons, big cliffs, a river bed that looks as though God hacked through the plain with a giant axe.

Grace, who loves all of this, maps the sites where we dig and correlates the strata to similar formations elsewhere. In the cliff walls, she reports, the relics are arranged by age, youngest at the top and oldest at the bottom, neat as a filing cabinet: the clearest possible demonstration of the ideas you and Caleb shared. The fossil skulls and shinbones we stumble across on the basin floors are more difficult to place, and we have to guess at how they were arranged above.

My work is the usual: interpreting for her as necessary, otherwise helping as I can. Everything she chips out with her chisels and hooks I pack and ship to Dr. Leidy, the vertebrate paleontologist in Philadelphia. He tells us who the bones once belonged to—a gigantic quadruped with three pairs of horns, an antique camel, miniature horses, saber-toothed felines, a ruminating hog. He is writing a book ("Of course," I can hear Caleb saying wryly. "Of course he is writing a book.") A complete account of the extinct local creatures, classified and given Latin names. He promises acknowledgment in a footnote: "Thanks to Miss Grace Dietrich, who gathered these specimens."

She doesn't complain, so neither will I. The lithographs of her finds are beautiful, and we both understand, every day, how lucky we are to be able to do this. . . .

Here Miriam stops, not sure what else she wants to say. She and Stuart are separated now by more than geography; the letters they've exchanged since her departure from Pittsburgh are friendly but also constrained. She takes pains to present Grace's accomplishments in the most positive light, as if to justify their absence. In turn, Stuart amplifies every sign of progress at the Academy. She suspects he is at his desk even now, a pile of student papers before him and a glass of lemonade nearby. Still he teaches part of each day, although it tires him. And still, after all the years they worked together, her feelings about him are complicated. He's her oldest and in some ways her closest friend, now that Caleb is gone. Yet they have often quarreled and hidden things from each other.

Are there not always conflicts, though? The best friend and the second wife of such a well-known man; they were bound to disagree. After Caleb's death, Miriam had felt burdened by Stuart's pleas that she continue to share the responsibilities of the Academy with him. In turn, Stuart had been hurt by the speed with which she and Grace detached themselves from their duties, proposed their project to several eminent geologists, and found a place at the unofficial edge of this surveying expedition in the Bad Lands.

"I wish you wouldn't," Stuart had told her. "All Caleb's hard work, the work we have *all* put in—we have twenty-three pupils, what about them?"

"They'll be fine," Miriam had replied. "William is anxious to take on a larger role, and you know what a good teacher he is. Both his sisters are coming along nicely. And you've been Caleb's essential lieutenant . . ." She'd tried not to flinch at the expression on Stuart's face.

Why has he always been surprised by her? The day they met, when he first saw her and Grace conversing, he had stared as if they'd fallen from the moon. She can't imagine what he thought when Caleb explained the idea behind his plans—that the deaf might have a particular *affinity* for the study of plant and animal shapes—or when, after Grace's friends arrived, the angry parents took their hearing children away.

Whatever Stuart felt during that tumultuous time he confided to Caleb, not her. From the moment their first new pupil walked through the door, his hands signing a greeting while his anxious eyes said, *What if no one understands me?*, she had known that they were doing the right thing. She couldn't worry about Stuart's feelings, or wonder what it cost him to set aside his own plans and throw himself into Caleb's grand project.

Miriam rises, sets aside the board on which she's been writing, and considers the jagged landscape surrounding her tent. One formation, not far away, looks like a giant molar waiting to be pulled and would, she thinks, delight Caleb nearly as much as would her and Grace's presence here. Ignore the gossip, he would tell her. Concentrate on your work. But it isn't always easy being the widow of such a man; everyone has opinions about his life as well as hers. In the schools that their former pupils have founded, portraits of Caleb hang in the halls, along with miniature biographies that might refer to someone else's life.

No one knew him, Miriam thinks. Not as she and Stuart did—and no matter how the two of them disagree, this crucial bond remains. She picks up her pen again.

> You should see Grace's face and hands: very brown, dotted with freckles. Against these her hair, powdered with rock dust, is

so white that strangers sometimes take us for twins. They ask what we are doing, where we have come from. Sometimes, when they persist, I pretend I'm as deaf as Grace.

As I write, she's at the base of a ravine. Big birds whirl around above her; I should go call her, dusk comes suddenly here. I miss my dear children, I miss the Academy, I miss all of you. I know my life doesn't make sense to you. It makes sense to me and to Grace; it would have made sense to Caleb. Please ask my William to write and tell us how things are with him and his sisters, also how many new students he has enrolled for the autumn classes. I think of you often, always fondly.

Miriam

The Origins of the World

In Pittsburgh, as Miriam knew, people continued to talk about Caleb after he was dead. They spoke of the great swerve he'd made in mid-life and the dedication his family showed to his cause; of the visitor from Hartford he corralled into training them all and the pupils who became such a credit to him. But no one spoke of the years that laid the course for those events. The obituaries made no mention of Caleb's original family in Philadelphia, nor of his adoption by the Bernhards. Samuel Bernhard appeared only as the Academy's founder and Caleb's father, never in the context of his other work. And Caleb's best friend, Stuart, who might have corrected certain mistakes and omissions, kept his secrets.

Before Miriam set off for the West, she too had refrained from adding to the accounts of Caleb's life. A few private moments she hoarded for herself. Other things she was not equipped to speak about. Caleb was fifteen years her senior, a young man before she was born. And for all they shared in their years together, he never told her much about his first home, or about the endless nights, after he moved, when he stayed up with his new father.

He was in a house in Pittsburgh during those nights, his feet cold and his eyelids drooping while the river at the end of the block murmured *Ohio, Ohio*. Everyone else was asleep. Rosina, his new sister, was too young to be up so late; Mrs. Bernhard, his new mother, went to bed early, still mourning the children who, if they hadn't died as infants, would have been the rest of his new family. Behind the house was Bernhard's Academy for Boys, which Samuel Bernhard ran with a single assistant—but there were neither dormitories nor boarders then; those pupils went home at the end of the day. As Caleb turned eight, then eleven, then twelve—1800, a fresh new world—he bore the brunt of Samuel's enthusiasms alone.

Listen, Samuel said to him. *Listen to this*.

What Caleb heard was new and often enchanting, despite his exhaustion; it helped distract him from all he'd lost. Unlike his first parents, who had been farmers, Samuel talked about geology, theology, the origins of the world and all its creatures. About fossils, which some people called figured stones. In the old days, Samuel claimed, when he was a boy in Germany, rocks formed like animals or plants had been grouped with those shaped like axes or pots or hats.

With the rest of the household fast asleep, in a room cold except for a space near the stove, Samuel would hand over gray slabs that dusted Caleb's fingers. "That shape like a fern," he said, "is a miracle of nature."

"Where did it come from?" Caleb asked. In his old life, people had talked about the weather. "How did it get here?"

"There is only one true and simple explanation," Samuel said gravely. "But despite this men have had many notions. I keep track of them in these pages."

As Caleb admired the basswood box containing the papers, Samuel eased forward a single sheet. "Here is one idea," he continued. "Perhaps the figured stones are sports or jokes, which a capricious God developed in the rocks."

Perhaps, Caleb heard, *perhaps, perhaps*. Swooning with lack of sleep, still he struggled each night to be a worthy confidante. There were vapors, he heard, which might have risen from the sea, bearing the spawn of organic life and then condensing into rain. Or God might have endowed the earth itself with some extraordinary plastic virtue, capable of imitating existing forms. Some men, Samuel said, believed that in the secret, hidden parts of the earth, fossils might have been created as ornaments, just as tulips and roses, also useless, had been created as ornaments for the surface.

"Suppose they grew," Samuel said, smiling as if the idea had a savor on his tongue. "And reproduced accordingly—as plums beget plums, so might a stone bearing a snail-like figure beget a second snail."

All those stories, all those words, swirling around in Caleb's mind.

When he admitted his confusion, Samuel said, "You must learn not just to listen, but to think for yourself."

Am I to listen? Caleb thought then. *Or am I not?* On another night, after carefully considering more of Samuel's stories, he asked, "But what is the *truth?*"

"The truth," Samuel said quietly—it was very late, and dark red halos shimmered around the coals—"is that fossils are relics of the Flood, the petrified remains of creatures drowned in the Deluge. When God punished the sinners and the waters rose, the earth's surface was converted into a fluid jelly. Think of the jelly around the pickled pigs' feet your mother makes."

"I like that," Caleb said, although he still had trouble thinking of Mrs. Bernhard as his mother.

"While the jelly is warm and still liquid, she can stir in bits of meat. But once the jelly cools, everything is set in place. Exactly so," he continued, while Caleb's stomach rumbled, "was everything living frozen into the rocks when the Flood receded. The just along with the unjust; plants and fishes and snails, who after all had committed no sins, petrified equally with the humans who offended God."

"But that's not fair," Caleb said indignantly. "Why should the in-nocent be punished?"

Instead of answering, Samuel led Caleb to a long, heavy arc of gray rock resting on the windowsill. "From an elephant, who did no harm," he said. "This is part of a rib. A man I know found it at a salt lick in Kentucky." As Caleb held his candle closer to the petrified bone, Samuel raised his hand and cupped Caleb's chin. Since Rosina's birth they seldom touched; Caleb leaned into the unfamiliar warmth.

"We cannot know what God sees," Samuel said. "Nor how he judges. We can only accept that all he does is both just and merciful."

Sometimes, in the following months and years, Samuel read to Caleb from the Bible. Sometimes he read from his growing pile of pages, in which—the better to set off his true knowledge—he detailed the erro-neous theories of the past. And sometimes he read from the papers of other men who studied the secrets buried in the ground. Although no one had ever seen the giant creature called Megalonyx, it was not ex-tinct, simply undiscovered. "For if one link in nature's chain might be lost," Samuel read, "another and another might be lost, till this whole system of things should vanish by piecemeal."

Caleb wondered if he might not vanish himself, his former ways and habits buried beneath the flow of Samuel's ideas. He felt most in danger of disappearing, but also most intrigued, on the nights when Samuel put down his papers and stared into the fire, describing his own vision of the Deluge.

When the rain ended, Samuel said, when the great masses of cloud finally parted, how astonished Noah and his family must have been! The water shimmering under the first pale sun, the clouds first black then gray and then finally white in an open and radiant sky. Under the water, Samuel said dreamily, lay lost cities, drowned mountains, entire forests uprooted from their tenuous hold on land to float horizontally.

The Flood sounded lovely then; Caleb listened raptly. Only during the day, when he paused to consider the stories he'd heard in the dark, did he think of what Samuel hadn't mentioned: the lost people also floating through that calm liquid, tangled with lizards and birds among the branches.

One of Samuel's gifts was his power to conjure such vivid pictures in Caleb's mind. But Caleb had a gift as well, which he discovered during those years: he could pick out secret shapes where others distinguished nothing. Where had this come from? Not from Samuel, whose eyesight was very poor. Perhaps his first parents had shared a similar sharpness of vision. Outside, along the cliffs and streambeds, Caleb was drawn to the hidden fossils as if they were iron and he a magnet. When he found a new specimen, his joy made up for his gritty eyes and the way his classmates mocked him for his old-fashioned speech and his love of rocks.

Bernhard's heartburn, some of them sang. *Headmaster's bonehead son.*

He shrugged them off, they were ignorant. For friends, until he met Stuart Mason, he had his much younger sister, Rosina, and a bent-tailed yellow dog.

On a rainy spring afternoon in 1810, when Caleb was twenty-three, he visited Dr. Mason's office on behalf of his mother and left with a prescription for a tonic.

"See my nephew," Dr. Mason said. "Next door. He'll make this up."

In the space between the two low buildings Caleb, already wet, was so thoroughly drenched that even the roots of his hair felt refreshed. Behind him, as he ducked through the door, the rain fell and fell for the third day in a row. The streets were streams, the empty lots were ponds, the river was pushy and loud. The yellow dog was dead by then; Rosina, who'd turned from an eager, long-legged girl who liked to run through the woods into a miniature copy of her mother, hated to get muddy now and would never go out on a day like this.

Caleb, who liked the rain, shook himself off. Inside the cool dark room, perched on a stool before bottles of rhubarb bitters and witch hazel, hanging dried herbs and mysterious twigs, was a compact, sweet-faced young man he'd met briefly several times but not yet gotten to know. After they reintroduced themselves, Stuart inspected the note and said, "For your mother?"

How clear and frank his eyes were. "The rain makes her melancholy," Caleb replied, stifling an impulse to add that she wasn't actually his mother. Recently he'd been startled by how little he resembled his adopted family, and how sharply his long, wiry limbs and his consuming curiosity set him apart.

He looked down at the newspaper lying open on the counter, leaning closer when Stuart pointed out an article and asked, "Did you see that?"

The Rappites, Caleb read—hardworking religious ascetics, calmly awaiting the end of the world—had built a new woolen mill. What could it be like, Caleb wondered aloud, to work a loom in the expectation of being lifted bodily, any minute, into heaven?

"Unnerving, I imagine," Stuart said. "Every time you heard a strange sound you'd be thinking, *This is it.*"

When Caleb laughed, Stuart offered a tale about a man named Symmes, who claimed that the earth was hollow and filled with nested concentric spheres, each one habitable and awaiting settlement. In Russia one might find mammoths in the frozen river deltas. In Egypt there were mummies underground, in Oregon relics of ancient tribes— and so who could say for sure what else might not be hiding inside the earth?

"You'd like to travel?" Caleb asked. "So would I."

The lines of a possible life fanned out—two companions exploring here, adventuring there—and just as quickly reeled themselves in: Stuart was already married, Caleb learned. Already tied to the infant fussing in a basket at his feet.

"Talk is my form of travel," Stuart said wryly. "At least for now. That, and reading whatever I can." As Caleb pondered the contrast in their situations, Stuart bent over the basket and then deposited the squalling bundle in Caleb's arms.

"Elias," he said, as Caleb inspected the infant's charming ears. "He's teething. He wants to be held, and I need both hands to work."

While Stuart ground and stirred, he said he'd meant to be a doctor but now made a living compounding potions for his uncle and experimenting with leaves and roots. A sharp smell rose from some herb he crushed. "My father's legacy to me," he said, wincing. "An over-sensitive nose." What would it be like, Caleb wondered, to *know* who had given him certain traits—his sharp eyes, his cowlick, his sense of not quite fitting in anywhere? The smell of living blood, Stuart said ruefully, was what had turned him away from medicine.

Caleb jiggled Elias gently and eyed a huge tooth lying behind the bundles of willow twigs. "Mastodon?" he asked, prodding the conical cusps with his foot. "My father has part of a rib, from a place down the river."

"The salt lick in Kentucky?"

Caleb nodded. "His speculations about the Elephant of the Ohio are almost the first things I remember."

A lie, already; no way to make a friend. He crouched, balancing Elias, and touched the tooth's curved roots. What he first remembered, hazily, was an entirely different life. If his true parents had not died of the yellow fever when he was a child, he thought. If the Bernhards, making their way from New Jersey to Pittsburgh, had not stopped near the smoking heap that until that morning had been his home; if their eldest son had not died a few weeks earlier and if he himself had not been been pulling against the hand of the doctor, shrieking as his first sister, Lavinia, was placed in a wagon with two women. . . . *Grateful,* the doctor had said. *Always, to this family willing to take you.* He'd been five when he was chosen. He had never seen Lavinia again.

"My father told me the ground near the salt spring is filled with giant bones, all mixed together," he said. At least that part was true. "Some from creatures that no one has ever seen."

Stuart looked up and nodded. "The great American incognitum, now extinct."

"Or simply, as my father believes"—Caleb had his own doubts about this—"a living nondescript we haven't seen *yet.*"

Stuart raised his eyebrows, which Caleb found both reassuring and alarming. "So where are these behemoths now?"

"Out west," Caleb said cautiously. He returned Elias, who had fallen asleep, to the woven basket. "Or at the tip of South America, or hiding in the arctic. Somewhere, my father contends, mastodons are still roaring."

"That's one possibility," Stuart said. "Myself, I think they are long extinct—and I don't mean by the agency of any biblical event." Through a rolled cone of paper he poured a stream of ground bark. "I heard from my uncle that your father is writing a tract about fossils."

"He is," Caleb admitted. "An historical overview of all the old theories, followed by his own account." Was this a betrayal?

"I'm interested in the relationship of fossils to geology," Stuart said. "My uncle lets me borrow from his library. I'd be glad to share some books with you, if you're interested."

They talked for another hour, a rush of ideas that left Caleb both grateful for all he'd learned from Samuel and, as he wandered outside through the last feeble rain, afraid of his new friend's opinion of Samuel's work.

In Stuart's company, among the delectable rows of Dr. Mason's excellent library, Caleb developed his own ideas about the earth's beginnings. Stuart passed books, stuffed with scribbled notes, to Caleb; in turn, Caleb passed the least objectionable of these on to Samuel. After all, Caleb told his father, the earth's crust did not so much resemble a fluid pudding in which raisins were randomly mixed. Rather it resembled a squashed and tilted book, each page bearing a different form of writing. And this sequence of strata might *mean* something; the neatly stacked layers, all bearing their characteristic fossils, a signal that different kinds of life had over time appeared and then disappeared. Not one Deluge, Caleb suggested. But a long series of inundations.

Although Samuel dismissed that idea with a laugh, their arguments, which often included Stuart, in general seemed to please him. "I have always kept up with the times," he said proudly. "I have always been open-minded. Reconcile your theories with the truth of Scripture and you will have my full attention."

It was enough, Caleb thought, to see Samuel caught up again in the pursuit that had once been his greatest pleasure. In recent years he'd grown sluggish, seldom going on the collecting trips that had punctuated Caleb's childhood. Work on his book had slowed as well; he was growing old, and sufficiently vague that his assistant master, exasperated, had recently resigned. Caleb, with little warning, now found himself teaching half the classes.

What a relief, in light of this, to see some of Samuel's old energy and enthusiasm return. Once again he was scouring the local cliffs and creekbeds, and if at first he returned with the same familiar fossils, still his ardor was touching. A small, solitary figure climbing clumsily up a rockface, scarf flapping over his shoulder as his bruised hands fumbled for treasures: how could this pleasing sight lead to so much pain?

During the weeks when Samuel found the first of the peculiar stones, Caleb, who was swamped with teaching duties, knew only that his father vanished at awkward times and seemed gleefully secretive. He would have been horrified to see Samuel on that cliff, charting the positions of his finds before removing and secreting them, like nuts. Had Caleb known what was going on, he would have asked the questions that became obvious later: why did Samuel find only counterparts—the impressions, the prints—and no corresponding parts? Why were all the impressions intact, and all of the same depth? But Samuel saw, instead of these problems, a grand solution.

His stones, which depicted bees caught in the act of sipping nectar, birds frozen in mid-flight, a spider consuming a fly, were not mingled together but layered, birds above bees above the spider until, near the top of the cliff, the sequence was crowned by pictures of the sun and broken shapes that resembled letters. Relics of men, Samuel decided. A civilization drowned in the Flood. Without telling Caleb anything, without showing the stones to a soul, Samuel commissioned an artist to draw illustrations of all he'd found. Only then did he confide in Caleb.

What was it like, that first sight of the stones? Like a blow to the head, like the onset of a fever. Caleb knew, he knew right away; Stuart agreed with him instantly. The stones are fake, Caleb told his father. Can't you see?

But Samuel locked himself in his study, emerging with fresh chapters for his book. These discoveries, he claimed, proved that fossils were arrayed in layers not because they'd been laid down over time, during successive inundations, but as a result of their differing degrees of intelligence and closeness to God. Little creeping things had drowned in the first days of the only Flood, while the more intelligent, flying or fleeing uphill, had been caught by the water later. Of course human beings had drowned last. By this arrangement, God demonstrated order even in the midst of chaos.

By then Samuel wasn't speaking at night, pacing before the fire; by then he was preaching to his family or bursting into Caleb's classroom. Nothing has altered since the Deluge, he claimed, nor will it ever, as God's first plan was perfect. Consider the sturgeon, that very odd fish. "From the Monongahela," he told Caleb's history class, "I once pulled a specimen five feet long, with a mouth like a hose." Who could have expected God to fashion such an improbable creature?

All this, and more, he wrote down. Soon his book assumed its final shape and a title that, repeated on brown calf covers, would haunt Caleb for years:

GOD'S HAND APPARENT
IN THE FIGURED STONES
OF THE ALLEGHENY AND MONONGAHELA VALLEY REGION;
ILLUSTRATED WITH FOLIO PLATES
OF THESE MARVELOUS CREATIONS.

Eighteen months after finding the first stone, three months after he'd sent copies of his book to all the best scientific societies and journals, Samuel found, in a crevice at the top of the cliff, a flat slab inscribed with his name.

In the schoolyard, among the whispering boys, were a few who betrayed the culprits: three recent graduates who, before leaving the Academy, had carved the impressions into bits of soft shale. Caleb tracked them down and made them apologize to Samuel. They'd never meant, they said, for Mr. Bernhard to take those stones seriously. They had thought he'd see their joke at a glance. Their bland blank faces and calloused hands, their fumbling explanations: Caleb had wanted to strike them.

Samuel stopped teaching, he stopped going out, soon he stopped leaving his bed. He spent all he'd saved, and more he borrowed, buying back copies of his book. During the days Caleb, now running the Academy by himself, could not be with him. But at night he sat by Samuel's bed, the two of them once more awake together while the rest of the household slept. This time it was Caleb who read: at first out loud, when Samuel could still listen. Later, near the end, he read to himself.

The Academy of Sorrow

A herd of schoolboys dropping books, reciting their lessons, bungling grammar and simple sums while exuding a smell—not unpleasant, completely definitive—that hadn't changed since he was a boy himself: for a decade, except for a brief, glowing year, this became the shape of Caleb's life. He worked to restore the Academy's reputation and to repay the debts which, along with a tower of brown books, and a clear sense of his father's errors, he'd inherited. To the curriculum, which he'd also inherited, he slowly added algebra, astronomy, a smattering of geology. Still he wasn't teaching what he wanted, but each small change was a revolution to the parents he courted and couldn't afford to offend.

Young Harry Spires, who joined the Academy as assistant master seven years after Samuel's death, was all for tossing Livy and Horace aside completely and adding botany, chemistry, French and German. Patience, Caleb counseled. We must move cautiously. He didn't say what he sometimes thought: that he'd inherited a kind of factory, stamping out adequately learned, sufficiently tractable young men. Men like him. He'd loved teaching, when he was younger and had first started helping his father. Now he sometimes dozed in class, waking to find suggestive drawings on the slates and the boys smirking as if he'd turned into their last, collar-frayed visions of Samuel. A *widower*, parents whispered, excusing his lapses.

Briefly, through his courtship of Margaret Harper and their simple wedding, through the lush days of August and the months when Margaret was carrying their child, he'd felt as clear and radiant as a glass bowl lit by a beeswax candle. Then something snapped or fell or cracked, a wind blew, a storm raged—who ordered this?—and he was sitting in the kitchen, staring at Stuart while his son struggled and failed to be born and left Margaret burning with fever. He roasted straws in the stove and removed them, burning holes with the fiery tips in a sheet of paper. From the pattern of charred holes, letters emerged: *The Academy of Sorrow*. Stuart seized the paper; Caleb singed spots on the back of his hand. Stuart seized his hands. During the rest of that terrible week, Stuart left his own work to help Harry with the classes, while Rosina managed the house so that Mrs. Bernhard could tend to her daughter-in-law. Caleb prayed, everyone prayed; and still, Margaret followed her son four days later.

After that Caleb turned away from whoever tried to help him. His pupils' well-meaning mothers—the widows especially—sometimes asked why he didn't remarry; it wasn't right for a man to be alone. He might have replied that the Academy, and his remaining family, required his full attention. Or he might have told the widows the truth: that once, not long after he and Margaret were married, he'd complimented her on a pot of yellow blossoms near the front door. She'd laughed, and blushed, and then confessed that weeks earlier, watching him walk around the vegetable garden, she'd slipped out, dug up a brick-sized clump of earth which held the clear impression of his right foot, and tucked it into a flowerpot. In that earth she'd planted a chrysanthemum, hoping that as it bloomed year after year so would his love for her. How should he marry again, after that?

He told the widows nothing. In the constant absence of Margaret he worked, and looked after his mother and Rosina, and missed his old lively friendship with Stuart; Stuart had two more children now and when they met they spoke wryly of the tasks—the endless, tedious tasks—that kept them, almost all the time, apart.

The spring of 1825, they agreed, was more than usually harassing. Stuart's daughters both had the measles; two of Caleb's pupils were caught stealing and had to be expelled. Rosina, who for years had managed the Academy's accounts and helped her mother with the housekeeping, was suddenly useless. She and Harry, surprising everyone, had decided to marry; she was so happy she wandered around in a daze. While she stood in the hall outside Caleb's classroom, smiling down at the bust of Homer beneath her unmoving feather duster, he led his youngest pupils in a geography lesson and imagined giving her away. Rosina's hand relinquishing his arm for Harry's, Harry moving into the house with them, sharing the family duties so that his own burdens finally lightened—why, then, did he feel so unsettled?

To the boys in his classroom, he read, "For what is Asia remarkable?" The boys said:

It is the division of the Earth that was first inhabited.

Who were the first persons on Earth?
Adam and Eve, who were placed in the Garden of Eden.

At what time was the Deluge?
Nearly seventeen centuries after the creation of man.

What then became of all living beings?
All living creatures died, except those that went with Noah into the Ark.

A sharp tight pain, which resembled a cramp, seized the base of his lungs just then. He dropped his eyes to the textbook, which he'd used for more years than he cared to remember. In the back of the room, Ian Berger pushed his lank brown hair aside, revealing freckles that merged into coin-sized splotches over his nose and left cheek.

"Question," Ian said, as someone did each term. "Where did the water go *after?*"

Caleb had no answer. Wasn't this endless repetition, wrestling each day with the same tasks, same words, same weak and squalid self, enough to make anyone yearn for change? After the boys had gone home, he made his way to Stuart's house. There he found his friend in equally bad spirits, sitting on the brick stoop and prying loose scraps of mortar.

"Tired?" Caleb asked.

"Of every single thing," his friend replied. He flicked a scrap disdainfully into the air. "I'll be thirty-eight next week—my father was dead by then. Yours has been gone for a decade. And here we're still stuck in the same place, doing the same things, never seeing anything more than this tiny corner of the world—look at this stoop, it's falling apart."

"Something could change," Caleb said. "*We* could change."

"Our natures don't change," Stuart snapped. "If you had children of your own, you'd understand." As Caleb flinched, Stuart reached for his hand. "Forgive me," he said. "I wasn't thinking."

He went into the house and returned with a bottle of rum, which a grateful patient had given him, and a single glass, which, like their discontent, they shared.

Classes ended at the Academy and the boys disappeared; Mrs. Bernhard and Rosina, absorbed by the wedding plans, failed to notice the anniversary of Margaret's death. As the trees leafed out and the dense heavy heat descended, Caleb spent hours down at the wharves, fascinated by the jumble of boats and barges. He saw Frenchmen, and Indians, and a group of emigrants heading west—where was everyone going?

The movement and bustle cheered him briefly, as did Rosina and Harry's wedding, but afterwards, watching the new couple settle contentedly into their household routines, he couldn't help thinking of the life that he and Margaret had lost. All summer he dreamed of Margaret; often he saw her holding his sister Lavinia in her arms. Lavinia's face, which had dimmed in his memory as he'd grown up, had mysteriously regained its color and definition after Margaret's death. Now he saw both of them clearly, the tiny scar on his first sister's chin as vivid as the dark speck Margaret bore on the rim of one hazel iris.

Those dreams brought a cloud of melancholy that even the start of the new term couldn't dispel. Stuart was downright gloomy; in November, when Caleb brought him a book they'd both coveted, and couldn't afford—Rembrandt Peale's *Historical Disquisition on the Mammoth*—Stuart only shrugged. The long, intense conversations of their youth, their arguments over philosophy, history, the nature of science: how these had shrunk, Caleb thought. Shriveled to almost nothing. He set the precious volume on the table.

"What we need," he said, "is a trip."

"I can't go anywhere," Stuart said flatly. "How could I? Barbara, the children, my uncle, my mother: everyone needs me."

The crumpled skin around his eyes, the softness below his jaw—how old they'd gotten, Caleb thought. "A few weeks?" he asked.

He tried to convey to his friend the ferment he'd detected in the air. At the wharves he'd glimpsed an enormous keelboat, still under construction, that belonged to a group of naturalists and teachers headed for Robert Owen's utopian community on the Wabash River. Other boats were crowded with emigrants headed for Illinois, merchants loading and unloading goods; everyone had a plan. The papers were thick with appeals—for a Fourierist phalanx, a haven for freed slaves, a rational utopia; for asylums to benefit the deaf, the blind, the insane. Even the Rappites, less than twenty miles away, had established a new community called Economy. Couldn't the two of them step back from the history of their own lives and embrace the larger history of the earth?

"I had a thought," Caleb said. "We could go to Kentucky together and visit the Big Bone Lick. I'd love to gather some fossils for the classroom, I think I'd have better luck teaching the boys if they could actually *feel* one of those giant tusks. And I'm curious to see for myself how the fossils lie where they haven't been disturbed."

Stuart reached for the book on the table, but offered no comment. And why should he? Caleb thought. Even to his own ears, the excuse for the trip sounded feeble. Something else was pressing at him: a sense, which he couldn't articulate, that in rummaging through that bone-filled pit he might finally make sense of his history with Samuel. More forcefully, he continued, "At the right site, we might be able to demonstrate a clear column of succession."

But still Stuart looked at him wearily. *Our natures don't change,* he'd said: but he hadn't meant that, he wasn't himself. Not so many years ago, they'd argued happily about the possibilities of a world still developing, still in progress. But if the world was fixed as God first created it, forever immutable; if nothing ever changed or became extinct but persisted and persisted—

"I know it's winter," Caleb said. Was that what Stuart was worried about? "But the lick is south of here, and the ground is saturated with salt. If it's frozen at all, it will only be on the surface. And no one else will be there—a great advantage."

"I really can't travel now," Stuart said. "I just can't. But why don't you go?"

Traveling alone seemed unappealing, but if he could bring back something that would cheer his friend. . . . Caleb jumped when Stuart smacked both palms against the table.

"*Go somewhere,*" Stuart said. "Harry can take care of the Academy for a few weeks. Learn what you can and come back and tell me everything. I'm so tired of being stuck here—bring me something *new.*"

Everything happened quickly after that. A pupil's father, a commission merchant, owned a flatboat being loaded with linen and ginseng and nails, which was leaving for New Orleans; Caleb was welcome, the merchant said, to passage as far as he desired. A three-week break was scheduled for the end of term, and although Caleb expected to be gone at least six weeks, Harry said he could manage with a temporary replacement. Surely that small inconvenience was nothing in light of the useful and instructive fossils Caleb might bring back. "If you happened to find any plant fossils as well, that would be excellent," Harry said enthusiastically. "And when you return, maybe we could order a new globe, and some botany manuals."

Rosina, leaning up against Harry, said to Caleb, "But don't be gone too long, will you? There's so much to do here."

While Caleb packed shirts and socks and waterproof boots, a gun and a measuring stick and two shovels, he considered, and then set aside, the fact that Samuel's bitter last months had also begun with a fossil-gathering trip. Yet at the wharf a few days later, shivering in the cold wind and regarding the roughly built boat heaped with kegs and tarpaulin-covered mounds, he felt an instant's panic.

Why was he leaving? A smell he couldn't name rose from the river, and in the confusion of saying his farewells he dropped a trowel into the water and then failed to thank Stuart for the book pressed firmly into his hands. Sally, Stuart's youngest, had brought a gift as well: three sprigs of holly tied with a white bow. With the crisp green leaves in his buttonhole, Caleb stepped onto the boat. Once not he but Samuel had said, teaching the boys some local geography, *If we could fly, we would see from the clouds the clear waters of the Allegheny flowing down from the north, the muddy waters of the Monongahela flowing up from the south, two rivers merging into the Ohio at our home and forming a great Y. By that enormous letter we are meant to understand. . . .*

He'd forgotten the rest, the most important part; always he remembered the wrong things. At the railing he watched a band of black water expand between him and the shore. In some language, an Indian language, Ohio meant "beautiful river." From the sky something cold, part rain and part sleet, began to fall.

Beautiful River

A few miles past the Rappite settlement of Economy, a farmstead set back from the river housed an informal school quite different from the Academy. On this December afternoon all the pupils—Grace Dietrich, her two older brothers, and four little girls from the neighboring houses—were walking toward the water, intent on their weekly nature lesson. Forget the snow, forget the cold. Or so said Miriam, who was their teacher. If the animals pranced about in it, why shouldn't they? Every week they made this journey, in every kind of weather. On this day they romped in the woods for an hour before they emerged at the river's edge and saw a boat being pushed toward the shore by rafts of ice. Men were shouting and long oars were flailing while the bow ground against tree roots already tangled in ice. The other pupils exclaimed at the noise and confusion, but Grace heard nothing.

Had the boat not appeared, Miriam would have pointed out deer-scat, or a woodcock's feather, or a fallen cardinal bright against the snow. Instead, as a man jumped from the boat to the ice to the ground, a rope in his hand, a hat on his head, Miriam directed Grace's gaze to the scene unfolding before them. Twice the man passed the rope around a tree, tying a complicated knot before he opened his mouth and spiraled a finger through the air. Another man lowered a plank from the deck to the shore. On the deckhouse roof a third man, tall and thin, stood amid the bristling oars and looked curiously down at the scene.

Grace held her arms straight out, in imitation of the oars, and then pulled them in and asked her sister a question. Miriam said, "Travelers," at the same time shaping a gesture with her hands.

"Going where?" asked three of her pupils at once.

Miriam called a question to the man who'd secured the boat.

"St. Louis, then New Orleans," he called. Once more Miriam turned to Grace and gestured.

"Where's the nearest village?" asked the man who'd lowered the plank. Carefully he made his way across the gap between the boat and the riverbank.

Miriam stepped toward him, drew a map in the snow—the river here, a farmhouse there, a stand of willows, the sandbar—and told him where he might buy flour and cheese. The sun was setting, the children were cold. Grace, who was watching her actions intently, was shivering.

"We won't be here long," the boatman said cheerfully. "I'm sure the ice will break up soon."

"I wish you good luck," Miriam said. Everyone was busy with something, she saw, except that odd figure still peering down from the roof. Uneasy beneath his inquiring gaze she herded her students together and began the long walk home.

Caleb had been tagged as an oddity even before his boat was forced ashore; not in the old, familiar way, but in an unexpected way. Only those with a purpose, he'd learned—traders transporting cargo, families looking to settle new land—traveled at this time of year. What, the boatmen asked him, was he thinking? They were unimpressed by his account of the fossil graveyard awaiting him downriver.

"You want to dig in this weather?" one asked. "For petrified bones? Good luck."

Caleb slept alone in the first and smallest of the cabins, while the boatmen, crowded into the other cabin aft of the big space heaped with cargo, laughed and talked and smoked their pipes, never inviting him to join them. On their fourth day out, when ice forced the boat to halt, they pushed him aside and moved through their tasks in an easy synchrony.

Unable to find a single useful thing to do, Caleb had watched the children racing like rabbits across a small clearing, the slender woman who spoke to the boatmen, and the little girl whose hands moved rapidly in the air. The woman's hair was almost white; the girl's hair was equally pale; they looked, not like the sister with whom he'd grown up, but like his real, lost sister. He'd raised a hand partway, a hesitant greeting, but they didn't respond and a minute later they vanished.

Later that afternoon, while the crew settled into a routine of chopping wood and playing cards, Caleb fiddled with his equipment and worried about the weather, so much colder than he'd expected. The river seldom locked up like this, one boatman said. But they'd probably be freed in a day or two. After dinner Caleb wrote a letter to Stuart describing his predicament: which included the fact that the mail wouldn't move until the river had thawed. *I could walk home in two days,* he wrote. *But it's too soon to give up.* Then he stuffed the letter in his satchel, wrapped himself in his blankets, and went to sleep.

When he woke the boat was still frozen in, and the boatmen were still playing cards. Determined to be useful, Caleb left very early with his gun. The birds and bushes and trees near the boat were the same, he saw, as those he'd left less than twenty miles behind him. Also the same were the rocks poking up through the snow and the hawks spiraling through the sky. Farther away from the river's edge, where the snow was deeper, he found the tracks of deer and possums and pheasants. Enormous trees, black and bare, and the sun so low in the sky; he walked for miles, beguiled by the light and shooting at nothing. Only when he crossed his own tracks did he realize he'd traced a great circle.

Off he went again, on a line diagonal to his first route. Near noon he came upon a modest house, where he thought to beg a few minutes by the fire. The young woman he'd seen near the river a day earlier opened the door.

"Oh!" she said. "You—was that you on the roof of the boat?"

"I waved," he said. "You didn't see me."

Her face colored slightly. "I was talking to my sister. I didn't have a free hand."

He took off his hat and introduced himself, both confused and touched by her embarrassment.

"Will you come in?"

Behind her was the girl he'd glimpsed, along with six other children. Twining among them were a black cat, a tortoiseshell cat, and a large splotched dog. From the kitchen an older woman, Mrs. Dietrich, came forward to greet him. Miriam took his coat and gun and settled him by the fire.

"Grace is deaf," she murmured as her mother withdrew. Then she continued with the introductions, Grace's hands following her words. For her older brother, who had large ears, Grace pinched her right earlobe gently and tugged it. For her younger brother she stroked her eyebrows: his were dark and full, the most striking thing about him. She had similarly eloquent gestures for the girls Miriam introduced as their neighbors and her pupils. As she shaped them Grace studied the stranger who'd finally arrived.

Not a stranger, exactly: she'd seen his awkward gestures on the boat. Along with the fresh smell of snow and the deeper notes of his wet boots and woolen clothes, he carried an odor of sadness. As he stretched his boots toward the fire, Miriam pointed at him and raised her eyebrows in a question. Grace put her hand to her forehead, palm out with two fingers raised and curled forward, imitating his tuft of springy hair.

"What does she mean?" Caleb asked.

Miriam laughed and repeated the gesture. "She told you her names for everyone here; then she gave you a name-sign as well."

Clumsily he tried to imitate her movement. "This?"

"Turn your wrist," said Miriam. "That."

"How do I make her name?"

Miriam passed her left hand, palm in, over her left ear and then her mouth, as if with that gesture she sealed them both shut. Caleb shaped the sign for himself, correctly this time; then pointed to Grace and smiled and shaped the sign for her. Mrs. Dietrich appeared with a tray.

"Your daughter has a whole language of signs?" Caleb asked. Mrs. Dietrich nodded.

"We do," Miriam replied, helping her mother pass around cornbread and coffee and peach preserves. The children stared at him and the splotched dog licked his hand. "Our whole family."

She did most of the talking; Mrs. Dietrich was quiet and the gestures she used to converse with Grace were cramped and halting. Soon she excused herself and returned to the pies she was making.

"Grace lost her hearing when she was two," Miriam offered. "Most of our signs she invented, though we also use some she's picked up from her friends." She passed Caleb the last fragments of the cornbread. "But tell me about your journey," she said. "Where you're headed."

Even as he tried to describe his plans—the salt lick in Kentucky he hoped to visit, with its famous graveyard of ancient bones; his hope of digging out some of these relics—part of his attention was also with the children, who'd returned to their lessons. A schoolmaster's trick, pounded deep within. As he spoke he eyed the few worn books they shared and the open picture-primer, its oversized words paired with drawings: HAT, RAT, POT, CAT, HEN, TOP, BOY. At the moment Grace was drawing a map of Pennsylvania while the others shared the history text. With a gentle word, Miriam quelled the fit of giggling that swept through the room when the big-eared boy dropped the book on the floor.

"Forgive them," she said. Her attention too was split, Caleb sensed. As it should be. "We're taking three days off from our lessons for Christmas, and they're so excited they can't concentrate."

"You do very well with them," Caleb said. He looked down at his wet boots, imagining himself back at the Academy a few weeks from now, pushing the younger boys through their readers and ignoring their yawns. "I'm a schoolmaster myself."

"You enjoy the work?"

He nodded and then, encouraged, described the Academy. He barely mentioned Samuel and at first, flattered by her attention, didn't notice how little she offered about herself. Nothing about how Grace had lost her hearing, nor how she'd started this school. As he spoke, Grace continued drawing her map.

With her beloved colored pencils she made a blue river, brown mountains, patches of green forest. This river, her river, without the ice but with Caleb's boat. The cat walked to the window, placed her front paws on the glass, and stood staring sway-bellied out at the snow until, without transition, she was perched on the sill and the dog was walking back and forth below her, considering all that the cat might be seeing. The dog moved toward the door and waited for one of the boys to release her. Their visitor, whose crest resembled that of a female cardinal, crossed and uncrossed his legs. What would her father make of him? Over her map she unconsciously shaped her father's name-sign, one hand holding and guiding an invisible chisel while the heel of the other pushed. He'd gone to a neighbor's to build them a table but would soon return. When the cat pressed a paw to the window, trying to touch a passing crow, Grace pinched the air near her upper lip with two fingers, drawing them in an eloquent movement through the place where her whiskers would be, if she were a cat.

Caleb, who'd been watching her, laughed and said, "Even I can understand that." The children, or the fire, or the fragrant woodsmoke, Miriam's easy conversation or Mrs. Dietrich's restful silence, the sight of Grace—perhaps especially Grace—had cheered him. Only now did he realize how off-balance he'd felt since leaving home. Through the window he saw the dog leap up in a startling curve, snapping at something beyond the frame. A beautiful day, one of those days for which the world had been created. He had almost missed it entirely.

He rose, flexing his toes in his nearly dry boots. "I should head back," he said reluctantly. "Thank you for making me so welcome."

"We're glad for the company," Miriam said. "The bad weather's cut us off from everyone." The children waved and the cats serpentined around his legs. Mrs. Dietrich, who hadn't spoken directly to him since they finished their meal, came forward, smiling, to offer a pair of mince pies.

He shared these with the boatmen on Christmas Day, when they asked him to join their quiet celebration. The captain led the men in some hymns; Caleb read from the Bible when asked; rain fell, harder and harder, melting the snow until it seemed that they must soon be freed. But after their dinner of pheasant and biscuits and pie, the rain stopped, the sky cleared, and a cold wind swept down the river, freezing everything again. Caleb excused himself from the boatmen's cabin and retreated to the pleasures of Stuart's farewell gift: John Filson's essay on the natural history of Kentucky. A book older than he was, but still very useful—and how like Stuart, he thought fondly, to give him not the most up-to-date scientific volume but this early description of the area. Stuart had marked one page with a piece of paper; the passage described the salt lick—still so far downriver that Caleb could hardly imagine it—and the finds of astonishing bones.

The celebrated Dr. Hunter, Caleb read, had observed from the form of the giant teeth found there,

> that they must have belonged to a carnivorous animal. . . . these bones belonged to a quadruped now unknown, and whose race is probably extinct, unless it may be found in the extensive continent of New Holland, whose recesses have not yet been pervaded by the curiosity or avidity of civilized man. Can then so great a link have perished from the chain of nature?

Where had Stuart found this book? And when—and why hadn't they read it together? Perhaps they had: there'd been long stretches, during Samuel's last months, when Caleb had sat by his father's bed with the books Stuart loaned to him, passing the words before his eyes but registering nothing.

Every morning, Caleb thought, Samuel had eaten the same kind of porridge at the same time, from the same bowl; then washed his hands and said a prayer and entered the same classroom full of boys essentially if not actually the same. After teaching the same Scripture lessons he dissected the same passages from Horace and Virgil and ate the same mid-day bread and cheese, eagerly awaiting the late-night hours when, surrounded by his trays of fossils, he might seek an answer to the riddle of Creation. What kind of a life was that? The same kind, Caleb feared—he was back in his bunk, unable to sleep—that he'd been leading himself.

Yet look what happened when he tried to broaden his horizons. In Pittsburgh, a few months earlier, he'd gone by himself to a party. The room had been filled with strangers, most from the same group of teachers and naturalists whose keelboat Caleb had seen being built at the wharves. They were headed for New Harmony, someone said; they meant to change the world. Intrigued—where did they find the nerve?—but also hugely skeptical, Caleb had eavesdropped on several conversations. A Frenchman attached to the group, a naturalist named Charles Lesueur, spoke eloquently about his earlier travels. The astonishing falls at the Niagara River, new species of sturgeon and pike; proudly he displayed his sketchbook to Mr. Wright, their host.

Caleb, edging up to the circle of listeners, admired the beautiful drawings until Mr. Wright, to his embarrassment, pulled him inside the circle and presented him to Lesueur. After repeating Caleb's name, Mr. Wright added, "Caleb is the son of Mr. Samuel Bernhard, who some years ago published a remarkable book about the nature of fossils and their role in God's creation."

This again, Caleb had thought. Always this. What did Mr. Wright have against him? Lesueur pouted his lips and blew, a small explosive puff that Caleb would forever after think of as definitively French. "That book," he said. "I have seen that book. Your father. . . ."

Caleb flushed and looked at his shoes. The moment would pass, he thought, if he said nothing. He had lived through similar moments before. "My father is dead," he said.

"I don't mean to insult him," Lesueur continued. "Or this back-

237

ward country. Merely to suggest that we consolidate the truth in opposition to a knowledge of the false—and so your father after all had a role to play. Cuvier proved last year that Scheuchzer's famous fossil skeleton, the one he called *Homo diluvii*, was the front part of a giant salamander. Your father probably believed it was a man who drowned in the flood."

Caleb had made some clumsy excuse and fled; but the damage was done. It had taken Stuart days to calm him.

Still thinking about that party, and of the Frenchman who'd insulted him, he slept fitfully and woke with an aching head. After breakfast he went walking again, this time making a beeline for the pleasant house in the woods. Once more, Miriam opened the door. Both would remember this, later: her surprise, which deepened so quickly to pleasure. Gratefully he settled down again beside the fire.

"My parents are out," she said. "It is just us. But we're glad to see you."

Grace sat on the floor, busy with her colored pencils; after Miriam signed to her that she and Caleb were going to talk privately, her hands were still while they chatted. The weather, the moving ice; her mother's pies, which had been delicious, and her father's work, which was all around them: table, clothespress, walnut chest of drawers. The house itself. Grace and her brothers had been born here but Miriam was old enough to remember the journey from northern New York and the isolation of their early days, before they'd had neighbors. Her parents had taught her to read and write and later, when she'd proved to have a particular gift for teaching, had encouraged her to take in pupils.

Although Miriam's words flowed in a straight line, still Caleb thought they skirted something essential. About to ask a question, he subsided as she explained that the key to Grace's education was the language of gestures, which, mysteriously, she'd been able to grasp more easily than had her parents. Through it Grace had already learned so much.

"She's beginning to read," Miriam said. "It's a second language for her, written English—I explain it by way of signs, and by drawings. Her written vocabulary isn't very large but she learns new words every day."

"Astonishing," Caleb said.

"Is it? Some days it simply seems like what we make together. What *is*. Since she first lost her hearing I've been able to understand her gestures almost instinctively, even though my mother stumbles and my father can't express himself that way at all. I'm not good at re-membering ideas from books, but I remember shapes. It was her own idea to learn her letters. One morning she carried a book to me, point-ing at the lines, then herself, then the lines. She was holding it upside down."

The warm glow that lit her features made him think of Margaret. "She makes signs in her sleep," Miriam said. "I think she must dream in gestures. And when she's reading she sometimes shapes the corre-sponding gestures with her hands, as you or I might have moved our lips when we were first learning."

He repeated a story he'd heard over Christmas dinner, about a young man, born deaf, whose father had been a boatman here on the Ohio. "When the boatman drowned," he said, "a deaf beggar took the child to Philadelphia and used him to help solicit alms. There's a school for the deaf there—"

"I know of it," Miriam interrupted eagerly. "There's one in Hart-ford as well, we use their signed alphabet."

"—and someone from that institution saw the boy on the streets and took him in, where he learned to draw wonderfully. Later he was apprenticed to an artist and learned lithography. Now he makes his living doing that and is much admired, especially for his skillful ren-derings of fish."

"I have to tell Grace this part," Miriam said.

Caleb couldn't see, in her liquid movements, where one word ended and another began: how did one learn this? He and Lavinia had been separated before she learned to speak, when she was about the age at which Grace had lost her hearing. But he had always known what she was thinking.

When Miriam's hands returned to her lap Grace began to draw a school of fishes: red and green and blue and brown, with huge fins and beautiful golden eyes. "She's fond of fish," Miriam said. "She likes to wade in the river."

"My father was enchanted by fish," Caleb replied. In this warm safe house, it seemed possible to mention Samuel without betraying him. "Not only live ones, but the images of dead ones in the rocks. There was a book he loved, when he was old—I've forgotten the Latin title, but in English it was something like *Complaints and Justifications of the Fishes*. A Swiss naturalist named Scheuchzer wrote it."

How peculiar to say that name out loud, after all these years. After hearing it roll, so unexpectedly, from the mouth of the Frenchman at the party. When he was young he'd sometimes wondered if anyone but he and Samuel knew the contents of Samuel's old books.

Miriam was looking at him expectantly, and he continued. "The hero is an enormous fish who swims close to shore and addresses the humans. In excellent Latin, no less."

He paused while Miriam conveyed this to Grace. With a pencil Grace sketched a giant fish pushing his head above the water, open-mouthed and wearing a look of utmost concentration.

"Perfect." He smiled at Grace. "The fish complained that his ancestors had suffered the effects of the Deluge, although they were innocent themselves. That the tribe of fishes had paid for human sins, some being left to perish on dry land when the waters subsided. And that it was wrong for people, uncovering the impressions of their bodies in the rocks, to deny that those were the remains of actual creatures."

"Did people deny that?" Miriam asked.

"Some did," Caleb said. "My father used to study the different explanations men have come up with over the centuries. He was always convinced, himself, that the remains were relics of the Flood."

"And you? The bones you hope to find in Kentucky—how do you think they got there?"

Instead of answering Miriam's question, he looked down at Grace's drawing. She'd done something to the front fins, drawn lines suggestive of their movement—the fish was gesturing with his fins? The fish was signing?

Beneath it, in blue pencil, Grace wrote F I S T.

Miriam leaned over, changing the T to an H. Grace scribbled again: FISH.

"How well you draw," said Caleb.

Miriam translated Grace's swift reply. "She says she likes you, very much. And your story about the fish." She pointed at Caleb and made five slow, separate shapes with her right hand. Above the drawing of the fish, Grace proudly printed CALEB.

He tapped his chest and then formed the name-sign she'd given him at their first meeting. "Have you thought about one of the deaf-and-dumb schools for her?"

"My parents and I have talked about it. But she wouldn't want to be away from me, nor I from her. I try to teach her here the best I can, I have books and pamphlets from some of those schools but I know it's not enough." Her face clouded over. "I wish you could see how she is with other deaf children. The Rappites are taking care of a few, who've become Grace's friends. On Sunday we're going to Economy, where they live. Would you like to come?"

"I hope I'll be gone by then," Caleb said. Although he felt strangely at peace in this house, still he hated to see the point of his journey slipping away. With each passing day his goals were further deflected by the wretched weather, his own poor planning, his need to return to his duties by a certain date. How had he thought this could work?

"But if we're still stuck," he added, remembering the thickness of the ice and the morning's bitter cold, "I'd be delighted to join you."

Lightning

A ridge, a path, some black-barked trees. All of this was pleasing to Caleb, and helped make up for the fact that Kentucky lay hundreds of miles away, down a stalwartly frozen river. Mr. Dietrich, taciturn but kind, had saddled his own bay gelding for Caleb and then settled his daughters, Grace clinging to Miriam's waist, onto a sweet-tempered dappled mare. More trees, an open field. They neared a cemetery almost buried in snow. The horses walked side by side as Miriam tried to explain what she thought Grace had thought before she could understand prayers. How she'd conceived of death as coming from the moon, which until their dog had sickened and died she'd believed had watched over their family. Then she'd stood beneath the trees, a tiny, furious figure throwing rocks at the sky. Not until later, when they shared a language, had Miriam understood that gesture.

Grace rode with her cheek pressed against her sister's back, Caleb saw. With her head turned towards him. "How do you teach an idea like death?" he asked.

"By example," Miriam said patiently, as if speaking to one of her pupils. "By generalizing from the specific." Grace caught his eyes with her own, the green-gray irises uncannily flecked with gold.

As their horses stepped between rows of small stone tablets topped with sleeping sheep, Miriam talked and Caleb listened without listening. Under similar miniature stones, he thought, lay his stillborn son and the four children his second mother had seen born dead or watched die within days. Under larger stones lay Margaret and Samuel and his first parents, perhaps his sister—where was his sister? Samuel had prized a shard of English limestone, made entirely of fossil ammonites. Each the shape of a coiled snake but no bigger than a human eye, all of them pressed together without a scrap of plain stone show-ing—the fossils *were* the stone, the stone a mass of petrified shells. How could someone think that they weren't shells? Or that human na-ture might be ductile, when each season laid down another layer of stony compacted coils.

"You were right," Samuel had whispered on his last day. The fig-ured stones on the cliff were fake and he should have seen it; he should never have accused Caleb of being an unsympathetic son. But still there *was* a message in the stones: the forms inscribed by the boys had been wonderful in themselves, representative of the effects of the Del-uge. In them his pupils had incarnated exactly the knowledge he'd tried to transmit—and wasn't that, in itself, astonishing? A sign from God?

The reverse, Caleb had wanted to say. They were simply doing what they'd been trained to do. Brothers, the sons of an Aberdeen stonecarver, they worked hard in the family shop and were often late for their lessons. For them, already skilled at chiseling names and pairs of dates, scratching the outlines of spiders and bees into crumbling mudstone had been a simple exercise. In a few weeks they'd made the counterfeits, in a day salted the cliff with their work. Then hid their amusement as Samuel uncovered them.

"I failed you," Samuel had whispered. "I have failed everyone. My inability to reconcile the truths of Scripture with those of geology was God's punishment for my sins. I have gone over and over these in my mind, trying to understand the huge offense that merited such punish-ment. So many sins. My worst wrong was to you."

"You rescued me," Caleb remembered protesting. "You took me into your home and brought me up as your son."

"I *acted* toward you as toward a son," Samuel said. "But when I took you from the wreck of your parents' house and remade you in my own image, I acted out of pride. And in my heart—once Rosina was born and I had a living child of my own I could not conceal from God that I loved her more."

The feeling that passed over Caleb then, that feeling—he had known that Samuel spoke the truth, confirming something he'd always sensed. Rosina shared with her father few habits of heart and mind; a fossil for her was a dusty rock. She shared his blood.

Beneath him the gelding walked easily, keeping pace with the mare. The wind blew, the sun glanced off the snow, and he chatted quietly with Miriam, the smallest part of his mind engaged and the rest lost in the past. Economy, when they finally reached it, stretched along the river like a picture of a village. So clean, so neat; empty of people at first. "They're in church," Miriam said. "They'll be finished any minute." And suddenly there were people everywhere, pouring from a door and moving purposefully in their neat plain clothes. Despite the cold, Miriam moved not toward but farther away from the central buildings and the crowds.

A few people nodded politely; no one approached them. Long ago, on a day when four of Caleb's classmates had pummeled him, Samuel had wiped blood from his nose and told him about the Rappites, who strove to live in harmony with one another. Equal in their stations, possessing their property in common; their hard work in this world meant to prepare them for an easy transition to the kingdom of heaven. You might try to live a bit more harmoniously yourself, Samuel had said. The boys, Caleb might have replied, were mocking *you*. Years later, Stuart's jest about the Rappites had made Caleb want to befriend him. It was a consolation to see this place at last.

Without warning, Grace flew to the three children playing along the river's edge. Immediately their mittens were cast aside; their hands darted and leapt in the air, arms whirling, eyebrows moving, mouths open, laughing, frowning, set in every sort of grimace.

"The tall boy," Miriam said, "with the shock of black hair—that's Joseph, the one who's taught us so much. When he was small, his father gave him into the care of some charlatan preacher who claimed he could teach him to talk. Joseph ran away and was found by one of Mr. Rapp's flock in the woods; they took him in, and brought him here when they moved. At first he bit whoever touched him."

She waved at Joseph and returned his elaborate bow. "I've been able to act as an interpreter for him," she continued. "The things he's told me—people have such remarkable ideas about the deaf. His preacher believed that since the deaf are without a voice, which is the breath of God, they must also be without souls. That their language of signs is no language at all, but the mimicry of trained animals. He tormented Joseph, trying to get him to speak. Tubes in his ears, hot stones in his mouth, a long probe and hot water down his nose . . ."

"Terrible," Caleb said.

"It was a great thing for Joseph when this community took him in.

Although they couldn't understand him at first, they believed that his language of signs was itself a divine gift, permitting entry into his soul of the word of God."

Listen, Caleb imagined the Rappites saying. *To this.*

Still the children were conversing intently. "I don't know where Conrad and Duncan came from," Miriam said. "They're both so secretive. But I know Joseph taught them too. As he's taught us."

"You've been lucky," Caleb said.

"Lucky we live on this river," she said. "If nothing else. It gives me a chance. Boats stop here at Economy, and sometimes at the clearing where you're tied up. A few of the boatmen take an interest in the children. They bring them presents, and gestures they've seen other deaf people make."

Three crows soared up the river and settled into a bare box-elder. Without any warning Miriam added, "Shall I tell you how Grace lost her hearing?"

Caleb, startled, turned his gaze from the crows to her flushed cheeks. "If you want."

Moving her hands, she said, "We were at a neighbor's wedding. Me, my parents, my brothers, and Grace. She was two and a half, and I was fifteen."

As Miriam spoke, Grace ignored her gestures. This was a story she already knew—but here were Joseph and Conrad and Duncan, the four of them free, with so much to say. What had happened to each of them that day, that week, that hour. What they could remember of the time before they found each other; the ways the world appeared to them, then and now. I have learned to bake bread, I have read a book. On Wednesday I rode by the river and saw a snake. Rain falls down through holes in the sky, said Duncan; from clouds, Joseph said. From clouds. Then Duncan again, who had never heard: At night, when I could understand nothing, I learned that others saw in the darkness with their ears.

With her eyes cast down, and her voice so low that Caleb could hardly hear her, Miriam spoke of a hot August day, a heavy meal, pitchers of strong cider from which they all drank thirstily. Dancing, different games, her parents laughing with friends they seldom saw and Grace sitting in Miriam's lap and then toddling next to her when she rose and, with a friend named Harriet, followed an older boy into a broad meadow. An enormous hickory stood all alone in the center of the grass. So safe, so sheltering. They ran for it when the thunderstorm flashed; the leaves kept them almost dry. Miriam held Grace in her arms and turned her head from Harriet and the boy, who were embracing.

Her hands, apparently without her knowledge, had continued to move as she spoke. Now she looked down at them and paused. Joseph, who'd been watching her, asked Grace a question.

I remember sounds, Grace told him. Then I fell in a big white light and when I woke someone carried me. At home there were people but I couldn't hear them. The cat sat on my chest and meowed but I heard nothing, the dog barked and I couldn't hear her, a crow flew down beside my window and I saw her beak open and open again but everything was silent and has been since then and I didn't know what that meant.

She dropped her hands to her sides as Joseph nodded. Once he'd told her about the shining instruments of pain. So little time they had to catch up with each other—what was life and what was death and who was God and who were they; when the wind blew, what did that mean? Why did the mare have spots, or the pike such teeth? Somewhere, far away, were there others like them? All these thoughts passed through her hands and face and it was blissful, pure bliss to know herself understood and to feel, pouring back into her, other stories in such swift and shapely forms. Miriam was her sister, her life; but she signed slowly. The man who'd come to them couldn't sign yet at all. She flashed his name-sign at Joseph and explained that her family had taken him in, as they might a lost dog. Joseph laughed and beckoned toward the river.

"And then what happened?" Caleb said.

"And then a big bolt of lightning hit the tree." Miriam grasped her right hand in her left and held it still. "Harriet and the boy she was kissing were killed, although I didn't know that until later. I felt the lightning come up my legs, I felt it flow down my arm like fire and I tried to drop Grace before it reached her but my hands wouldn't work. When I woke there were people all around us. Harriet and her beau were gone, someone had covered their bodies with a blanket. I was unharmed except for one long burn." She rolled back her sleeve and exposed to the cold air a forked scar branded between elbow and wrist. "Grace had a bruise on her cheek where she'd fallen, but she seemed fine. Then after a while we knew she wasn't."

Always, he thought, the blow was felt after a while. After Samuel's death he'd continued to see the guilty boys in town—almost grown, then truly grown, then with children of their own. While the oldest one had trebled the family business, replacing his father's flat chiseled slabs with three-dimensional angels and willows carved in high relief, he himself had lost Margaret and their son.

"It should have been me who was punished," Miriam said. "Not her."

Before Caleb could object to this, a man appeared beside them, gliding up so silently that his greeting made Miriam jump. Gray-haired, rosy-skinned, too gaunt. Miriam introduced him as Brother Eusebius. "The schoolmaster here," she said. For a few minutes they talked politely, catching up on the past two weeks.

"And how are our wonderful children today?" Eusebius asked.

"As you see," Miriam said, gesturing toward the animated group streaming away from them.

To Caleb, still pondering the vision of Miriam electrified, the sky's fire pouring through her arms and into Grace's ears, Eusebius said, "You're enjoying your visit?"

"Very much."

"Any friend of Miriam's is welcome here."

While Miriam excused herself and followed the children, now running along the river and poking at the heaps of ice, Eusebius began to talk about the advantages of this settlement. Silkworms, merino sheep, the cider-press and the wine-cellar; he spoke too fast, his eyes were too bright. Caleb barely listened to him. The look on Miriam's face when she mentioned that boy she'd followed, when she spoke of him and her friend embracing—perhaps she'd wished herself in her friend's place. When Eusebius paused, Caleb asked how Joseph and his two friends had come to join the community.

"It is our tradition," Eusebius said obliquely. "To welcome all who arrive here destitute and ask for help."

"Everyone?" Caleb asked. "Even tramps?"

Eusebius frowned. "We prefer to call them pilgrims," he said. "Or unfortunates. But yes—we house and feed whoever arrives, no matter what their state, and even though some people think we're foolish and call this place "Tramp's Paradise." But better to take in a hundred unworthy than to turn away the one who is worthy. Some—like Joseph—have clearly been sent to us by God. When they ask for work, we give them work. If they ask to join us, we welcome them."

He peered more closely at Caleb. "You, for instance," he said. "You have not said why you arrive here on a Sunday, unattached to family and friends, accompanying our beloved Miriam and Grace—perhaps you are without a home?"

"I *have* a home," Caleb said, startled.

"Yet you aren't there," Eusebius said. He tucked his hands inside his sleeves, seeming at the same moment to tuck his lips inside his mouth. "You are not there, tending after your own, nor are you in church. I pray for your soul."

Who made you? Samuel had asked at prayers each night. *In whose care is your soul?*

"My soul is in the hands of my Maker," Caleb said.

"You could lose it this day," Eusebius replied. "This very hour. We expect the Second Coming at any moment, certainly during Mr. Rapp's lifetime. Then a general harmony will rule, as it did before disorder entered the world."

Caleb felt his face contort, the muscles twitching without his permission.

"You think we are fools to await the millennium here," Eusebius said angrily. He barely acknowledged Miriam, who had just returned to them. "But I tell you this: we are not so foolish as you who believe that the world is fixed as you see it." He stalked away.

"You upset him," Miriam said quietly. "I think he has hopes of me and Grace joining their group."

"Would you really think of joining them?"

"Would you?"

For a moment they gazed at each other curiously, and then she smiled. "I'm grateful for the interest they've taken in Grace. But to live here . . . I want a family of my own. And I don't share their beliefs."

She beckoned to Grace, who waved but stayed with her friends. *Inside me,* she was explaining to Joseph, *is a little person, the size of a thumb, who looks exactly like me. You have one too, yours looks like you. When we sleep they fly out of our chests and go here and there, then come back. When we die, they leave for good. These are our souls.*

"I want *more* for her," Miriam continued. "More than I can give her—look how her face lights up around her friends. Look how their hands fly. I want to start a school for the deaf near our home, I want someone to come here and train me and and a few other people, so we can teach all the children we can gather."

She turned toward a stand of willows, denying Caleb any hints he might have gleaned from her expression. Did he know then? Perhaps he knew. Beyond the willows a scraping, repetitive noise, which he'd heard faintly for some time, grew louder. He followed Miriam through the screen of hanging branches, toward a frozen creek framed by steep low banks. A solitary man was skating there. An enormous wild bird. No, a man. Moving forward at great speed and then, after a smooth pirouette, backward just as quickly, his hands clasped behind his waist and his head thrown back with pleasure. Just when Caleb was about to call out a warning—a hole in the ice, where rapids bubbled—the man spun again, took a few strong strokes, and leapt over the darkness. Landing, he reversed once more, slipping over the plain.

As Caleb moved forward, his arm was tugged backward: Grace, pulling his sleeve and gesturing at the skater's intricate patterns. She clasped her hands behind her back and leaned forward: *Teach me, teach me.* The skater slid backward, disappearing, as Samuel had disappeared, behind a bend. Caleb could not remember, anymore, the real details of their fiercest arguments, the language of his accusations, the precise texture and smell of the sheets beneath Samuel's wasting body. He could not remember all the pages he'd turned to distract himself, nor all Stuart had done to comfort him. *The Earth,* Samuel had once read to him, *was more fruitful before the Deluge. The temperature of the air was more equable, without burning summers or piercing winters; the air was more pure, and subtle, and homogeneous, and had no violent winds or agitations. The Antediluvians ate only vegetables; their lives were more equal, and vastly longer, than ours.*

From the creekbank, which Caleb found he was kicking with his right foot, a spray of smooth, reddish-brown stones tumbled down. Click, clack, clonking against each other and the ice. When one split, he knew what he'd find. The stone had cleaved neatly, revealing the impression of a palmate leaf. Beautiful, if not a surprise. He held the halves out to Grace, part and counterpart, and said to Miriam, "Would you help me explain it to her?"

She bent over her sister's hand. "What is it?"

"A fossil," he said, waiting while she finger-spelled the word. Joseph was watching her hands as well, although Conrad and Duncan had been diverted by a goose. "The word refers generally to anything dug out of the earth, and more specifically to the petrified remains of something once living, like this. Some are species that no longer exist."

He relied on her to translate accurately. "They're quite common," he said. "Not just the remains of plants, but shells and sea-creatures and larger animals, too, some of them enormous—at the place I'm headed to, people have found the fossil remains of a giant creature with the tusks of an elephant and the teeth of a hippopotamus. We call that creature *Mastodon* now . . ."

Miriam halted him with a raised hand. "And where," she said wryly, "should I find a name-sign for *that?*"

What a complicated smile she had! And still he kept talking, unable to stop himself. It was like being in the classroom of his dreams, saying exactly what he meant in the light of someone's full attention. He must have known then. As he spoke, Miriam's hands moved swiftly. Grace's eyes never strayed from her sister's gestures.

Beneath her feet, beneath the river, Grace thought, the world was as densely layered as a leek. Was that what Caleb meant? Her geography book had said nothing of this, that beneath the superficial film of dirt and vegetation were layers of fish and serpents and bugs and plants, frozen lives, life she hadn't known was alive—anything might exist in the rocks and that she hadn't seen it before was only because she hadn't thought to look. She bent down, searching through the rusty pebbles fanned across the ice and then cracking a smooth oval the size of her palm against a large rock. Shocked and disappointed, she held the pieces out to Caleb.

"They're not *that* common," he said gently, speaking to Miriam but looking at Grace. "Tell her they're only in special stones."

Joseph was staring at him, he saw. As intently as Samuel's pupils had once stared—what had those boys with their figured stones meant to say? He watched Grace crouch on the shore, inspecting the bank behind her. The boys might have forged the stones, he thought, as much for *him* as Samuel.

For years he'd listened without complaint as Samuel described, first to him, then to them, the earth's unchanging perfection. Some of the boys, clean and well-dressed, had listened attentively. But the shabby ones, those with dusty hands and shadowed eyes, missing parents, irregular households: what had they known of such order? Perhaps, Caleb thought, like him they'd seen evidence of a Maker whose attention wandered. One day, after taking over the afternoon class, he'd offered them an alternate view of the earth's history.

Not just *his* view, he said, regarding the boys' dropped eyelids and sullen mouths. The modern view, the *real* view. He'd presented to them what he'd just tried to share, in a simplified version, with Grace: a vision of an earth immensely old and subject to natural processes, the sea-floor heaved up into mountains, the mountains ground down by rivers and glaciers, evidence of change and movement visible everywhere in the strata. In the newest layers of the earth, he told them, barely below the ground on which they walked, might be found the bodies of mammoths and the bones of mastodons. Below those were other fossils, and still other fossils, each layer more ancient than the last. He drew on the stories Stuart had told him; the books they'd read together. The fossils that Samuel had shown the boys were, Caleb claimed, the remains of plants and animals which lived no more.

"From the Flood?" asked a boy to his left. And from the back bench, in a tone that might have been disrespectful, or merely tired, a voice Caleb had never pinned to its owner whispered:

At what time was the Deluge?
Nearly seventeen centuries after the creation of man.

What became of all living beings?
All living creatures died, except those that went with Noah into the Ark.

"There are different theories regarding the origin of fossils," Caleb said, trying to locate the voice. "Many of these my father has explained to you. He believes what you just suggested: that they're relics of creatures destroyed in the Flood. For myself, I think they are evidence of the earth's antiquity, and of the antiquity of life."

The boys whispered in twos and threes, one coming forward to ask what he was supposed to think when his teachers contradicted each other.

"Think for yourself," Caleb calmly suggested.

And a few months later there was Samuel, coat flapping in the wind, hair flapping over his eyes, happily grasping counterfeit stones which he wrapped in paper and hid from his son. After his death, when Caleb finally told Stuart about his impulsive lecture, and about the disturbing timing of the stones' appearance, Stuart had groaned and said, "Couldn't it have been coincidence?"

Miriam touched his arm. "What are you thinking about?"

He pointed to Grace, who was still rummaging through the stones. "Her."

He had not been honest with Stuart, either, when they first met. Why did he start this way?

When they left, the horses once more stepped quietly along the river. The trees were quiet. The birds were quiet. The sun had dropped, the sky was gray, and it was, suddenly, very cold. On the horses the riders were silent. Grace was clutching both Miriam and the handkerchief knotted around her cache of rocks. Miriam held the reins in one hand, with the other trying to imitate a new sign she'd seen Duncan make. Caleb, behind them both, stared down at his own hands as if they might suddenly begin to speak, revealing what he was meant to do with his life. So he'd once stared, when he was a boy, at a beautiful stone Samuel gave him, which was marked with coin-sized reticulated disks.

One minute these were decorations, elegant and mysterious. The next—the sun was glaring through the window, the cicadas were shrieking their hot-weather song; it was three days before his thirteenth birthday and his pants were itching the tops of his thighs—the disks were the stems of plants, seen in cross-section. What had happened to his eyes? The familiar turned strange and the strange familiar: Margaret's face would later turn overnight from an appealing arrangement of features into the countenance of the woman he loved, her skin enclosing blood and bone and a light he couldn't name, which had seemed like life itself. Lavinia, who'd been folded into a stranger's arms when he last saw her, her small self pressed against the woman's cloak, had twisted her head as the wagon began to roll and gazed directly at him.

He looked up from his hands, at the horse ahead, at Miriam's straight, slim back and her pale hair. At Grace, who had turned around and was looking back at him.

Fire

Out here, surrounded by the evidence of vanished rivers, Miriam thinks of that evening riding home along the frozen Ohio. At what moment had the stream of Caleb's life bent and merged with hers? The people she's left behind in Pittsburgh know nothing of this; nor does Stuart. When she finds herself signing, almost unconsciously—*Was it what you wanted, was she like a daughter, was she more to you than your own daughters?*—she is more reassured than surprised.

She and Caleb were married for twenty-five years, and although it is Stuart to whom she's been writing, she can't help but reach at the same time toward the companion of her heart. Caleb was proud, she knows, that he made the Academy for the Deaf into a place known throughout the country. Five of their first students have themselves become teachers of the deaf, one opening a school in Kentucky and another in Missouri. A long way from the early days of the children teaching her and Caleb and Stuart their home-signs while they taught back everything else they knew, history and geography and botany, the way to roast a joint or dress a loom. How bold they'd been, and what unexpected gifts Caleb had turned out to have!

In her opinion they were lucky despite meeting so late in his life: their school's success, and their three healthy children, more than many get. Was that enough? It was never like him to complain. She always knew that his fascination for Grace was part of his bond to her. As he always knew what she most wanted. And if he didn't feel for her exactly what he felt for Margaret, if his mind wasn't braided as closely with hers as it was with Stuart's—what did that matter? They worked together, they made a life. In the dormitory they built for the boarders, they sometimes found the children, late at night, huddled around an illegal candle with their hands flying urgently. Despite the risk of fire, Caleb could never bear to snuff the flame.

She walks to the edge of the bluff, lifts her skirt calf-high, and sits with her feet dangling into the cool, sweet air. It is almost dark, and although Grace has a lantern with her, and always works until the last minute, Miriam likes to watch over her sister's final ascent. She waves her arm, signaling across the ravine to where she can see one shoulder, one lifted arm, a fraction of Grace's gleaming head moving up the narrow trail. When Grace signals back, Miriam rises, shakes the dust from her skirt, and prepares to start a fire.

The people around them, concealed by the twisting bluffs and canyons but near enough as the crow flies, will read in the column of smoke, she knows, the news that they're still here. Soldiers uneasily surveying the Bad Lands under the eyes of the Lakota; the acquisitive geologist, meant to keep an eye on her and Grace, whom the Lakota call *picks-up-stones-running*; the Lakota themselves, with whom she and Grace converse in an Indian sign language somewhat similar to their own—all of them, Miriam thinks, wishing the inconvenient women would leave. Or perhaps they wish something else entirely, their true desires as hidden as the paths by which she and Caleb reached the decisions that shaped their lives.

Were you happy? she signs to Caleb. Under this vast and steely sky the world seems ancient, and very large. She feeds more grass to the little flame and adds this: *I was.*

CONTRIBUTORS

Elizabeth Alexander is the author of *The Venus Hottentot* (University of Virginia Press, 1990) and *Body of Life* (Tia Chucha Press, 1996) and *Antebellum Dreambook* (Graywolf, 2001). She is Visiting Lecturer in the Department of African-American Studies at Yale University. **David Altshuler**'s art is appearing in print for the first time. **Andrea Barrett** is the author of five novels and two collections of stories, the second of which, *Servants of the Map*, will be published by W. W. Norton in January 2002. **Stephen Benz** has published two travel narratives, *Guatemalan Journey* (University of Texas Press, 1996) and *Green Dreams* (Lonely Planet, 1998). **Diann Blakely**'s most recent collection of poems is *Farewell, My Lovelies* (Consortium, 2000). **Richard Blanco**'s first book of poetry, *City of a Hundred Fires*, won the 1997 University of Pittsburgh Agnes Starrett Prize. **Robert Bly**'s most recent books are *The Night Abraham Called to the Stars* (Harper Collins, 2001) and a book of translations (with Sunil Dutta) of the Indian poet Ghalib (Ecco Press, 1999). **Catherine Bowman** is the author of two collections of poetry, *1-800-HOT-RIBS* (1993) and *Rock Farm* (1996), both from Gibbs Smith. **Susan Briante**'s poetry has appeared or is forthcoming in *New American Writing*, *Quarterly West*, the *Marlboro Review*, and other journals. The poems, "Cintas," were inspired by translations of Aztec metaphors and proverbs. **Nick Carbo**'s latest book of poems is *Secret Asian Man* (Tia Chucha Press, 2000).

Jim Daniels' most recent books include *Blue Jesus* (Carnegie Mellon University Press, 2000) and *No Pets* (Bottom Dog Press, 1999). **Greg Delanty**'s latest books of poems are *The Hellbox* (Oxford University Press, 1998) and *The Blind Stitch* (Oxford Series, Carcanet Press, 2001; due out from Louisiana State University Press, 2002). **John Dufresne** is the author of *Louisiana Power & Light* (Plume, 1995) and the forthcoming *Deep in the Shade of Paradise*. **Denise Duhamel**'s most recent book is *Queen for the Day: Selected and New Poems* (University of Pittsburgh Press, 2000). She is a recipient of a 2001 NEA fellowship in poetry. **Peter Fallon** is the author of *News of the World Selected Poems* (Wake Forest University Press, 1993) and the editor (with Derek Mahon) of the *Penguin Book of Contemporary Irish Poetry* (Penguin, 1991). **Albert Goldbarth** is a recipient of the National Book Critics Circle Award. His most recent books are the poetry collection, *Saving Lives* (Ohio State University Press, 2001), and *Many Circles: New and Selected Essays* (Graywolf Press, 2001). **Eamon Grennan**'s most recent books are *Relations: New and Selected Poems* (Graywolf, 1998) and a collection of essays, *Facing the Music: Irish Poetry in the Twentieth Century* (Creighton University Press, 1999). **Vona Groarke's** previous collections of poetry are *Shale* (1994) and *Other People's Houses* (1999), both from Gallery Press. **Mark Halliday**'s books of poems are *Little Star* (William Morrow & Co., 1987), *Tasker Street* (University of

Massachusetts Press, 1992) and *Selfwolf* (University of Chicago Press, 1999). **Barbara Hamby**'s second book of poems, *The Alphabet of Desire* (New York University Press, 1999), won the New York University Prize for Poetry. **Kerry Hardie** is the author of the poetry collections, *A Furious Place* (1996) and *Cry for the Hot Belly* (2000), both from Gallery Press. Her first novel is *Hannie Bennet's Winter Marriage* (Harper Collins, 2000). **James Harms** is the author of three books of poems, *Modern Ocean* (1992), *The Joy Addict* (1998) and *Quarters* (2001). **Michael Hettich** has published two books of poetry and a number of chapbooks, most recently *Sleeping with the Lights On* (Pudding House, 2000) and *Singing with my Father* (March Street, 2001). **Tony Hoagland**'s most recent book is *Donkey Gospel* (Graywolf, 1998). He teaches in the University of Pittsburgh writing program. **Ben Howard**'s most recent books are a verse novella, *Midcentury* (Salmon Publishing, 1997), and *The Pressed Melodeon: Essays on Modern Irish Writing* (Story Line Press, 1996). *Dark Pool: Poems 1994–2001* is forthcoming from Salmon. **David Kirby**'s collection of poetry, *The House of the Blue Light,* was published by Louisiana State University Press (2000). His poems have been chosen for *Best American Poetry 2000* and a 2001 Pushcart Prize. **J. O. Lane** is the founder of the religious massage practice known as Johnnyatsu. **Li-Young Lee** is the author of three books of poems, *The City in Which I Love You* (1991), *Rose* (1993) and *Book of My Nights* (2001), all from BOA Editions, and the book-length autobiographical prose poem, *The Winged Seed* (Ruminator Books, 2000). **Lisa Lewis**'s two books are *The Unbeliever* (University of Wisconsin Press, 1995) and *Silent Treatment* (Pen-

guin, 1998). **James Liddy**'s recent books are his *Collected Poems* (Creighton University Press, 1995) and *Gold Set Dancing* (Salmon Press, 2000). **Kristina Martinez**'s work has appeared most recently in *Spoon River, Poetry Review,* and *Yemassee.* **Campbell McGrath** is a 1999 MacArthur Fellow. His most recent collection is *Florida Poems* (Harper Collins, 2002). **Medbh McGuckian** teaches creative writing at Queen's University in Belfast. Her most recent collection of poetry is *Shelmalier* (Wake Forest University Press, 1998). **Lissette Mendez** lives in Miami Beach, Florida, where she is at work on a memoir about the Mariel boatlift. **Nicole Moustaki** is the author of *The Complete Idiot's Guide to Writing Poetry* (April 2001, Alpha Books). **Jim Murphy's** chapbook, *The Memphis Sun,* won the Stan and Tom Wick Poetry Award and was published by Kent State University Press (2000). **Conor O'Callaghan** has published two collections of poetry in Ireland, *The History of Rain* (1993) and *Seatown* (1999). A selection from both collections, *Seatown and Earlier Poems,* was published by Wake Forest University Press (2000). **Mary O'Donnell**'s most recent novel is *The Elysium Treatment* (Trident Press, 2000). **Dennis O'Driscoll**'s five collections of poetry include *Weather Permitting* (Anvil Press, 1999). He received a Lannan Literary Award in 1999. **William Olsen** has published three collections of poetry, *The Hand of God and a Few Bright Flowers* (University of Illinois Press, 1998) and *Vision of a Storm Cloud* (TriQuarterly Books, 1996), and *Trouble Lights* (TriQuarterly Books, 2001). **Micheal O'Siadhail**'s ten collections of poetry include his most recent, *Our Double Time* (Bloodaxe, 1998), and a new selection of earlier work, *Poems 1975–95: Hail! Madam Jazz and A Fragile City*

(Bloodaxe, 1999). **David Rivard**'s most recent book is *Bewitched Playground* (Graywolf, 2000). He won the James Laughlin Prize from the Academy of American Poets for *Wise Poison* (Graywolf, 1996). **Polly Roberts**' work has appeared in the *Antioch Review, Another Chicago Magazine,* and the *Paterson Literary Review.* **Hugo Rodriguez** is a firefighter and paramedic in Miami, Florida. His poetry has appeared in *Mid-American Review, International Poetry Review,* and other journals. **Aidan Rooney-Céspedes** won the 1997 W.B. Yeats Po-etry Competition and the Sunday Tribune/Hennessy Cognac Award for New Irish Poetry. His poetry has appeared in *Poetry Ireland Review, Brangle, College English* and *Metre.* **Angela Schlaud** is an artist living in Evanston, IL. **Bill Tinley** has published widely in journals in Europe and North America. He won the 1996 Patrick Kavanaugh Award. **Eamonn Wall**'s most recent books are *The Crosses* (Salmon, 2000) and *From the Sine Café to the Black Hills: Notes on the New Irish* (University of Wisconsin Press, 2000). **David Foster Wallace**, author of *Infinite Jest* and other works, has recently been appointed Disney Professor of Creative Writing at Pomona College. **Martin Walls**' collection of poetry, *Human Detail in Care of National Trust,* was published by New Issues Press (2001). **Charles Harper Webb**'s most recent book is *Tulip Farms* and *Leper Colonies* (BOA Editions, fall 2001). *Liver* (University of Wisconsin Press, 1999) won the Felix Pollak Prize. **Lydia Webster's** work has appeared in *Quarterly West, Salt Hill, Puetro del Sol, Willow Review,* and *Story-Quarterly.* **David Wheatley**'s two collections of poetry are *Thirst* (1997) and *Misery Hill* (2000). He co-edits the journal, *Metre,* and writes on poetry for the *Times Literary Supplement, London Review of Books,* and the *Irish Times.* A native of Jamaica, **Debra Woolley** currently lives in Miami. This is her first publication.

Subscriptions
Three issues per year. **Individuals:** one
year $24; two years $44; life $600. **Insti-
tutions:** one year $36; two years $68.
Overseas: $5 per year additional. Price
of back issues varies. Sample copies $5.
Address correspondence and subscriptions
to *TriQuarterly*, Northwestern University,
2020 Ridge Ave., Evanston, IL 60208-
4302. Phone (847) 491-7614.

Submissions
The editors invite submissions of fiction,
poetry and literary essays, which must
be postmarked between October 1 and
March 31; manuscripts postmarked
between April 1 and September 30 will
not be read. No manuscripts will be returned unless accompanied by a stamped,
self-addressed envelope. All manuscripts
accepted for publication become the
property of *TriQuarterly*, unless otherwise indicated.

Reprints
Reprints of issues 1–15 of *TriQuarterly*
are available in full format from Kraus
Reprint Company, Route 100, Millwood,
NY 10546, and all issues in microfilm
from University Microfilms International,
300 North Zeeb Road, Ann Arbor, MI
48106.

Indexing
TriQuarterly is indexed in the Humanities
Index (H.W. Wilson Co.), the American
Humanities Index (Whitson Publishing
Co.), Historical Abstracts, MLA, EBSCO
Publishing (Peabody, MA) and Informa-
tion Access Co. (Foster City, CA).

Distributors
Our national distributors to retail trade
are Ingram Periodicals (La Vergne, TN);
B. DeBoer (Nutley, NJ); Ubiquity (Brooklyn, NY); Armadillo (Los Angeles, CA).

**Publication of *TriQuarterly* is made
possible in part by the donors of gifts
and grants to the magazine. For their
recent and continuing support, we are
very pleased to thank the Illinois Arts
Council, the Lannan Foundation, the
National Endowment for the Arts,
the Sara Lee Foundation, the Wendling
Foundation and individual donors.**